MADELEINE

A NOVEL

ALEX SIMONS

STRAW HAT
BOOKS

First published 2023
Straw Hat Books

ISBN 978-1-7394993-0-3

Cover design by Sheer Design and Typesetting
alexsimonsauthor@gmail.com

For AMP and HS with love and thanks

'No work or love will flourish out of guilt, fear, or hollowness of heart, just as no valid plans for the future can be made by those who have no capacity for living now.'

ALAN WATTS

CHAPTER 1

She watched him bounce, twist, spin down the cliff.
Three hundred feet below, circles rippled out across the sea.
Her scream echoed off the mountain and like him, disappeared.

Madeleine lay on her side, her knees drawn up, her body shaking, sweat soaking her nightie. Not that nightmare again. Please, not again.

She waited for the shower to warm and shuddered, remembering her Tinder date who'd left at two in the morning. He'd promised much and delivered self-centred tedium. The shower helped her shake off both the dream and the man. Brushing her teeth got rid of the sour taste in her mouth.

She felt the early autumn chill in the air as she opened the French windows. A blackbird hauled a worm into its beak and flew away. Sipping her coffee, she reflected, as she had done so often since their separation, on how she'd yearned to be free from Richard, imagining that being alone would at least be a deliverance from the boredom of living with him. She had her wish, and what was the result? Here she was, muttering to herself and staring vacantly at the remnants of the take-away in the sink and the empty bottle of wine on the drainer. A memory of her alcoholic mother lying drunk on the kitchen floor came into her mind. She picked up the bottle, dropped it into the bin with a satisfying crash, and walked through to the sitting room to lie on the red sofa, the coffee mug warming her hands.

After eighteen years of marriage, Richard had told her he was leaving her for Paul, his best friend. At first, she'd collapsed, numbed, abandoned again, plunged back into the darkness he'd rescued her from twenty-two years ago. She had opened up to him, trusted him totally with her deepest secret. He'd been a good Samaritan, but a lousy husband. Now it was over, it wasn't the marriage to Richard she was mourning. It was something else, something deeply buried.

The nightmares had re-started. She knew, for sure, the voices of the dead had the power to drive the living mad. She forced herself to think about Richard; at least he was alive.

Whatever trust she had slowly built after two decades with him had evaporated. That trust had been the main reason she had stayed so long in a comfortable but uninspiring, dull marriage. A lying, sham of a marriage. What an idiot she'd been, what idiots they'd both been.

Depression had eventually turned to anger. At first, she'd tried so hard to make the marriage work. Richard had always been non-committal about children, too busy with his business and his friends. She'd fallen out of love with him years ago and she knew now it must have been the same for him. His lack of interest in her made her shut down her desires. If only he had been honest with her, it would have saved so much time. He was a good man, kind, generous, but so uninterested. At least now she knew it wasn't personal.

Within a week of him leaving, she'd had the whole house re-painted in strong, primary colours. She had additional bookshelves built and filled them with the novels, Greek myths, biographies, and travel books she loved, which had been in boxes for ages. Gone were the dreary reproduction prints that Richard was so fond of, replaced by colourful abstract paintings she'd bought over the years. The table under the window held her collection of pottery, at the centre of which was a Lucie Rie bowl. She loved to hold it, imagining the potter's hands shaping its exquisite simplicity, fantasizing she was moulding the clay herself.

MADELEINE

They'd had little contact since he left. Madeleine was happy with that. She'd thrown out the grey dresses and suits she'd bought during her marriage and replaced them with lively, fun, colourful clothes that better reflected her determination to take control of her life. She'd signed up to various dating apps, though with little success. She had a job she loved, some great friends, did some volunteering from time to time but so much was missing at a deeper level, where it mattered, where there should be meaning. As much as she loved her friends and the intimacies they shared, she knew she had to find her own way to be free.

Emily, Shammie, and other friends had gently, lovingly, helped her through her sleepless depression, held her hand as she cried. Now the Decree Absolute lay on her bedside table, endorsed by a wine stain. She was aware of the material comfort she enjoyed from her divorce settlement, but it felt like no more than a carapace to hide her emptiness, her loneliness, her guilt. Material things weren't the answer. She knew she needed to come out of her self-imposed shell, to open to life again and make up for lost time. Maybe that would help to reduce the nightmares. Maybe.

The day the Decree Absolute arrived, Emily and Shammie came round to toast her freedom. To illustrate that the world was now Madeleine's oyster, they re-wrote the famous opening lines of books, each one making them laugh more.

'To Hell with Ishmael. Call me Madeleine.'

'Madeleine, light of my life, fire of my loins.'

'It is a truth universally acknowledged that a divorced middle-aged woman in possession of a strong libido, must be in want of good sex.'

If she did have a strong libido, Madeleine mused, it must have a chain and padlock on it.

She shook her head. Fuck. Freedom was terrifying.

CHAPTER 2

Madeleine walked down Albemarle Street, shopping bags in both hands, her phone jammed under her cheek.

"Shammie, I'm nearly at Browns. How long will you be?"

"About twenty minutes. I'll meet you in the bar and let Jacob know he can pick us up. Order some champagne my lovely, we've earned it."

She'd never been to Browns Hotel. She chose a table in the corner near the bar, put down her bags, took off her coat and settled into a comfy chair.

"A cappuccino, please."

"Yes, Madam." The waiter was halfway to the bar when she called him back.

"I've changed my mind. I'll have a glass of champagne." The waiter smiled. "I have a friend coming soon. When she arrives, will you bring one over for her too?"

"Of course, Madam."

Madeleine took a book out of her bag and started to read. Absorbed in the novel, without thinking, she finished her glass. The waiter came over to her table.

"Excuse me Madam, the gentleman over there would like to buy you another glass of champagne."

"Sorry?"

"The gentleman over there, Madam."

A young man was sitting at the bar, looking at her, smiling. He raised his hand to his mouth, imitating drinking from a glass. She shook her head. "No thank you."

The waiter moved away, and she started reading again.

"If I can't buy you a drink, may I get you something else?"

She looked up from her book. The man was standing by her chair.

"Thank you, but no. I'd just like to read my book."

"A coffee, perhaps?" His voice had an Irish lilt that she found disturbingly attractive. Something in her wanted to say yes.

Out of the corner of her eye, she saw Shammie looking around the room. She waved her over.

"Ah, there you are Maddy. I couldn't see you, tucked away in the corner. And who are *you*, you gorgeous man?"

She put several bags of shopping on the floor. The man helped take off her coat.

"I'm Finn," he said. "I was just offering your friend another glass of champagne. Can I get you one?"

"Well, yes, that would be lovely. Maddy, have one too."

"I've already said no. I don't want another glass. Or a coffee. Let's just have a quiet drink…?"

Shammie ignored her and looked Finn up and down.

"I'm Shammie. Sit down with us. We're waiting for my husband. He's late as usual."

He smiled. "Thank you. I rarely get the chance to sit with two such beautiful women."

Madeleine looked away. Shammie laughed.

"I know a player when I see one, Finn! But I'm always happy to talk to a charming man. My husband will assume I'm flirting anyway. We have an arrangement."

"An arrangement? Sounds intriguing…" said Finn, smiling.

"Shammie! Come on, not now," said Madeleine.

Shammie grinned and clinked glasses with Finn. "Finn, this is my friend, Madeleine."

"Madeleine, what a beautiful name. It's a pleasure to meet you."

Madeleine looked at him briefly. "Nice to meet you. Excuse me, I need to go to the washroom." As she walked away, she heard Shammie's laughter, but she knew the man was watching her.

* * * *

When Madeleine returned, Shammie was still laughing and flirting with the Irish stranger. A man in his fifties, out of breath and flustered, spotted them, and rushed over. Shammie introduced her husband to Finn. Jacob put a protective arm round his wife and kissed her on the cheek. The traffic had been horrendous; he'd managed to park outside and didn't want to get a ticket.

"Hello, Maddy. I'm sorry to rush you both but are you ready to go?" he asked.

"Trust you to turn up just when I was getting to know this charming young man!" said Shammie.

"Sorry Sham but we're in a hurry," said Jacob, nodding briefly in Finn's direction.

Finn put a hand on Shammie's shoulder.

"It was a pleasure and I hope we meet again." He handed her a business card. "Do call me sometime."

She winked at him and put the card in her handbag. Jacob picked up her bags and Finn watched as they walked out of the bar. To his surprise, it was Madeleine who turned briefly to glance at him as they left.

The clock had started. Tick.... tock....

CHAPTER 3

Madeleine didn't need to dress up for Shammie, but hell, why not? She had no-one else to dress for. She decided on the cream wrap-around silk shirt she'd just bought, tight blue jeans, short leather boots and a loose green jacket.

Shammie brought a superb red wine to go with the lasagne Madeleine had cooked for supper. They spent the meal catching up on news and gossip. Shammie always had outrageous stories to tell, and Madeleine enjoyed her sense of drama. It cheered her up.

"Let's open another bottle," Madeleine said.

"Great idea. I've something else to tell you. Something you're going to love, Maddy."

They settled on the sofa. Madeleine tucked her legs under her. "So…?"

"You remember that guy Finn, who we met in Browns? He wants to meet you again."

"Seriously?!" Madeleine said. "No, no, no. No way. He was outrageous! He tried to pick me up."

"Come on, Maddy. He was great. He's stylish, bright, professional, and bloody gorgeous. That smile, and that sexy Irish accent. He really likes you. He wants to meet you."

"How do you know that? I thought you'd be meeting him yourself!"

"I called him because I noticed his interest in you. Sure enough, he asked about you. I told him you're available. You know what, Mads of my heart? He's just what you need!"

"You did what?! There's no way I'm going to meet him. For a start, he's too young. And anyway, he's the kind of man I'd run a mile from! I want someone who'll respect me. All he'd ever want is a dirty weekend!"

"And what's wrong with that?" asked Shammie with a playful shove. You can't deny you could do with some good sex! And you must admit he was attractive!"

Madeleine remembered Finn only too well. To her shame, she hadn't been able to get him out of her head. Twice in the last week she had lain in bed, fantasising about him, imagining what they might do to each other. She'd had her first orgasm for a while.

"Maddy, it's up to you. But, come on, let go, have some fun! You'll have a great time. I know you will. Trust me." Shammie mock pouted.

Madeleine had been on a few dates, mainly with men in their fifties, usually bored and boring, married and trying their luck. The ones who weren't married seemed either lost or unable to forget a former love or get over the terrible injustice of their ex-wife's infidelity. She'd only dated a few men more than once, the ones who'd had at least a smattering of conversation, but they'd all been so disappointing in bed.

"Come on, Maddy. You're both single. Worth at least a meeting, no? You need to be open to new possibilities, my love. What have you got to lose? And it could be a lot of fun…"

Shammie had a point. For years before learning of her husband's betrayal, she had suffered the lonely agony of sexual incompatibility. Looking back at the last decade of her marriage, she was at her most lonely when she lay awake beside her sleeping, snoring husband after he'd had occasional, one-sided sex with her. She had stopped bothering to moan a pretence of satisfaction. Her body ached with frustrated desire, her heart with unfulfilled love. She longed for tenderness, to be able to say, *'I love you'* and mean it.

"You're insane, Shammie! Okay, okay, totally against my better judgement, I'll meet him. Just for coffee."

Shammie whooped and clapped and toasted the hot date to come.

"Oh, Maddy! I love you! Here's his number. Call him."

Madeleine sat back, shook her head, and shivered. What on earth was she doing? Charm usually belonged to bad men, the serial leavers, the ones that were always infernally irresistible to women. Perhaps a young man who liked older women would be a different kind of lover? One who listened and paid attention as he explored not just the obvious places. An intelligent man with confidence and patience who would give her goosebumps, make her feel beautiful, desired. But *this* man? He was a *charmer,* dammit... But then again, what if he really could...?

* * * *

For a week, Madeleine had done her best to forget about the card that Shammie had given her. But as hard as she'd tried, she hadn't been able to get Finn out of her head. Shammie's cajoling words kept coming back to her. She called his number.

"Finn, it's Madeleine."

"Hello, Madeleine."

The voice was soft, Irish, playful. Smiling. Seductive.

"I'm not sure this is a good idea, but would you like to meet me for a coffee?"

"Yes, but I think we could do better than that. Come and have dinner with me at Brown's." She could feel his smile. "The food's great. I'm really looking forward to seeing you again. Please say yes."

"Thank you, but I think a coffee will be fine."

"I promise you; you'll love dinner there. Please."

"Let me think about it," she said. "I must go. I'm running late for a meeting."

"Think about it, then call me. Bye."

She closed her laptop, put on her coat, and left the office. She went to the supermarket, wandering the aisles, unable to concentrate, that Irish lilt like a worm in her ear. She picked up a ready-made meal for one. Changing her mind, she went back and replaced the meal with fresh vegetables, organic chicken breasts and a bar of Green and Black's 80% chocolate. There was something else she needed. What else was it? Damn him.

She waited a few days before calling again. A part of her had wanted to resist, or even tell him to fuck off. But his voice, his unseen smile had disturbed, aroused her. Whatever her reservations, she knew she was going to meet him. Just for herself.

Would this Finn surprise her? Would she let him?

They spoke twice more on the phone. Short, practical conversations, finalizing arrangements. She couldn't deny being impressed by his confidence. She was so conflicted over this meeting, but filled with a nervous excitement she hadn't felt for years.

Tick.... tock....

CHAPTER 4

Evening shadows stretched along the pavement outside Browns Hotel as Madeleine got out of the taxi. The last time, she hadn't noticed the artistic black and white photos of glamorous, dramatic-looking women on the walls.

In the bar, three couples sat quietly gazing into their drinks. Madeleine noticed how elegant and confident they seemed, clearly used to luxury. A woman sat at the bar, laughing with the barman, her little black mini dress showing a glimpse of the top of stockings, high heels. A similar look to the women in the photographs. Is that how he'd be happy she'd dressed?

A hand touched her shoulder.

"Madeleine. Hello."

It was his twinkling eyes she saw first, and she felt her stomach clench. He took her arm, and they walked over to a table where a pair of champagne glasses and two bowls of olives were waiting. He pulled out a chair for her. She liked good manners. He beckoned the waiter, who brought Krug champagne. She looked at his curly hair, the ring in his ear. What on earth was she doing? She wished she'd asked the taxi driver to pick her up in an hour. Even that would be too long. But those blue eyes, that smile! That accent! Oh God.

The woman at the bar, evidently bored with the barman, crossed and uncrossed her legs several times in Finn's direction. At one point she smiled openly at him, but he did not return the smile. Nor had his eyes wandered across to admire her. Maybe he *was* different. When they'd spoken on the phone, Madeleine had had some unanswered questions. Now there were more in her mind. Had he lied to Shammie and was really another bored, married man? What was his body like? She could tell he was strong. What would it feel like to run her fingers through those curls? Along the faint scar on his cheek? How well did he kiss? For her that was the big test in a man. She had a feeling he would kiss superbly. Her belly clenched tighter.

"Shammie seems to think that I'm in need of a man. I'm not, you know," she said.

His quizzical look had the hint of a smile. "I'm sure she meant well.

"I hope you're not married," she said, surprising herself with her bluntness.

"Absolutely not. I much prefer to be single. My life is far too busy."

"I bet it is. You're a ladies' man, the type that mothers warn their daughters about. I can see why Shammie likes you."

"So, what made you come here, tonight?" he asked.

"I'm wondering the same thing," she said. "Well, am I right about you?"

"Don't judge me so quickly," he said. "I'm a successful businessman."

"What - a second-hand car-dealer?"

Finn stopped smiling. "Are you always this rude?"

Madeleine grimaced. "Yes, that was rude. I'm sorry."

"I'm an art dealer, Madeleine."

"Oh, that's interesting. My father was an artist and he never trusted dealers," she said.

"Was your father successful?"

"Sadly, not."

"Then maybe he should have trusted dealers," said Finn, grinning again.

"Maybe so… Can I trust you, Finn?" she asked.

"Trust in what way?"

"Trust that you won't…. oh, forget it. Why did you choose this hotel to meet me?"

"I love it here. It suits me."

"Have you always been an art dealer?"

He had. He'd loved art at school but was a mediocre painter. That had made him appreciate how talented the best artists are. He'd been to Trinity Dublin to study art history. He knew he wanted to deal. It allowed him to be close to artists and their work and get to know them. And to make a lot of money.

He was starting to be more interesting than she'd expected.

"Enough about me," he said. "What do you do?"

Against her will, her body was beginning to betray her, an animal lust taking over. Her head, her soul might not approve but her body was responding to this divine stranger. She felt beads of sweat at the base of her spine and sensations she had forgotten or, most likely had never felt.

She breathed deeply then told him about the literary agency where she worked.

"I'm not a writer, but I know how to improve and edit a writer's work. I love their thoughts and ideas, and the way they craft a novel."

"We have something in common, then," he said, pouring her more champagne. "Shammie told me you're divorced. What happened?"

"My husband ended up preferring men. It hurt and to be honest, I felt a total failure. With hindsight of course I should have noticed sooner. But you don't, do you? I trusted him. What an idiot. Anyway... I'm moving on," she said.

Subconsciously, she felt for the phantom ring on her wedding finger. He reached across the table, putting his hand over hers. "It must have been tough," he said, gently.

"I should never have married him. But I was young, in a mess, vulnerable, alone. He was an older man, kind to me. He sort of looked after me, and I looked up to him. I just slipped into it."

She pulled her hand away and looked across at the woman in the mini dress at the bar. "Is she your usual type?"

"Yes, she's an attractive woman," he said. "But so are you, and you're much more interesting."

"In what way?" asked Madeleine.

He hesitated for a moment. "Your obvious intelligence. And you're unusual," he said.

"Unusual?"

"Yes, unusual and intriguing. You've been persuaded by a friend who isn't exactly one of your 'married for better or worse' types, to meet a man you obviously didn't take to when you first met him. In my experience, most women on a first date dress in ways they think the man will want them to look. I get the feeling you've dressed just for yourself, not for me and I find that fascinating. Not only that, but I also found you really intimidating when we first met. I still do. So, yes, you intrigue me. I want to get to know you."

Madeleine shook her head and couldn't help smiling. "I don't know why I'm here, Finn. This is so unlike me. You aren't even my type!"

"Shammie said you'd be a challenge," he said.

"Did she now? And what else did she say? Actually, I don't want to know."

For a while, they sat in silence. Then she glanced at him, picked up an olive and flipped it into her mouth.

"I used to do that as a kid," he said.

"Do what?"

"Flip nuts into my mouth. My record was thirty-five," he said, with a childish hint of pride in his voice.

"What else did you do as a kid?" she asked.

He told her he played with friends, listened to music, read, was good at sport, but often spent time alone in his bedroom. For a moment he looked like a little boy lost, and she felt herself soften.

He wanted to know more about her work as a book editor. She told him about the authors her agency represented. She worked with nine writers, five of whom were published and one in particular she had very high hopes for. He asked about her colleagues.

"There are four of us. Catherine, who set up the firm, is the brains and all-round brilliant inspiration. Charlie is my co-editor and Helen our intern. We've got twenty-three published authors. We all muck-in together. I work four days a week."

And when she wasn't working?

Friends, cinema, theatre, restaurants, pubs. Reading. She admitted to too much unoccupied spare time and immediately regretted it.

He looked straight into her eyes and said, "That doesn't sound good for you."

He was right, of course. He wanted to know more about her marriage. Had she had affairs, lovers? She looked down, embarrassed.

"No, I never did. I believed in marriage, for better or worse. Affairs, being unfaithful, can be very destructive."

For better or worse. Ha! How she'd longed to marry Justin before Richard all those years ago. What on earth would have happened if she had? She shuddered and pushed thoughts of him away.

"Richard and I separated three years ago. We're now finally divorced."

Finn smiled and then laughed.

"Why do you find that funny?" she asked, annoyed. Divorce was no laughing matter.

He apologised; he was not laughing at the divorce; it was what she'd said before. For some reason, he said, her strait-laced attitude to marriage made him laugh. "I'm not laughing at you, Madeleine. It's just something I haven't come across much," he said.

"Tell me more about you," she said.

"I love art, of course. Poetry too."

"Poetry? I somehow didn't expect that. I'm glad. I like surprises!"

"Good," he said, grinning.

"So, what else did you like when you were young?" she asked.

"Hurling," he said.

Madeleine laughed. "Hurling? What's that?"

"It's a mixture of hockey and lacrosse. Said to be the fastest and most skilful game in the world. Bray Emmets is my team. Bray's outside Dublin. I still look for their results."

"I've heard of Bray. Aren't there film studios there?"

He nodded. "Yes, there are. They make a lot of movies and TV shows. Braveheart, for example."

"I assume you liked that movie."

"Why?"

"It's about a man taking control."

"True."

"You like control, don't you, Finn?"

His smile broadened. "I like to make things happen," he said.

"Why do you think that is?" she asked.

"I had a weak father. I vowed never to be like him." He grimaced.

She nodded. "I can understand that."

She reached across and touched his hand. "I'm sorry I was so rude earlier. It's just, well, this is new to me," she said.

Softly he asked her, "What's new to you?"

She fiddled with her hair and looked down. "Knowing how to react to a man I'm attracted to." She looked up into his eyes. "It's been a long time, Finn."

He took her hand. "Thank you, Madeleine. I'm attracted to you too. Very much." He took his hand away.

"So, what are you looking for now?" he asked.

"To widen my horizons, I guess."

It wasn't a fully honest answer. She knew what she wanted. Sex. With him.

She wished she'd eaten properly before she came out. Champagne was an aphrodisiac for her, and this was good champagne.

"Tell me more about widening your horizons."

His voice was mesmeric. For a moment she closed her eyes. She felt dizzy and glanced across at him. He was looking concerned. He called the waiter over and asked for a large bowl of mixed nuts and a bottle of sparkling water. When they arrived, he waved the waiter away and poured a glass for her.

"Are you okay?" he asked.

She swallowed some water.

"Thank you. Yes, I'm fine. Okay, to answer your question, I'd like to travel more. I've been to the States a few times. I especially love France and Italy. I went to Greece a long time ago. I've never been to Africa or India or South America."

She told him how they'd bought a house in France, but Richard wanted to keep it for himself and his boyfriend, so sadly she didn't get there anymore.

"There are so many wonderful places to go to. I wished I'd travelled more. I guess there's still time," she said quietly. "Anyway, what about you, where have you been?"

"I haven't travelled that much either and what I've done is for work. So, the States, Greece, Italy, France, Germany, Spain. Anywhere that art thrives."

She smiled. "Sounds like you could do with widening your horizons too, Finn."

"Madeleine, I think we could be good for each other...."

For a moment, they gazed at each other. Madeleine broke the silence. "Finn, I'm getting hungry. Can we eat?"

The maître d' greeted them warmly, addressing Finn by name, and showed them to a table at the end of the room. Finn pulled a chair out for her, and she sat down. The waiter filled their glasses with Chablis and set down a stand of oysters on the table. Finn looked at her a little nervously.

"I hope you don't mind, but I've already ordered."

She felt herself flush and shook her head with irritation.

"Please don't be cross, Madeleine. You won't find better oysters anywhere. I know the food here." She softened her gaze and shrugged. This wouldn't be an ordinary night.

They each selected an oyster from the ice. She knew just what he'd be thinking. Despite herself, she closed her eyes as she swallowed. God, it felt good.

He looked around the room and asked if she'd noticed the art on the walls. She hadn't. Richard Hopkinson and Rachel Grieves. They were excellent young British artists, and he represented them both. The hotel was a client of his.

She was leaning forward as he talked. The champagne had warmed her. And now the Chablis. Finn was gazing at her, fully confident again. Those blue eyes. That smile. His self-assuredness. Maybe he wasn't so arrogant after all, just relaxed in himself. She was finding him more and more tempting.

She liked his casual, well-cut clothes. His collarless, white cotton shirt unbuttoned enough to show the hairs on his chest, his dark blue linen jacket, designer black jeans and immaculately polished shoes. His hands were strong, wide, with very long fingers, immaculate nails. She had never slept with a man on a first date.

The waiter cleared away their plates.

"I checked with Shammie that you're not a vegetarian, Madeleine. They cook this next course especially for me. I hope you like it."

A waiter arrived with a succulent Chateaubriand steak and a béarnaise sauce with broccoli and triple cooked chips. The sommelier poured them each a glass of Cabernet Sauvignon. Watched over by the Maitre d', the slices of steak were laid carefully on their plates. She tasted a small piece.

"Good?" Finn asked.

"Exquisite."

They ate in silence, occasionally glancing at each other, smiling. Ever discreet, the waiters re-appeared, cleared their empty plates, and refilled their glasses.

"Would you like dessert?" he asked.

She knew exactly what she wanted for dessert. She held his gaze and felt her cheeks redden. She reached behind her, pulled out a couple of pins, shook her head and her hair tumbled down to her shoulders.

"Yes. Definitely," she said.

★ ★ ★ ★

The next morning, she switched on her phone. Five missed calls and voicemails from friends. Her phone pinged. *"I want you again."* She had just left the hotel room and already he was texting her. With a smile, she tucked the phone back in her bag and strode off across Green Park. London was looking glorious in the late morning sunshine.

Tick.... tock....

CHAPTER 5

"How was everyone's weekend?" Catherine looked at her colleagues round the conference table, sipping their coffee.

Charlie was in her thirties, newly engaged. "Ewan and I ended up in Dorset. Found a great pub that brewed its own ale. We should have spent more time in the bar!" She giggled. The others glanced at each other. Sex. Nothing but sex.

Helen, the intern was doing an OU Degree in English. Her weekend was spent in a library writing an essay. Madeleine tried to remember when she'd last been in a library. She envied Helen's dedication.

"Maddy? What about you?" Catherine asked.

"Oh, I met a strange man in a posh hotel and if I told you what happened next, I'd have to kill you."

They all laughed. "Come on. What did you really do?"

Madeleine smiled. "I told you. Anyway, what's on the agenda today, Catherine?"

Catherine was in her fifties, nearly six foot tall. Her short-cropped hair suited her face. She wore blue dungarees and a white t-shirt, with her signature large, colourful, jewellery. She rarely talked about her private life or socialized with her colleagues, but they all respected and liked her. She supported them and they were loyal to her. They assumed she lived alone. She never mentioned a partner and seemed to live for her work. As usual, Catherine's weekend was not discussed. Instead, she ran her team through the weekly diary. They had a lot to do. Madeleine's priority was to get the final draft of Julia McGuigan's novel ready for submission.

Back at her desk, Madeleine opened her emails. There were several from authors, a couple from fellow editors, the usual promotions and invitations. Her mind kept returning to Finn. If anyone had looked closely, they'd have seen a small smile on her lips that hadn't been there before. She knew she'd see him again. He had called once and texted twice more since yesterday morning, but she hadn't answered. She didn't know what to say. He was insistent that he wanted her again. And she wanted him. So much. Normally, she was totally focussed. Now she was struggling to concentrate. Her body was on fire and her mind absorbed by desire. She'd never experienced anything like the sex with Finn. It reminded her of the scene the day after sex between Brad Pitt and Geena Davis in *Thelma and Louise,* where Thelma's massive grin reveals she has 'finally had some good sex.' How she'd envied Thelma! And now she had her own Thelma moment. In one of the erotic novels she'd read, they said sex always improved after the first time. She shivered. Could it possibly get any better?

She loaded Julia's novel onto her screen and started to read from where she'd left off. She heard the ping of an email arrive. Another invitation. Her phone rang.

"Have you opened it?"

"Opened what?" she said.

"The invitation."

"Finn…."

"Open the email. It's an exhibition I'm putting on in Liverpool," he said. "It opens on Friday with a private view at the Walker Gallery. I've booked us into the Titanic Hotel, so we can make a weekend of it. Have you seen the Gormley statues on the beach at Crosby?"

She told him she was out with Shammie on Friday.

"Postpone it! You can see her anytime. I'll meet you at Euston. I've got reservations on the 12:43. See you at the ticket office at 12.15."

For a second, she was silent. "Did you say the Titanic Hotel?" she said.

"Yes, and I promise, no icebergs."

Any iceberg would melt if Finn smiled at it. There was no point in playing hard to get.

"I've never been to Liverpool," she said.

"Brilliant! I'm so pleased. You'll love it. See you on Friday," he said, and ended the call.

Madeleine stared at her phone. "Fuck!"

* * * *

Julia's novel was beautifully written. It was full of suspense with a terrifying twist at the end that even Madeleine with all her experience had not seen coming. Julia had taken on board the suggestions she had made. It was nearly there, and Madeleine knew it would be a success.

She rang the author. "Jules, I love this latest version. Can we meet to discuss some final changes? A couple of hours should do it."

"That's great. I'm so happy. Can you do Friday? Then I'm away on holiday."

Madeleine hesitated. "I'm usually off Fridays. Can you make it work any other day?"

Julia couldn't. She had three deadlines to meet by Thursday, and her partner Maxine was coming down with some bug.

"Okay," said Madeleine. "Friday it is. Can you make 8am at the St Pancras Hotel for breakfast?"

Julia snorted. "That early? I'm usually still asleep."

"I'm sorry Jules, that's the only time I have."

Damn. Madeleine had wanted a leisurely Friday morning to get ready. She didn't want to risk Julia seeing her with Finn. Or anyone else for that matter. The St Pancras Hotel was far enough away from Euston for that not to happen, but close enough for her to walk to.

She wondered what Liverpool would be like. She googled the Titanic Hotel. Finn obviously never stayed anywhere that wasn't stylish. God, she was looking forward to this trip. She also felt anxious. Should she have slept with him on that first date? Could she really expect a second helping of such magnificent sex?

Tick.... tock....

CHAPTER 6

Madeleine arrived at the St Pancras Hotel in good time. It seemed like a fairy-tale castle to her, and she loved going inside. She hoped that for once, Julia would turn up on time.

She'd bought a well-fitted rose-pink wrap dress for the gallery reception. The neckline was revealing and when she sat and crossed her legs, the dress fell open at the side, revealing her thigh. It would work for the gallery reception and for dinner. She'd packed jeans and a couple of tops and a sweater for the beach walk. What to wear for both the meeting with Julia and the train journey with Finn had been more difficult. She'd eventually found a flowing, long blue shirt dress that buttoned from top to bottom. Perfect to be adjusted for both. At Browns, she and Finn had stumbled into his hotel room, unwilling to break the passionate, desperate kisses. He'd struggled to get off her tight polo-neck dress. She'd wanted him to rip it off. This time it would be easier.

She was deep in these thoughts when Julia arrived, ten minutes late. At first, she didn't see Madeleine but then realized that the woman in a blue dress sitting at a table in the corner with the suitcase was her. She looked different, more open somehow. Attractive.

"Hello, Maddy. I'm so sorry I'm a bit late. Maxine isn't well and I had to sort a few things out."

Madeleine stood up and kissed her on both cheeks.

"I'm sorry to hear that, Jules. I hope she'll be okay for your holiday. Where are you going?" she asked.

"Lanzarote. A colleague of Max's has an apartment there. Just what we both need."

Julia ordered Eggs Benedict and coffee, Madeleine coffee, soft boiled eggs with soldiers and an orange juice. She felt light-hearted, excited, childish, and hoped it didn't show.

Julia was in her late twenties, with blonde hair that fell to her shoulders. A simple, small, dark blue pendant hung round her neck. Her sweater slipped off her right shoulder, showing a delicate blue rose tattooed on the top of her arm. Madeleine hadn't noticed it before and wondered if she had other tattoos. What would they be, and where? The tiny little flutter in her belly, surprised her. She hadn't felt this before. She liked it.

Madeleine loved hearing about Julia's life. It was so different from hers and she found it exciting. Julia had told her that since she'd been a girl, she'd created stories and invented characters, curious figments of her imagination that placed people in strange, unworldly situations. As she got older, the characters became more real, based on people she knew or observed, and often the stories bordered on the erotic. There was more to the stories than sex, but it was the lens through which Julia often processed her past.

Her first self-published story collection touched on the intersection between religion and the body. Julia's parents were devoted Irish Catholics whose families had come to Liverpool after the Famine. Their faith was central to their lives, but in her teenage years Julia had started to doubt. Life for her was about fun, and if there was a bit of sinning, so much the better. At school, she'd been popular with the boys. She wrote about how she'd developed early and allowed them to explore her breasts. If the thrill of being touched was a sin, then bring it on. Occasionally, she'd go to confession and tell the hidden priest what had happened. She didn't go for absolution, but to hear the priest's voice catch as her descriptions became more lurid.

She wrote about past male lovers, some of whom were into some strange stuff. But she also detailed the sleepovers she used to have with her best friend, Alison. Lying naked together in

Julia's single bed allowed them both to discover everywhere that gave pleasure, and they learnt from each other how to build that pleasure until their bodies shook with relief. Julia once told Madeleine that it was only when she had met Maxine that she had re-captured the level of excitement that she'd experienced with Alison.

Madeleine had devoured Julia's short stories a while ago and had wanted to suggest her to Catherine, but erotica was outside the company's remit. Madeleine had thought she'd only ever be able to enjoy Julia's fiction as a fan, and maybe a friend. But then Julia had told her the plot for a novel she was planning. It was a thriller set in Liverpool that involved the church, politics, and lots of lesbian sex. Her take was innovative, and despite the racy content, Madeleine knew Catherine would go for it. The first three chapters had been enough to win both of them over.

Julia pointed at the suitcase. "Are you off somewhere? Who's the lucky fella?"

"I'm going away for a couple of days. I need a break too," she said.

"Anywhere special?" asked Julia

"Your hometown, Liverpool."

Julia clapped. "Lucky you! I've hardly been back since Max led me astray in London. How come you're going? By the way, you look amazing, Maddy. Gorgeous dress!"

"Thanks. I'm going because I heard a lot about Liverpool when it was European City of Culture. I've never been."

Julia reached for her bag. "I'll give you my parents' number. They'd love to meet you and show you round. I've told them what a boss editor you are." She pulled out a notebook, tore a page out of it and scribbled their names and number down.

"Thanks, that's great. Let's see how the weekend goes."

By 11.30, they had discussed all the points Madeline wanted to cover. Julia had agreed to most of the changes and promised to have the next draft ready by the time she got back from holiday.

"I hope Max gets better and you have a great time," Madeleine said.

Julia squeezed her hand as Madeleine hugged her. "Have a great time in Liddypul. I want to hear all about your adventures."

Madeleine watched as Julia left and felt a little shiver of excitement again. In the washroom, she checked her make-up, added an extra layer of lipstick, spritzed her neck and breasts with her favourite Acqua di Parma perfume and undid three buttons at the top of her dress. Then a fourth. She felt light-headed as she walked the short distance to Euston station.

Tick.... tock...

CHAPTER 7

Madeleine walked onto the station concourse towards the ticket office. She spotted Finn looking at his watch and came up behind him. He turned and she was enveloped in a bear hug. "Maddy, you look stunning! I've missed you." She felt his breath on her neck and tilted her head to kiss him deeply.

"Hello...."

That smile. She wanted him again. There. Then. Anywhere. She stepped back and looked at him.

"I love that suit. And you've had a haircut. Well, well. You're a gorgeous surprise, Finn!"

She did a twirl and her dress billowed out around her. "Like it?" she asked.

"Maddy, you're stunning. I love it. And so many buttons, too!"

She put her arms round his neck again and kissed him hard.

"Missed me, then?"

"You have no idea, Maddy. I'm so glad you came!"

He took her hand, and she squeezed his. A few people stared at them. Did Finn look like her toyboy? Did she care? Hell, no. The train was at the platform, its doors open.

"We're in Coach H."

She knew it would be first class. They sat at a table, side by side in the direction of travel.

"I hope no-one else sits opposite us."

"They won't. I reserved all four seats."

Madeleine looked at him. "You're something else!"

"You're beautiful, Maddy," he said. "Glass of prosecco?"

"Why not?" She felt so relaxed, she surprised herself. Finn made even the ridiculous extravagance of the seat purchase seem normal - as if she deserved nothing less.

She snuggled against him as the train left Euston.

"It's good to see you again, Finn. Sorry if I was a bit hard to get hold of. I've been trying to get my head straight after our night together. A lot to think about. Most of all, I loved it. For the first time in so long, I felt alive. I want to feel it again this weekend."

"Maddy, it was amazing for me too. To be completely honest, I hadn't expected it to happen. I thought you'd have a quick drink and leave."

She turned towards him. "You know what I fell for? Your smile. It melted me. You're a wonderful lover, Finn. But I imagine you know that. And full of surprises."

Finn raised his glass. "Thank you. You're a fantastic lover too. And I don't mean just the sex. I love your mind and intelligence. And I think you have some deep needs that are yet to be explored."

"What do you mean?"

"Well, I couldn't help noticing that when I made love to you in front of the window, you loved it... you did, didn't you?"

Another surprise for Madeleine; being understood so quickly by this intuitive devil of a man. "Yes. Knowing that anyone could see me naked, watch us having sex. I loved that feeling."

Finn squeezed her hand. "I know. Now... go to the toilet, take off your bra and undies. Bring them back and give them to me."

"Finn! No, I can't. You want me to do that? Now?"

"Yes."

"For fuck's sake. I can't."

He turned towards her, took her face in his hands, and whispered in her ear. "Do it for me."

She came slowly back to her seat, moving with the train, her eyes on him as others in the carriage eyed her. She put her underwear on the table in front of him and sat down.

She raised her glass. "To a fun weekend!"

"To a fun weekend! Kiss me, beautiful."

She settled into the seat by the window and undid another of her buttons. London slipped away behind her. She gazed out of the window, her face not reacting as his hand slipped inside her open dress and stroked her thighs. She closed her eyes and opened her legs as his fingers explored.

★ ★ ★ ★

The Titanic Hotel had been developed from an old redbrick warehouse in Stanley Dock, a run-down undeveloped area of the city, full of the ghosts of sailing ships, trans-Atlantic liners, gamblers, gin joints, horses and carts, dockers, sailors and brothels. Madeleine felt the vibrations from the cobblestones as the taxi approached the hotel.

"Maddy, I'm sorry. I'll check us in but then I must get over to the Walker. After tonight, we have the entire weekend to ourselves. I promise, no distractions. Just us. We'll just play things by ear. Okay with you?"

It was okay with her.

They walked hand in hand into the foyer, a bellboy following with their cases. She looked around and spotted tables outside by the water.

She gave him a kiss on the cheek. "I want to sit outside and have a coffee. Then I'll need a siesta. With you."

She sat in the sun at one of the tables next to the water. A wedding party was gathering at the end of the colonnade. She stretched her legs to let the dress open and the sun warm her thighs. A waitress came over and she ordered a coffee. When it arrived, the waitress bent over as she slowly and carefully put the coffee, sugar, and milk on the table. To make sure that Madeleine saw her full cleavage? She was liking Liverpool.

Finn came over and stroked her hair. "We're checked in. Come and have a quick siesta."

"Let's sit here first. I'm enjoying my coffee and the view. Keep going. I love my hair being stroked."

She wondered how many other women he'd brought here. Right now, she didn't care. This was her moment and hers alone. The sun broke through and the water in the dock dazzled her. She closed her eyes as Finn took her hand. She knew the waitress was watching as Finn kissed her, holding each side of her face with his hands. She pushed her lips hard against his and opened her mouth to his tongue. She hadn't acknowledged this about herself before their night in the hotel, but she was beginning to realise that she enjoyed putting on a show.

As soon as they were in their room, Madeleine took off her dress. "Let's fuck!"

"It'll have to be a quickie, my lovely. I must go soon."

"I don't care how long it takes. Do it!"

Something about the authority in her voice aroused him.

"Yes, Ma'am."

She lay on the bed, her legs spread. There was no kissing, he was straight in, and her body shook.

"Fuck me, more! Oh, God!"

He didn't hold back. She wanted it; she'd get it. It took him ten thrusts to come inside her. No condom. She pushed him out and fingered herself. She came almost immediately. They lay apart on each side of the bed. She looked across at him.

"I've never come so quickly before. Fuck, that was good... Okay, you can go now!" she said in a tone she'd never used before.

She rolled over and snoozed as Finn showered and dressed. He bent over her and kissed her gently.

"I'll order a taxi for you. 6.45. Sleep well, gorgeous."

Tick.... tock...

CHAPTER 8

Madeleine was deeply asleep when her phone rang. She hadn't meant to sleep so long.

"Hello, sleepyhead…time to get up. A taxi will pick you up from the hotel in an hour. I've left some clothes out for you to wear tonight." Finn sounded business-like.

"Where are you? What clothes?"

"I'm at the gallery to check everything's in place for tonight. Look on the divan at the end of the bed. One hour, Maddy."

Black briefs, a bra and a garter belt were laid out for her. She looked at the label. La Perla. The black stockings were silk and seamed. Next to them was an Agent Provocateur little black dress, on the floor a pair of silver ankle-strap Calvin Klein shoes. She sat on the floor and stared. What on earth was Finn up to? The possibility of wearing clothes like this had never crossed her mind. She could never have afforded or thought for one moment to have chosen them. Was being treated this way offensive? Should she be angry? But she wasn't angry, she was intrigued and excited to be suddenly in the role of a sex goddess with a man who knew his way around sex and goddesses. This unexpected situation made her feel the last thing she expected – powerful.

An hour later, the bedside phone rang. "Good evening, Madam. Your taxi has arrived."

As she came out of the lift, Madeleine knew she'd been noticed, and it felt good. The receptionist stopped in mid-sentence, the waitress stared, and no taxi driver had ever leapt out of a cab for her before.

At the Walker Art Gallery, a trio of string players serenaded the guests as they arrived. The grand marble lobby was filling up. A waiter approached with a tray of champagne, and she took a glass. She looked around as the bubbles tickled her throat.

She saw Finn standing at the top of the marble staircase, a woman she recognised as Rachel Grieves on his arm. A man in a smart blue suit started to clap, and the other guests joined in. Finn and Rachel were both beaming.

The Lord Mayor welcomed Rachel back to her home city. Madeleine realized that when Finn had said this was a big exhibition for him, he hadn't been exaggerating. She noticed he stood to the side, leaving the limelight to his artist and the guests. She caught his eye and he smiled.

As soon as the speeches finished, she made her way to where Finn was talking to the Lord Mayor and Rachel. Finn put his hand out to her, and she squeezed it, smiling, then turned and joined the guests who had moved into the gallery. Rachel's work was bold, full of colour and life. She was the talk of the art world, an artist who mixed large abstract works with small intricate drawings of herself with lovers. The overt sexuality and explicit intimacy of her work stirred Madeleine. This is what it must be like to feel free and at ease with one's body. It reminded her of Julia's writing. She spotted Finn in the corner of the room in deep conversation with a beautifully dressed woman. He pointed out some aspect of the painting they were standing in front of. She watched as the woman laughed and wondered how well Finn knew her. The man in the blue suit was hovering behind them. There was something oddly intriguing about this man that Madeleine couldn't quite work out.

The guests looked at the paintings and gathered in small groups with their drinks, chatting with the air of people who value their own opinions, nonchalantly preening for the busy photographer.

Finn came up behind her and put his arm round her waist. "Maddy, I'm so sorry I've neglected you. You look gorgeous."

"Do you supply complete outfits for all your women?"

He laughed. "I'm glad you wore it. How does it feel?"

There was a smile on her lips too. "You're incorrigible, Finn. After I got over the astonishment - okay, I admit it, it feels sexy, and I love it. Thank you. Do I get to keep it or is it for one night only?"

Finn squeezed her hand. "Of course, you keep it. I want you to wear it on special occasions. You are the star of the evening, Madeleine. All the other women are mere shades of grey. Give me fifteen minutes, and we'll get a taxi. I just have to check in with Rachel. Sadly, she's not joining us. She and her husband are meeting friends. So, it's just you, me, Joanna and Mike, and a few people from the Walker."

"Who are Joanna and Mike?" asked Madeleine.

"Oh, Joanna's one of my biggest clients. I'm sure you'll like her. And Mike is my business partner."

★ ★ ★ ★

A private table was set aside in the Titanic Hotel dining room. Painted on the wall was a quote by Jacques Cousteau, *'The sea, once it casts its spell, holds one in its net of wonder forever.'* Was this what had happened to her? Was she a captive in Finn's net? Madeleine was deep in thought when she felt a tap on her shoulder. Finn was standing with the man in the blue suit and the elegant woman.

"Madeleine, I want you to meet Joanna. She's very interested in buying Rachel's work. And this is Mike."

For an instant her eyes locked with the man in the blue suit.

Then Madeleine smiled and turned to Joanna. "How wonderful. Are you a collector?"

"I am now. This astonishing man has opened me up to many things, art included. I trust him totally."

Finn laughed. "She's the perfect client."

"How wonderful to have one of Rachel's paintings. I love them. It was such a good exhibition," said Madeleine.

"Wasn't it just!" said Joanna.

"We're hoping Joanna will find her way to buying more than one." Mike's voice was deep with a strong Scouse accent. The suit was well cut, and his tie immaculately knotted.

Joanna laughed. "I'll want a good deal from you boys. Let's eat. I'm hungry."

At the dinner table, Madeleine sat next to Finn with Joanna opposite them. Mike was deep in conversation with the other guests and something he said made them laugh out loud.

"That Mike, he's a hoot! What do you do, Madeleine?" asked Joanna.

"I'm a book editor. I work with a small literary agency in London," said Madeleine.

"Oh, that must be so interesting. Would I know any of your authors?" Joanna asked.

"I doubt it. We haven't made a huge breakthrough yet, but the writer I'm working with now is fantastic and I'm very hopeful that this will be the one. She comes from Liverpool."

"What's her name? I might know her."

"Julia McGuigan."

"Which part of Liverpool is she from? I know some McGuigans."

She hadn't read the note Julia had given her with her parents' address. "I don't know, I'm afraid."

"Ah well, never mind. If she makes it, I'd love to meet her sometime."

"I'd be happy to introduce you both," said Madeleine.

Joanna reached across the table and took Madeleine's hand. "I love your outfit. Are you here with Finn?" she asked softly.

"Yes, he invited me."

"Lovely. How's it going?"

"Fine, thanks."

"Good. He's a lovely guy. Have you met Mike yet?"

"No. Well, not until this evening."

Joanna grinned. "You will!"

Madeleine pulled her hand away. "What do you do, when you're not collecting art?" she asked.

"I own a property development company here. We're expanding fast. It's non-stop!"

The conversation round the table was buzzing and Mike had become the centre of attraction. He was a good raconteur, though Madeleine was struggling to catch everything he was saying with his strong Scouse accent. From time to time, he glanced across at Madeleine and smiled. She tried to pretend not to notice, hiding a smile behind her hand, but her eyes betrayed the attraction she was feeling. The waiters kept filling everyone's glasses and Madeleine wished she hadn't drunk and eaten so much.

The meal over, a couple of the guests got up to go and Mike gave them both a hug. Joanna went over to him, and he embraced her, whispering in her ear as he looked over at Madeleine. Joanna laughed and went across to Finn who threw his arms round her. Madeleine got up from the table as Mike came over to her.

"Madeleine, it's a pleasure to meet you. I'm so sorry we didn't have time to talk. Hug?"

He embraced her with a bear-hug that took her by surprise, but that she had no intention of resisting. Over Mike's shoulder, she saw Finn grinning.

Joanna took her leave. "Mike, Finn, thank you both for a great night. Can't wait to have those paintings on my walls. Madeleine, it's been a pleasure. I hope we meet again. Good luck!" Joanna turned and tottered across the room, arm in arm with one of the waiters.

Finn put his arm around Madeleine. "Was that okay? I hope you weren't too bored. Tomorrow, it's just us. Mike and I need to spend a few minutes on a bit of admin. Do you want to go up? I won't be long."

Madeleine was asleep when Finn came into the room. She stirred as he got into bed and felt him kissing her gently on the cheek. Her hand sleepily brushed him away.

"No, Finn. Let's go to sleep. We'll talk in the morning."

Finn made a sad face and turned over, his back towards her. After a few minutes, she heard him snore gently and she fell asleep again.

★ ★ ★ ★

Falling, falling, faster into the dark void.

A look of horror on his face...

Madeleine twisted in the bed and screamed.

"Maddy, hey, I've got you. It's okay..." She was shaking, sobbing.

"What is it, baby, what did you dream?" He held her, stroking her hair. "Breathe deeply, Maddy, breathe..."

She wiped her eyes and sat up.

"I'm sorry. It's a nightmare I get. I'm okay now. Let's go back to sleep."

"Are you sure? Can I get you some water? Do you have nightmares often?"

"Yes, occasionally."

"Poor you. I'm sorry. What do you dream about?

"I'd rather not talk about it. I'm sorry I woke you. Go back to sleep. It's fine."

He put his arms round her and she snuggled against him. "Sleep well," he said.

The next morning, Madeleine woke early. Finn was still asleep. She was dismayed that the damn nightmare had come while she was here, on her weekend away. Watching Finn sleep calmed her, and she felt her strength coming back, along with the languorous sexiness of the day before. She bent over Finn and pressed a nipple against his mouth. He instinctively sucked, then bit hard. She gripped his hair and threw her head back.

For an hour they fucked, made love, fucked, building an appetite for breakfast.

In the shower, they soaped each other and kissed under the power-jet. In front of the mirror, she noticed how her body was both bruised and glowing as she pulled on her jeans and a sweater. Her skin tingled, and she felt totally fulfilled. Fuck the nightmares.

In the dining room, they ordered the Full English and a big pot of coffee. After they had sat for a while in silence, savouring the relaxed, contented feelings in their bodies, Madeleine tapped his plate with her knife. "You know, you really hurt me. I don't think my body can take more war wounds. Why do you bite so much?"

He carried on eating, not looking at her. "You responded to it. You liked it. Especially on your breasts and nipples, as I recall."

"Look at me, Finn. You like doing it? Hurting someone?"

Finn was thoughtful. "I wouldn't say I enjoy hurting. I do like playing with domination and submission. That inevitably includes giving and receiving some degree of pain. It's about both partners' enjoyment. It's not hurting; it's a sensual pain... didn't you feel that?"

Madeleine thought for a moment and said, "Yes, I think I did".

"Anyway," he said. "Tell me about last night. Did you enjoy the exhibition? Anyone you particularly liked?"

Madeleine nodded. "Finn, it was spectacular. Joanna was fun. Very interesting. She's obviously done well. I only had a brief chat with Rachel. I have to say, she was the one person I'd have loved to have come to dinner with us. I'd have enjoyed getting to know her a bit."

"Yes, that was unfortunate. But hopefully, you'll meet her when we have the London exhibition. Anyone else you liked?"

"I didn't really get a chance to chat with anyone else. But they seemed like a fun bunch. Oh, and Mike seems an interesting guy."

Finn leaned forward and grinned. "You liked him?"

"He's a bit larger than life!"

"Yes. He's a great guy. I'd really like you to get to know him better."

"Yes, I think I'd like to," she said.

Finn looked at her intently.

"Mike and I go back a long way. He's a sort of father figure to me. When I was at university he came and talked to us budding art historians. When he discovered I wanted to deal in art but was hopeless at business, he offered to help. We just clicked immediately. He was a financial consultant who loved art, so it was a good match. Now we're business partners and he's given up his practice. I know the art, he knows business. It works. And as we got to know each other, it turned into a close friendship as well."

He paused, then said, "We share everything."

She sat back. "What do you mean, you share everything?"

"I mean, we have no secrets."

"None?"

"None."

"So, what does he know about me?"

Finn held her gaze. "I told him what a great lover you are."

"What we do is private between us. I don't want you to discuss me like this." Her voice was serious.

"Are you upset?" he asked.

"No. But I don't think I like it, and I don't want you to tell him anything more."

"Sweetheart, Mike and I share everything. It's part of our relationship. He's completely discreet. He likes you."

She shook her head. "Okay, well. I'm glad he likes me. But please, Finn. I don't want you to talk about me with him anymore. And this may seem odd, but can you ask him not to wear Vetiver aftershave when I'm around? My ex, Richard, wore it. It was weird for me, smelling it again."

"Oh, okay." Finn smiled, wiped his mouth with his napkin, and stood up. "Now let's go and see the naked Anthonys on the beach at Crosby!"

CHAPTER 9

Finn took her hand as they walked between the dunes and onto the beach. The family groups, dog walkers and couples enjoying the warm Sunday, melted into the vast expanse. In front of them were the 100 life-sized cast-iron statues that stretched along the beach and a kilometre into the sea. The figures gave the impression of walking into the water. The deeper into the sea they got, the more barnacled they were.

"These are extraordinary. Another client?" she asked.

"I wish he was. Every time I come here, I feel moved and inspired. Come, let me show you."

Finn watched her face light up as she looked around. He was enjoying making her happy. It had been a long time since he'd felt like this with a woman. He enjoyed her company, her conversation. She was interesting and intelligent. And sex with her was total. No half-measures. A breath-taking intensity.

Ever since their meeting in Brown's, she'd been impossible to get out of his mind. She didn't seem aware of her sexual power. The memory of that incredible night had not diminished. Her passion and abandonment had left him breathless, drained, exhausted. She had taken everything that he could give, and she wanted more. It was not only wild sex; she had a loving gentleness that embraced him when he lay in her arms. Then she'd turned into a tigress, using his body for her pleasure, shaking as orgasms cascaded through her. She was full of so many surprises. He remembered how she had got out of bed to go to the bathroom, then drawn back the curtains, standing naked in front of the window for several minutes, exposed to whoever might be looking from the buildings across Albemarle Street. He'd watched her silhouetted in the window and come up behind her as she spread her legs and bent over, grasping the sides of the window. This time there was no foreplay, no gentleness, no waiting. His turn to take. They had both instinctively switched roles, ceding control and taking it back over and over, through the night. And here they were, together again, so relaxed.

He had to remind himself that this was meant to be a game for him. And for Mike.

★ ★ ★ ★

The Gormley figures stretched for three kilometres along the beach. Finn and Madeleine walked hand in hand, stopping to kiss every few minutes. They stood beside the erect figures and took selfies. Finn asked her to embrace one of them and she laughed as she posed with him.

"Lift up your sweater."

"Seriously? But there are people…?"

"No one will see. And if they do, what does it matter? You have beautiful breasts."

Slowly, nervously, excited, she raised her sweater.

"You know what? I'd love it if you didn't wear a bra when we're out. Come here."

He removed her bra, bent down, and took a nipple in his mouth. She looked around. No one was close, and she held his head tight to her breast. She felt him suckling her, drawing her nipple into his mouth. His teeth started to nip her, and she held his head tighter.

"Please Finn, not so hard. My nipples are so tender. It's too much."

He nipped her gently one more time and stood up. "Don't move. That's perfect. Look over towards the sea." He had taken several pictures on his iPhone before she realized.

"I don't I want you taking pictures of me like this. Stop it," she said.

"They're just a great memory of an amazing weekend. And they're private. I promise you."

"I mean it, Finn."

"So do I."

He took her hand, and for a while they walked on along the beach in silence, the seagulls swooping and weaving on the air currents before coming to land on the sand, hopping, searching for small crabs and food carelessly thrown away. A gull spotted a bag of chips in a child's hand and swooped. The girl's scream and the feeble flapping of her mother's hands didn't stop the bird as it soared, swallowing a huge chip.

The tide was out, and they walked barefoot, skipping in and out of the water, splashing, laughing. Anyone watching them might have assumed they were on their honeymoon.

An occasional cloud passed over the sun and with it came a cooler wind that whiffled around them, bringing them together for warmth. Small swirls of sand shuffled around their feet. He stopped walking and pulled her close.

"I love that sound."

She looked around. "What sound?"

"The sound of sand breaking free and rushing alongside us." He put his finger to his lips. "Listen."

They stood together, unmoving, silent. After a minute, he broke into the quiet.

"We miss so much when we don't listen properly, don't you think? It's the same for me with looking at paintings. They aren't only visual. They have sound too. When I stand in front of a painting, I can hear it as well as see it. There's a conversation going on between the people you see, between a boat and the water, between a river and the riverbank, between the sky and the sea. If you stand long enough, you can hear the conversations. When I go into a room full of paintings, I wonder if they are happy together, if they like each other. If one is taken down, do the others feel sad? Do they wonder who will take its place? Does a landscape wonder if the woman in the portrait next to it enjoys what she sees, and would like to walk along its road? Would the woman be disappointed if she couldn't take that walk?"

She looked at him quizzically. "Hmmm. Interesting. I've never thought about that. Let's walk on. I want to hear more."

"I could talk about art for hours, Maddy. But I want to know about you. Where were you born?"

His question took her by surprise.

"In Oxfordshire. Why do you ask?"

"I'm interested. I suspect we have very different backgrounds."

"Maybe. Were you born in Dublin?"

"No, in Bray."

She grinned. "The world's capital of hurling and filmmaking."

"You remembered! So, come on, tell me about your childhood."

She looked down and kicked at the sand. He felt her body stiffen.

"It was pretty uneventful, really. Apart from the fact that my mother was an alcoholic. My father abandoned us when I was five. I was sent away to school, which I quite enjoyed, mainly because I couldn't wait to get away from home. Both are dead now."

"Poor you. Do you have any siblings?"

She looked away. "I had a brother. He died young. There, that's my potted childhood story. What's yours?"

He took her arm, and they started walking again.

"Well, I told you my father was a weak man. My mother was a total monster. She dominated him. When he tried to stand up for himself, she'd lay into him."

She turned and looked at him. "What, physically?"

He nodded. "Yes, and verbally too. She was a control freak. I used to run up to my bedroom and slam the door shut, trying not to hear. They're both still alive. Still together. God knows why.

I've cut off from them, but my sister for some reason, still sees them. I wasn't sent away to school, but I had a lovely diversion in my teens called Moira. I thought she was the love of my life!"

Madeleine stopped and twisted away from him.

"Maddy, what's the matter? You okay?" he asked.

She put her head in her hands and took a deep breath, then turned back to him.

"I'm sorry, thinking about my parents and my past always rattles me. I'll be okay." She took his hand. "Is that why you don't want to commit to relationships?" she asked.

"Never seen the point. Life is much more fun without it. Anyway, I don't think I'd know where to start. Maddy, what's the matter? You had a terrible nightmare too last night. Was it about your past?"

"Yes...no. Look, do you mind if we don't talk about it?" She squeezed his hand. "Seems like neither of us has had it that easy."

"Of course. Let's change the subject," he said.

"Yes please."

By the time they reached the end of the long beach and walked back, they had discussed music, argued over the importance of football, explored tastes in art, recited poems, Finn had shown off his prowess at handstands, and Maddy hers at building sandcastles.

★ ★ ★ ★

It was late on Sunday night by the time she got home and ran a bath. A weekend she'd never forget. She'd loved Liverpool. Not just Crosby beach, but also dinner in Wreckfish and brunch in Queen's Bistro the next morning. He'd taken her back to the Walker and shown her a painting he'd loved as a child, *'And when did you last see your father?'* It portrayed a small boy from a Royalist family being interrogated by Cromwell's troops. She'd wondered if Finn felt connected to the young boy who might innocently give away his father's hiding place.

On the train back to London, she had rested her head against Finn's shoulder as he played with her hair, curling it around his fingers. Even in first class, the carriage was full, and she was glad he'd again booked the seats opposite. A man had tried to sit down in one of them. Finn had told him they were reserved. The man had started to argue, saying there was no one sitting there. Something about Finn's tone of voice had made the man leave. Maybe she really was worthy of such extravagance, maybe their privacy as they kissed and cuddled *was* the most important thing in the world at that precise moment in time. He made her feel cherished, pampered, wanted. They parted at Euston promising to meet again soon. He held her head tight as they kissed, his eyes smiling in that way he had that made her tremble.

As she lay in the bath, she could still feel his fingers exploring her, how their kisses changed from gentle to demanding in a moment. Her body felt so raw and tender. It would take a few days for the bruises to disappear. She didn't know how she felt about the red weals on her body, but she knew it was something new to her, and surprisingly in a good way. She needed time to reflect on the weekend and her eyes closed.

Tick.... tock....

CHAPTER 10

Madeleine tried hard to focus on her work. She deflected the questions from her colleagues about her weekend and got away with glowing descriptions of the statues on Crosby beach and how much Liverpool had impressed her.

Lots of emails had come in over the weekend, as well as several manuscripts. She settled down to answer them. Nothing from Finn. A text arrived from Julia.

'So how was my lovely Liddypul? Did you get in touch with my parents? Writing going well though Max is better and very demanding of my time!!'

'Loved Liverpool. Glad Max is better, but make sure you get that draft finished! No, sorry, I didn't get in touch. Maybe next time. Let me know when you're back. Good luck with the writing! Can't wait to see what you've done.'

'Can't wait to show you. I'm really excited.'

'I've been meaning to ask you. Where did you get your tattoo done?'

'You noticed it! That's nice. In Liverpool years ago. Have you got one?'

'No, but I might.'

'Please do. I can help if you want.'

'I'd like that. See you on Tuesday ☺'

She got her coat and went out into the street for a walk round the block. The Plane trees were starting to let their leaves go. They cartwheeled along the pavement in gusts from the wind. Madeleine skipped along with them, a spring in her step.

By Tuesday there was still no contact from Finn. Several times her finger had hovered over his number. She'd resisted and called Shammie instead; they arranged to meet in their favourite pub.

Shammie had already drunk a glass from the bottle of Prosecco when Madeleine arrived.

"So, my lovely, tell all!!" She filled Madeleine's glass and topped up her own.

"It was a great weekend. Couldn't have been better! You were so right about Finn. So, thank you. I feel revived, renewed, alive. I'd forgotten what it's like to abandon myself. Finn is everything you said he'd be. He's an interesting guy, an art dealer. Liverpool's a fun place too. There are things though that make me uncomfortable."

"Like what?"

"He bought me a very expensive, sexy outfit to wear in Liverpool. Things I'd never wear normally."

"Did you wear them?"

"Yes, I did. I couldn't resist trying them on and I felt and looked good in them, strangely powerful, which really surprised me. I think though, in doing that, I've gone too far, made him think I'm something I'm not. It's a misogynistic, controlling thing to do to a woman, don't you think?"

"Maybe. But the important thing is, you felt good in it. If you hadn't you wouldn't have worn this outfit. Right?"

"True."

"Then by choosing to wear it, you were choosing to because you felt good, and you wanted to. Remember that. It wasn't him dictating what you do. You chose to do it, for your pleasure."

Madeleine took a sip of wine and nodded. "Thank you, Shammie. I needed to hear that. It's been worrying me."

"Remember, you're the one in control. Enjoy him, have fun, see where it goes. You deserve it. When are you seeing him again?"

Madeleine was hesitant. "We haven't made any plans. I've got a pile of work to do anyway, so probably just as well. I'm torn between seeing him right now and waiting...you know...making him wait."

Shammie remembered a past encounter and grinned. "I love making a guy wait. Make him beg!"

"Haha! You know, Finn did that to me, in bed. He refused to let me touch myself and then, well...brought me so close and then stopped. I was screaming."

Shammie laughed. "Yay!! That's wonderful. So, what else happened?"

Madeleine told her about meeting some friends of Finn's and Rachel Grieves at the exhibition. Shammie had read about her. "What's Rachel like?"

"She seems very down to earth but she was very busy, and I didn't really get a chance to talk with her. I loved her paintings, especially the small drawings. They were so intimate. I met Finn's business partner, Mike."

"I didn't know he had one."

"Nor did I. But he does. And it seems they share everything."

"What do you mean, share everything? Sounds interesting."

"I don't know. It's all a bit odd."

Shammie leant forward and took her hand.

"I wouldn't worry. You can look after yourself. But don't put up barriers, my darling. Nothing quite like opening new doors in my experience. And you can always say no."

Madeleine sat back in her chair. "Thanks. I'll remember your words of wisdom. So, what have you been up to?"

"You know, Maddy, it's easy for Jacob and me to take our relationship for granted, especially as it's open. But sometimes, like this weekend, we have magical times, just the two of us together, feeling so close. We're soulmates. I'm really lucky."

★ ★ ★ ★

Madeleine was deeply asleep when her phone rang. One in the morning.

"I want you."

"Finn, it's the middle of the night." He had interrupted a dream.

"You loved it when I woke you up in the night. I'm missing you. I can still taste you and feel you. I want you, Maddy."

Madeleine could feel herself stirring. "Okay. Come over."

"I'm outside your house."

Madeleine's thoughts and worries disappeared in a blissful few hours of Finn time. Their lovemaking once again moved from gentle to abandoned and back again. They kissed for ages, giving and taking, absorbed by each other. They explored each other's bodies, and for the first time in years, she had an explosive orgasm from oral sex. He whispered in her ear how he wanted to watch her having sex with other people, and this to her surprise, aroused her too. They lay in each other's arms and gently kissed, drifted to sleep, and woke up smiling. Before he left, she insisted they make love again, even though she knew she was still sore, and it would probably hurt. She didn't care. Telling her lover what to do and when to do it felt so good. She lay in bed, smelling him on her and in her.

Tick.... tock....

CHAPTER 11

Mike woke with a hangover. He groaned as he pushed his feet into his slippers and got up unsteadily from his bed. Slowly he made his way to the bathroom. A face he barely recognised looked back at him, baggy, with bloodshot eyes. Still handsome, he thought, but the grooming was not what it should be. He stuck his tongue out. Furry. He filled a glass with water and slowly drank it down, immediately needing a pee.

At fifty-five, he was as fit as any man in his thirties, but he felt he'd let things slip recently. He flexed his muscles. Not bad, but his belly had expanded a bit. He'd have to get back to a gym regime and tone up his muscles. He would get his head shaved again.

He had dreamt about Finn's new friend, Madeleine. What a delight she had been! He hoped he'd get a chance to see her again. She was probably the biggest challenge Finn had presented him with in the ten years they'd known each other, and he was determined not to fail.

He put on his big heavy dressing gown, one of the few things he'd kept from his marriage all those years ago. In the kitchen, he put coffee in the percolator and stood waiting as the gas burner did its work. The percolator and the lovely bowl he used to drink his morning coffee were gifts from his sister. They had a good relationship, and he was glad she lived nearby. They had grown up in poverty in the Dingle, but both now lived in the fashionable part of the city, near Sefton Park and Lark Lane.

They'd come a long way, but he wasn't ashamed of their past. He was proud of it. Now his sister looked after their aged mother, and he paid the bills. The two women both nagged him to find a wife and many of his sister's friends had tried to snare him. But having had the worst divorce possible in which he'd lost nearly everything to a woman who had never loved him, he wasn't going to fall into that trap again. His relationship with Finn, both business and personal was all he needed.

He'd met Finn in Dublin where he'd moved twelve years ago for a fresh start. He knew a Professor in the Department of Art History and Architecture at Trinity who wanted to try and get some business acumen into her students' heads.

Finn was his most interesting student; he had immediately grasped the opportunity he was being given. Over many pints of Guinness, they developed a friendship that turned into a business relationship. They knew they complemented each other's strengths; and, it soon became clear, their weaknesses too. Finn had introduced him to his girlfriend at the time, and he had quickly noticed that Finn did nothing to stop her flirting with him. When Finn had gone to the bar for more drinks, she had whispered in his ear that Finn got off on her flirting with other men. She'd then leant over and kissed him hard. From the corner of his eye, he could see Finn at the bar looking at them almost gleefully. Mike had slept with her that night. He'd never come across this fetish before, but he wasn't going to complain. It wasn't long after that Finn had let slip his other sexual interest. He had the same one. It had built into a great relationship.

He took a shower, dressed, and sat at his desk going over the figures for their business. They had over-spent in the last year and he was worried about their lack of working capital. They had already used half the large overdraft he'd negotiated with his friendly bank. Finn would have to face the fact he couldn't just spend with impunity. They were on a knife-edge with a potential exhibition in Athens. Finn had discovered a new Greek artist and loved her work. He was sure she'd be a huge success. Against his better judgement, he'd agreed only after Finn's coup in getting Rachel Grieves as a client. Selling eight paintings on the opening night in Liverpool had been a great result and would bring in nearly £250,000. If it was all for them, there'd be no problem, but it wasn't. From experience they'd sell another two with luck. Probably the cheaper small drawings. Then the exhibition would move to London where he had no doubt they'd sell well. But until then, they needed to be careful. Finn had developed great contacts in the art world. He was a consummate salesman. But they were going to need the Greek artist to be as successful as Finn predicted for the finances to balance.

He picked up his phone and looked at the message Finn had sent him, detailing his night with Madeleine. He'd been pleasantly surprised when he'd first seen her in the Walker. Sophisticated, self-contained, confident, intelligent, fascinating. Nice legs, thick auburn hair with a hint of red falling to her shoulders, a full, beautiful, mature body. He guessed, early 40s. Not Finn's usual type at all. And she'd worn The Dress. It fitted perfectly. Finn had done well in getting the right sizes from her clothes while she showered after their first night together.

He had seemed unusually protective of her, but Mike knew exactly what buttons to press. Playing them both for a while would be fun. If he played it a bit cool with Madeleine now, he'd soon have Finn begging him to make a move on her. So delightfully predictable!

He now had to contact the buyers to arrange payment as soon as possible. And that bloody Athens exhibition to pull together. Athens… maybe a trip to Athens could include Madeleine. She too was worth investing in.

CHAPTER 12

It was a Sunday, but Madeleine was determined to concentrate on her work. As well as finishing Julia's novel, she was under pressure from Catherine to take up more book launches and book events. The agency needed more good writers to develop and publish. They were doing alright but money was tight, and Catherine carried the financial burden. Madeleine loved the job and respected Catherine as an agent, editor, and boss. She'd agreed to promote the agency further and accept more invitations. They knew that Julia's novel was potentially a huge commercial success, and the agency would receive a lot of kudos. She was going to have to get Finn to give her more notice in future. She didn't want to have to say no to him, but she needed her time, too.

After lunch, Madeleine spent some time in the garden cutting back the plants that had died off. She was careful not to disturb the beautiful webs where large spiders sat immobile, waiting for an unsuspecting fly to land in their trap. Which was she, the spider, or the fly? She shuddered. Never again would she allow herself to be controlled. Final groups of swallows gathered on the telephone wires, ready to escape back to Africa. A dove fluttered onto the birdbath and sipped from the water. In the hedge, a quarrel of sparrows chattered at the top of their voices. She stood still, listening to the songs of the birds. She envied them their freedom. For her, Autumn was a depressing time of year. Any distractions were welcome.

Julia called.

"It's done, it's done! When can we meet up?"

"Wonderful! I'm so excited. Can you come to the office on Tuesday, say 11.30? I'll get Catherine to join us."

She went back into the garden, dead-headed more plants, and pulled out weeds. After a couple of hours, the garden looked better, ready for the shorter days and the approaching long sleep. She felt better too, and noticed with satisfaction that the garden looked a lot better than when Richard used to do it.

She called Finn. An overseas dial tone. She hung up.

★ ★ ★ ★

Catherine loved Julia's book. The three of them spent a morning discussing the latest draft and planning which publishers to send it to. The twist was even more devastating than in the early drafts. Above all, it was beautifully written. It fit into several genres – crime, romance, thriller - which wouldn't make it easy to place, but Catherine shared Madeleine's gut feeling about it. If she could place it with a publisher with vision, it had a real chance; Catherine was even thinking awards.

Over lunch, Madeleine and Julia toasted the future success of the book, fantasising about the perfect casting for a film adaptation; Jennifer Lawrence, Lesley Manville, Suranne Jones, Cillian Murphy, David Tennant…

The second novel would be much harder to write; readers would expect her heroine to return and continue her nefarious ways. Madeleine and Julia worked well together, bouncing ideas and plots between them. By the time the bottle was empty, they had worked through some interesting and very dark storylines, almost vying for who could be the most outrageous.

Julia reached across the table and took Madeleine's hand. "I'm so glad I have you as an editor. We have fun, don't we? I really like you, Maddy." Madeleine held her gaze for a fraction too long and blushed. "I really like you too."

Tick…. tock….

CHAPTER 13

Tourists still flocked to Athens in early autumn. The cafes and restaurants were full, and the air beautifully warm. Finn loved the way of life here. He and Mike were sitting outside the Blue Bear in Exarchia Square enjoying a Mythos beer. They'd had a long day planning the exhibition in a trendy gallery in Kolonaki, and this was their last evening before flying back to London. Kolonaki and Exarchia were geographically close, but miles away in every other aspect. Exarchia was edgy, the anarchist centre of Athens, full of refugee squats and anarchist banners hanging from lampposts and trees. The statue of a young boy was sprayed in pink paint. Street food vendors sold felafel, souvlaki, and chicken kebabs. Graffiti was everywhere in Athens and Exarchia had some of the best.

Kolonaki, by contrast, was chic, sophisticated, expensive. Finn loved both, but it was the chaos of Exarchia that attracted him most and he hoped Madeleine would like the edginess of it too. He'd look up some suitable poems for her and wondered if she'd read any Cavafy or Kazantzakis. The way they were opening to each other excited him, sharing their interests, feeling free to express and share even their most deeply buried desires.

As they drank their beers, Mike expressed his doubts about Madeleine. "Yes, she's attractive, intelligent, sexy… but I doubt if she'd ever be persuaded to come to the Club. It's a pity because she'd be popular. When are you seeing her next?"

"I'm not sure," Finn said. "She rang, but I was asleep. I'll call her when we get back."

"Are you sure you're not falling for her, my friend? That's not allowed to happen. You know that don't you?" said Mike. Finn gave him a friendly punch on the arm. "Have I ever let you down, Mikey boy?"

"Okay, but be careful, Finn." They finished their beers and walked back to the hotel to pack for their flight home.

The Heathrow Express took them back into London and Mike made his way to Euston for the Liverpool train. Finn was glad to be back in his Paddington flat; small, cosy but elegant. One bedroom was all he needed for now. It was his private sanctuary.

He showered, made some scrambled eggs, and had a catnap before starting work.

In the evening he went to his local pub and called Madeleine. She sounded pleased to hear from him but was out at a book launch and couldn't talk long. She asked him where he'd been.

"Athens? Hmm. You must tell me all about it. Let's talk in the morning. I'd love you to come for dinner one evening this week," she said. They arranged for Thursday.

He turned to the young woman sitting next to him at the bar and smiled. "Hello, I'm Finn."

⋆ ⋆ ⋆ ⋆

Finn decided to walk part of the way from Paddington to Putney to see Madeleine. A brisk walk would help build up an appetite for the dinner she was cooking. It was dusk and the air was pleasantly autumnal.

As soon as she opened the front door, he could smell something delicious coming from the kitchen. It mingled with her scent as he kissed her and stroked her face.

"I've missed you, Maddy."

She took his hand, and they walked through the hall and into the kitchen. Candles were burning on the table. He showed her the wine he'd brought.

"I hope red is ok."

She handed him a corkscrew and turned to the hob where a sauce was simmering. He pulled the cork, put the bottle on the table and came over to her, standing behind her, his arms around her waist, nuzzling her hair.

"You smell gorgeous! It's the same scent you were wearing when we first met," he said.

She turned to him, her eyes twinkling. "Yes, it's Acqua di Parma. I wore it in Liverpool, too. I hope you like fish. It's a Nigella recipe."

"A beautiful woman cooking another beautiful woman's dish. What's not to like? I'm feeling very hungry now."

She kissed him deeply. "So am I."

They'd eaten the meal greedily, both yearning for the main course. And it hadn't disappointed. They lay in each other's arms, the duvet pulled close around them. He felt so good with her, as though they had known each other for years.

Finn stroked Madeleine's back and shoulders as she snuggled closer to him. "I want you always to be honest with me. Can you do that?" she asked.

"Yes, of course," he replied.

Madeleine propped herself up on her elbow and looked at her lover. "Tell me what you meant about sharing everything with Mike."

He turned to face her. "Ah...okay. Mike and I go back a long way. He's been a bit of a mentor to me, and we don't have secrets from each other. I guess that's what I meant."

"Nothing else?"

"Er…no, not really. What makes you ask?"

She told him she thought it might mean they would share her. Finn propped himself up with pillows.

"Would you like that?"

"So, you did mean that, didn't you?" she said.

"Yes."

"And if I say no? Is that the end of our relationship?"

"Are you saying no?"

He watched her as she answered.

"I don't know what I'm saying. I know nothing about Mike. But… yes, okay, he's an attractive looking man. I can see that. Finn, this is all so new to me. I've always been a one-man woman." She ran a finger over his lips. "Okay. I'm not denying I find the idea exciting. But I'm not saying yes. Nor am I saying no."

He felt himself harden and pressed himself against her thigh.

"So, you'll think about it," he said.

Tick… tock…

CHAPTER 14

The bouncer outside the Club recognized Finn and opened the heavy door for him. Finn saw Honey behind the desk, taking the names of members as they arrived and remembered how submissive she had been when he played with her. That had been a while ago now. Too long.

He felt at home in the familiar surroundings with the soft, dim lighting, sofas, and chairs along two walls, the stage at the far end with three large wooden crosses, the fourth wall with the vaulting horses and a table full of equipment for sale. He felt a thrill of pleasure as he inspected the floggers, canes, whips, paddles, nipple clamps, collars, cages, wrist and ankle cuffs and other toys for pleasure and pain laid out there. He mingled with the hundred or so members. He knew most of them and enjoyed their company. The Dominant men and women wore leather, rubber or latex. Submissives wore little and sat or stood quietly next to their Dominants. Many were collared, some wore masks. He could smell the excitement and expectation filling the room.

This was an exclusive club and members could only join on the recommendation of two existing members and payment of a large annual fee. He remembered the first time Mike had brought him here. They'd come with Jenny, a submissive woman wearing a very short, revealing dress with no underwear. Mike had introduced him to friends there and he'd been surprised at how friendly and interesting everyone was.

On the stage, two men and a woman were tied to the crosses. They were being flogged and had red, swollen welts on their bodies. The men on the crosses had erections and the woman seemed similarly aroused. A very large woman was tied face down on a vaulting horse, her huge breasts falling each side of the horse. She had clamps on her nipples and a Dominatrix caned her bottom, taking her time, teasing the moaning woman. As each stroke landed, she cried out and her body shook. She hadn't used a safe word at any point, so he knew for certain that she was a willing participant. Everything here was consensual.

In the middle of a group of people was his friend Mistress Jasmine and her male submissive, Number 1. Jasmine was holding court, a Queen Bee in the centre of the room, chatting with a couple he didn't know. She spotted Finn and beckoned him over.

"Mistress, a pleasure as always. Your outfit is magnificent," he said.

She was dressed from head to toe in red rubber. Three-inch metal spikes protruded from wide shoulder pads. She wore deep-red lipstick and thick false eyelashes. Her black hair was tied in a tight bun. She held out her hand to Finn and he kissed the huge red ring on her wedding finger.

"Finn, meet Peter and Isabella. They're new members. I want you to make them welcome. My dears, Finn is one of our Dominants and I'm sure you'll both enjoy his company."

Finn grinned. "Thank you, Mistress. You look great, Isabella."

She was wearing a man's shirt open all the way down, undies, stockings, suspenders, and high heels. He noticed with pleasure how large her nipples were. Her long brown hair fell halfway down her back. Finn guessed she was about 35, Peter much the same age, with a shaven head. His leather trousers were tight, and he wore a sleeveless black t-shirt.

"Peter and Isabella came to one of my parties. Peter thinks he's a Dom but I'm not so sure. Isabella is wonderfully submissive, aren't you my dear?"

Isabella nodded respectfully. "Yes Mistress. Thank you."

Mistress Jasmine took Finn to one side. She wanted to know if he had any new friends to introduce to her.

"Not yet Mistress, but I'm working on it."

She looked sternly at him. "Good. It's been a while. Now take Isabella over to the sofa and get to know her. Peter, you come with me. It's time to play."

Jasmine pulled at the lead connected to the collar on Number 1 and Peter followed them. They went across to a vaulting horse.

"Peter, strap Number 1 to the horse and flog him. I want to see you in action."

From the sofa, Finn noticed Jasmine was not particularly impressed with Peter. He hadn't flogged Number 1 hard enough and had not been accurate. He had missed No 1's backside three times and flogged his upper thigh instead. He had taken too long to build up to the heavy, sustained flogging she expected. Worst of all, he had flogged him once over his kidneys. He had a lot to learn. Finn turned his attention back to Isabella.

"When they've finished, it's your turn, Isabella." She squeezed Finn's hand.

Finn strapped Isabella to the St Andrew cross on the stage. Jasmine told Peter to come and watch how it should be done. Isabella was held tight by the straps on her wrists, ankles and around her belly. Her head hung down and her hair partly covered her face. She was still wearing the open shirt that had been tied back but all other clothing had been removed and her body was totally visible to everyone. Anyone new to the club was of interest to the members and a large group was standing in front of the stage watching. Finn knew he had to be at his best. He lifted Isabella's head and looked deep into her eyes. They were distant, lost in another place. She moaned as the first nipple clamp was tightened. Peter tried to approach Finn but was held back by Mistress Jasmine. Playing with a man's wife while the husband was forced to watch was a pleasure Finn didn't often have the chance to enjoy. He made the most of it, making great play of attaching a clamp to her other nipple and weights to her labia. On Jasmine's orders Peter went up on stage to feel Isabella and tell everyone how wet she was. It was enough to prove that

Peter, as the Mistress had thought, was submissive. Finn knew that Jasmine would develop him herself.

Finn held the flogger to Isabella's lips, and she kissed it. Then, starting softly, he built up the strength of the strokes until by the fiftieth he was flogging her as hard as he could. He made her count the number of times the flogger kissed her breasts, belly, and thighs. Her body was covered in sweat and red welts. He wiped her armpits with his fingers and smelt the arousing pheromones. As Finn applied the vibrator, the audience applauded her willing helplessness and multiple orgasms. When Finn signalled he had finished, Jasmine ordered Peter to remove the clamps and weights and untie his wife. She slumped to the floor and Peter held her. Isabella was breathing deeply. Her face was beatific. Jasmine nodded towards Finn, acknowledging his abilities. The audience applauded, and he bowed. Two new submissives for the Club. They needed a third, and Finn knew exactly who he wanted it to be.

* * * *

The next day, Mike called. He was furious. The gallery owner in Athens had emailed asking them to postpone the exhibition for a year, citing administrative problems. Greece was a hard place to do business in, and all the concerns he had had from the beginning were coming true. Finn had been too confident. It was a disaster. Finn waited until Mike had finished, then quietly reminded him that Helene was a very good up-and-coming artist and was working on paintings especially for the exhibition. It was a risk, but it was worth taking and they would sort it out by going to Athens and talking to the gallery and Helene themselves. And how about they took Madeleine with them? Kill two birds. But Mike wanted to pull out. They needed to save money.

"Come on Mike, it's not like you to give in so easily. Even if the exhibition is postponed a bit, it won't matter too much. In fact, it might help. Come on, let's make this happen. If it doesn't, we'll know for sure where we stand and we can move on. I'm feeling good about Maddy. I think she'd come with us."

"I'll think about it. I'll call you later."

Mike would come round. He'd been excited about Helene's work as well, and the bait of Madeleine in Athens would be too much for him to refuse. The trip to Athens would happen. It was time to take Madeleine to dinner at Browns Hotel again.

The dinner had been excellent, and Madeleine was so relaxed this time. Without him saying anything, she had arrived wearing the clothes from Liverpool.

She lay snuggled up with him in the big bed. They had abandoned themselves to each other and were exhausted. She played with his chest hairs as he caressed her. He leant over her and nuzzled her breasts.

"Maddy, you know, I feel so close to you, it's amazing."

She sat up. "You promised you'd tell me the truth. If I come to Athens with you, will Mike be involved? Is that what you want? Tell me straight."

"Would you like him to be?"

"That's not what I asked, Finn. Tell me."

He sat up and took her hand. He had something to tell her. Ever since he was a teenager, he'd had this thing about wanting to see the woman he was with, having sex with another man. He didn't understand it. But it excited him. He'd tried to stop the feeling many times, but it had never gone away for long. Mike knew about it, and he was turned on by sleeping with other guys' wives and girlfriends. It was a power thing. So yes, if the woman was willing, they always shared her.

"Does it shock you?" he asked.

Madeleine looked at him and stroked his cheek. "No, it doesn't shock me. I'd guessed. Remember how I responded to you telling me how you'd like me to have sex with a stranger?" she asked.

Finn squeezed her hand and kissed her. "Yes, I do."

"I have something to tell you, too," she said. "I've lived an unadventurous and, frankly, repressed life. I've had some awful times, times I never ever want to repeat. But I'm not a total innocent. Meeting you was the catalyst I needed to make this happen. I'm having great sex with you and even in my wildest fantasies, I never imagined myself so open and abandoned. I feel very close to you. But I'll decide on my own if I want to have a threesome with you and Mike. If it happens, it's on my terms, not yours. Mike's an attractive guy and he's more my age. I'll want to meet him alone and get to know him better if anything's to happen."

This was just how Finn wanted it, too. Knowing Madeleine was with another man, kissing him, getting turned on while he waited at home - wondering, fantasizing, feeling helpless, excited.

She turned her back on him and he stroked her shoulders. In a few minutes Finn heard her breathing deepen. He gently stroked her hair as she slept.

CHAPTER 15

Madeleine thought long and hard about going to Athens with Finn and Mike. The last thing she wanted was to be a pawn in their sexual game. But did it have to be like that? She trusted Finn enough to know anything that happened would be with her agreement. From everything he had said, Mike was a decent guy and had no interest in anything non-consensual. She was free, single, mature. She was loving letting go. And she was still learning delicious new things about herself, about grown-up sex. But...Athens? Why did it have to be Athens? Maybe if she exposed herself to Greece again, it might help with the nightmares. She wouldn't be going anywhere near the island. There'd be time over the weekend to explore the city on her own and deal with any feelings it might bring back while Finn and Mike were working. At the very least, there was a free weekend in that lovely city. And perhaps a completely new experience.

* * * *

She chose the window seat, disappointing Finn who had wanted her to sit between him and Mike. Mike sat beside her and soon had her in fits of laughter, telling stories of his childhood and jokes that left her wiping her eyes. His Scouse accent still took some adjusting to. Finn joined in the craic, and it became even funnier. She had to stop them so she could catch her breath. She could see why they got on so well.

The sky was clear as they followed the Croatian coastline and its islands, down through the mainland of Greece. The plane banked over the deep blue sea and made its approach to Athens International

Airport. Madeleine realised this was a new airport, thankfully not the same one she'd arrived at all those years ago. Never had a four-hour flight passed so quickly and been so much fun.

In the taxi, Finn took the front seat and she and Mike sat together in the back. Finn and the taxi driver made small talk and Mike told her about the best places to go to in Athens. He had a favourite spot from which to see the Acropolis; the best thing she could do while they were working was to just wander. She let him talk, telling her more about Athens. As he talked, she forced her mind not to go back to all those years ago when she'd come here for the first time with Justin.

The taxi arrived at the King George Hotel in Syntagma Square; two rooms had been booked for them. The receptionist looked quizzically when Mike got a coin out of his pocket and spun it in the air, catching it heads up.

"Well, you're a lucky boy, Finn! Anyway, I need to pop out for a moment so you two get settled into your room. Finn, I'll meet you in the lobby in half an hour."

Mike gave Madeleine a hug. She felt good in his arms. She was realising this might work. He'd changed his aftershave, too. Whichever way the room-coin had landed, she was going to sleep with Finn the first night. After that, she'd see.

She unpacked and took a shower. The room was comfortable, elegant, and well equipped, looking out onto the square. She read the information about the hotel and previous guests Grace Kelly, Marilyn Monroe, Frank Sinatra and Aristotle Onassis. What fun!

Outside, the sun was shining, and the warmth in the air embraced her. Wearing a sun hat and a short, flowing white cotton dress, she walked out into Syntagma Square and set off for nearby Plaka, which the concierge had suggested was a good place to start exploring the city. In the old narrow streets, people were wandering as though time didn't matter. The pavement cafes and restaurants were full. She felt herself relaxing, put her map away and walked slowly, taking whichever turn felt right. She caught glimpses of the Acropolis above her and wondered if she'd have time to climb up to the Parthenon. In a small square, she came upon the Dionysos cafe and restaurant. The God of wine and debauchery, with his endless appetites. She was in the right place to have the freedom to explore.

She stopped outside a tiny church and peered inside. It was dark, and it took a while for her eyes to adjust. There were icons everywhere and a lingering smell of incense. She sat down on one of the pews. She hadn't been inside a church of any denomination for years. The stillness enveloped her. The only sound was the creak of the pew when she leant forward to get a clearer view of the small dome above her, painted with saints with gold halos. She couldn't tell who they were or if one of them was Christ. She heard footsteps and someone sat down behind her.

"It's beautiful, isn't it? Where are you from, Madam? Russia? France?"

She turned and saw a small, stocky old man looking at her.

"I'm English."

"Ah madam, you are in Greece. Therefore, today you are Greek. Do you like old things?"

She looked at him over the top of her sunglasses. "It depends on what the old things are."

"Madam let me recommend you go to the Archaeological Museum. It has the best old things in the city. It's not far away. You will not be disappointed. There's a taxi rank close by."

Maybe she would. Maybe the Gods were sending her a message.

A crowd of children surrounded their teachers in the entrance hall of the National Archaeological Museum. She got her ticket and walked into the first room she saw, full of statues. The bodies were astonishingly perfect. She turned right and stood in front of beautifully carved funerary reliefs. Into the next room and there was the famous bronze statue of Poseidon, his arms widespread. The tourists surrounding it were taking photos and selfies. She stood quietly to the side, taking him in. What a perfect-looking man. The groups moved on and she slowly walked around him, having him, just for a moment, to herself. So beautiful. So powerful. She had never seen a statue so viscerally alive; just how she felt. She knew she would not forget this moment, this encounter with a God of the sea. She wondered if the old man in the church had sent her specifically to see Poseidon.

She took a long deep breath and walked on slowly, turning to look at him one more time before leaving the room. Across the central hall was a room of Cycladic art. So different in style. She stood in front of a small collection of bowls. One of them was delicate, translucent marble of a simple beauty that reminded her of her Lucie Rie bowl. She sensed someone standing close beside her and froze. That scent, *lemon, cedarwood, musk, vetiver.* Richard. It must be. It couldn't be.

"It's beautiful, isn't it? If I was able to create that, I'd be happy for the rest of my life."

She turned and saw a tall woman, much her own age, wearing a brightly coloured Kaftan, smiling at her.

"Are you alright? I'm sorry I didn't mean to startle you."

"No. It's okay. I smelt your perfume and it gave me a shock. I'm the one who should apologize."

"Ah. A bad memory?" The woman looked concerned.

"I guess so. My ex-husband used to wear it."

"Oh dear," said the woman. "Sorry. I promise I won't wear it again!"

Madeleine laughed. "So, you like pots too?"

"I should do. I'm a potter. I get inspiration from ancient art, especially Cycladic. It's nice to meet you. I'm Barbara."

"I'm Madeleine." She held out her hand and the woman grasped it with both hands. "I collect pots," said Madeleine. "Do you live in Athens?"

"No." Barbara replied. "I have an apartment on one of the islands in the summer and sell my work. In the autumn I go back home to the UK, to Ledbury where I have my pottery. Over winter, I make enough pots and jewellery to bring back with me for the summer."

"Sounds like a great life."

"It works for me. How about you?"

"I'm just here for the weekend with a couple of friends. I work in London. I'm a book editor."

"Interesting. Look, I don't want to disturb your visit to the museum, but would you like a coffee?"

The cafe in the large open square outside the museum was busy. All the tables outside were taken. As they arrived, a family of four saw them and standing up to leave, waved them over. The waiter cleaned the table and brought over a bottle of water and two glasses.

"I love how this always happens here. Water is essential to life and should always be free, don't you think?"

Madeleine nodded. "I guess so. Is there a water shortage here?"

Barbara shook her head. "Not so much here. There's a lot of rain in the winter but on some of the islands, water is short mainly because so many people have swimming pools now. It's getting a bit out of hand."

Madeleine sighed. "I guess we don't think about that. We look in the brochures at the idyllic houses and pools and just imagine lazing by them for a couple of weeks without a care in the world."

Barbara nodded. "Yes, it's easy to forget. So, Madeleine, have you been to Athens before?"

"Yes, just over twenty years ago. It wasn't a happy experience, I'm afraid."

"I'm sorry. What brings you and your friends to Athens now?"

"They're putting on an exhibition here for a Greek artist. They invited me along."

"Who's the artist?"

It suddenly occurred to Madeleine how little she knew why Mike and Finn had come here. She'd only thought about the fun they wanted to have with her.

"I'm afraid I don't know. Nor do I know them very well, to be honest."

"Intriguing. Tell me more."

Madeleine laughed. "Let's order coffee. Maybe I'll tell you later."

"Even more intriguing." The waiter came over and Barbara ordered coffees in what sounded to Madeleine like fluent Greek.

"I've been coming here for twenty years. For the first five, I had a Greek lover who turned into a husband. He didn't speak any English, so I learnt Greek. I'm always amazed at how many people live here and don't bother to learn the language."

"So, what happened to the Greek lover/husband?"

"Oh, the usual with Greek men. After a while they want their woman to turn into their mother. I wanted a man, not a son."

"Do you have children?"

"No. You?"

For a moment Madeleine looked away.

"No. My ex-husband never wanted them and then he turned out to be gay. Not that that was the reason he didn't want kids. Our sex life just disappeared after a while. Makes it a problem to have kids without sex."

"And now? You could still have a child, couldn't you?" Barbara asked.

"I could technically but no, it's too late. Anyway, I don't think I want one. I'm enjoying my independence. Tell me about your pottery. Which island do you live on?"

Barbara explained she had a small shop with a flat above it on Naxos that she'd bought in 2011 during the economic crisis. The owner was forced into a quick sale, and she'd got it for a song.

"It's embarrassing because I see him from time to time and he always gives me a rueful look. I know how lucky I am."

Barbara rapturously described the main port, the Castro with its labyrinth of narrow winding streets above the port where she had her shop and flat. She made a simple living, which was all she needed.

"Then I have my house in Ledbury, just behind the high street. My wheel and kiln are in the basement and that's where I disappear like a mole in the winter."

"Do you live alone?" Madeleine asked.

Barbara brushed back a lock of hair that had fallen over her face. "I have an on-off lover. What about you?"

Madeleine leaned back in her chair and fiddled with her coffee cup.

"Well, it's complicated.... Actually, no, it's not complicated. It's very simple. A friend set me up to meet this much younger guy. We had some great sex. Then he introduced me to his business partner. I have a feeling I might be going to have some great sex with him too." Madeleine surprised herself by how relaxed she felt in this woman's company; she felt she could say anything to her, a kindred spirit.

Barbara was grinning. "And these are the two people you're here for the weekend with?"

"You got it."

"Wow. Well done you. Brava."

"I'm making up for lost time."

"What a way to do it. Where are you staying?"

"The King George."

"I had my wedding night there!"

"Which room?"

"God, I can't remember. We could only afford one night but it was a truly memorable one. May yours be as good, Madeleine."

Laughing, they high-five'd across the table. Barbara's bracelets jangled. Madeleine resolved to wear more jewellery.

"So, tell me about your on-off lover. Is he here or in Ledbury?"

Barbara's eyes twinkled. "Actually, it's lovers. She's in Ledbury and he's on Naxos. You see, one on and the other off."

"Crikey. They know about each other?"

"Oh yes. Dimitri works on Naxos during the summer and goes back to his wife in Athens in the winter. Stella travels a lot in the summer, mainly in India. In the winter we come back together and hibernate."

"Have you always been bi?"

"No. But when I met Stella, five or six years ago, we just got on so well. The truth is she seduced me, and I just let go. But we're all a bit bi, don't you think?"

Madeleine ran her tongue over her lip. "I did have a crush on a girl at Uni, but that's about all. We kissed a lot, I remember. Both of us were a bit nervous of going any further." For a moment she thought about Julia and the lunch they'd had together.

"Do you have time for another coffee?" Barbara asked. Madeleine looked at her watch.

"God, I need to be getting back to the hotel. I'm sorry, I'd have loved to. Can we keep in touch?"

"I insist upon it. I want to hear all about your weekend."

"Okay! I'm so glad to have met you, Barbara. Here's my card. When are you back in the UK?"

"I'm flying back on Tuesday. I have a great friend here who I'm staying with for a few days."

Barbara opened her bag and gave Madeleine her card.

BARBARA BECKWITH
Potter

"It's got both addresses on it. Please call me next week. And this is my treat."

They got up and Barbara left six euros on the table. "I'll walk you to the bus stop. It's just over there. The trolley goes straight to Syntagma. You don't need to pay. No one checks."

"Will you come too?"

"No. My friend lives just round the corner. I always have a siesta in the afternoon. Maybe you should too." Barbara grinned. "You might need it."

Madeleine hugged her. "It's wonderful to have met you! I'd love to see your work sometime."

"Well, you have two places to choose from. Have you been to Ledbury?"

"No. But I've heard it has some great restaurants. It's a bit of a foodie place, isn't it?"

"Yes. And a poetry festival in the summer. It's sad I'm never there for that because I love poetry."

"Me too. And pots."

"Well, that's three things we have in common."

"Three?"

"Poetry, pots and unusual love lives."

"A threesome!"

They laughed and hugged again. Barbara whispered in her ear.

"Enjoy yourself."

The Gods were smiling.

* * *

Mike and Finn were in good spirits. The meeting had gone well and the date for the gallery opening had been finalized to everyone's satisfaction. Oikeio restaurant was filling up as they sat down at their table. The restaurant was intimate, ornately decorated with colourful ornaments, rich, red wall hangings, a scattering of chintz and discreet white fairy lights. Strings of garlic bulbs and peppers hung from the ceiling. A round chandelier bedecked with flowers reminded Madeleine of the Wicker Man movie.

"What an interesting place," she said.

Finn replied. "Yes. It's one of our favourite restaurants. Oikeio means Home in Greek. We normally sit up in the mezzanine. Gives a good view of everyone else. But tonight, with such a beautiful woman with us, let everyone look at us."

"It looks a bit like a souk," said Madeleine. "I love the oriental wall hangings."

"It looks more like a bordello to me," said Mike. Finn laughed.

"Have you been to a bordello?" asked Madeleine.

"Madeleine, what happens in a bordello, stays in a bordello," Mike answered.

Madeleine raised her eyes and shook her head. "Men!" she said. And then added, "You can call me Maddy, Mike".

"I will! Maddy. I love it!" said Mike.

"The restaurant caught fire a while ago," said Finn. "Started in the kitchen. They've made a great job restoring it."

"Well, if the food is as good as the restoration, it's going to be amazing!" said Madeleine.

Their table was in the corner, and Madeleine sat between them. A heavily tattooed waiter brought them a bottle of water and three menus in English.

"Are you okay to share, Maddy?" Finn asked.

"He means the food. It's usual to share dishes in Greece," said Mike.

Madeleine looked from one to the other and shook her head.

"I know. And I know what I want. Let's order."

The electricity in the air between them crackled.

The food was excellent. They shared a Greek salad, a slow-cooked rabbit stew and chicken souvlaki.

"Now I have you both here, I want to know what drives you both. About art, I mean. I assume you love art too, Mike. Am I right?"

Mike laughed. "Simple. It's the money. Doesn't mean I don't like art. I do." He looked at Madeleine. "I love owning beautiful things. But yes, it's the money. We're running a business."

Madeleine raised an eyebrow. "What about you, Finn? I know you love art."

"I like making money, too. I'm lucky I can make it from art."

She expected that reply from Mike, but Finn surprised her. She'd grown fond of him, and his response disappointed her. After their conversations in Liverpool on that magical beach, she had hoped he would say that art was his passion and money a side-line. Although she loved the pleasures of occasional luxury as much as anyone, she doubted she could ever be close to a man driven primarily by money. She'd had too much of that with Richard. But she brushed her doubts aside; after all, Finn was giving her a great time and was fun to be around.

She had a long night ahead of her. As they left the restaurant and walked past the heavily guarded British Embassy, she took their hands.

Tick.... tock...

CHAPTER 16

Finn woke up after a disturbed night. It had shaken him when Madeleine kissed him in the hotel foyer and then turned to Mike and told him to take her to bed. Mike had looked triumphantly at Finn as he put his arm around her, and they walked towards the lift. This was what Finn had wanted. It was what they did. But to his astonishment, this time felt different. For the first time, the usual excitement was laced with a stinging pain which made it even more intense. Jealousy. He could guess what she and Mike would do, the same opening up, sharing, swapping, alternating who was in control. She had texted him from Mike's room. '*Sleep well. Think of me!*'

Finn had thought of nothing else and had masturbated twice to relieve the clench in his stomach. He put his ear against the wall, but this was not a cheap dive. He wanted to go to Mike's room and claim her back. His imagination was teasing him, playing with him. He wanted her with him. But he also trembled with the familiar thrill. By now, they would probably have finished, and she would be lying in Mike's arms. She would come back to his room, come and snuggle with him, tell him she'd missed him, and he'd take her, ravish her, reclaim her.

But she hadn't returned, and he'd woken alone. His phone pinged. A text.

'Good morning! Followed by a smiley face.

He replied straight away. *'Please come back.'*

No response.

At last, there was a knock and he jumped up from the bed and opened the door. A waiter was standing there with a coffee and a croissant.

"Your friend ordered this for you. He asked that you meet him and the lady on the rooftop in an hour."

For fuck's sake.

An hour later, they hadn't arrived at the rooftop restaurant. When they finally did, Finn was glad that at least they weren't holding hands. She had showered and her hair was still damp. She was looking tired, but relaxed. They spotted him and came over. She sat next to him and kissed him on the cheek, then looked around and gasped at the Acropolis opposite.

"Wow. This must be one of the best views in the world!" she said.

He felt her hand on his thigh, and it moved closer to his stiffening crotch.

She looked at him, smiling, and asked, "How was your night?"

He touched her lips with his finger. "Long. How was yours?"

"Wonderful."

She turned to Mike. "I want lashings of yoghurt, honey, fruit, and a large coffee for breakfast. What are you having?"

"The same."

Mike looked across at Finn's sullen face. "You look like you got little sleep, my friend. We need to get your energy up. We've got a big day ahead."

Finn looked at Madeleine. She was enjoying this. A collared dove fluttered down onto the rooftop balcony.

★ ★ ★ ★

On the flight back to London, Madeleine sat between them both. Not much was said. They were quietly reflecting on a weekend that had amazed them all. After that first breakfast, she had gone back with Finn to his room. He had consumed her, reclaimed her, made love to her with a passion that had devoured her. They had slept for several hours in each other's arms, only woken by the sound of knocking on their door. Mike had come in, undressed, and joined them. She had lain between them, and they had kissed her, explored her, and taken her. Never had she felt so needed, so wanted, so wonderful, so powerful. That night she had slept with Finn, both too exhausted for sex. They had come up to the rooftop together for breakfast. A couple who'd been there the previous morning had looked at each other quizzically as they walked past hand in hand and joined Mike at the table. Had this experience been just as good for Finn? She hoped so.

The taxi dropped Madeleine at home in Putney. Her neighbour was in the front garden, deadheading roses. He noticed her suitcase.

"Hi Maddy. Good weekend?"

"Hello, Aaron. The best."

Shutting the front door behind her, she dropped her case, kicked off her shoes, did a jig round the hall, went to the bathroom, and sang in the shower at the top of her voice.

Finn slept deeply and woke early. He made coffee and turned on the Today programme. Fucking Brexit. Thank goodness he had an Irish passport. He wondered what Madeleine thought of it. He wanted to get to know her a lot better, get to know her friends. They'd talked a bit about their lives, but not as much as he wanted. He imagined this was not just about sex for her. It rarely was for women. It unnerved him that it might not be for him either.

He wasn't in the mood for Mike, but he knew the call would come. It didn't take long. "She's amazing. Just the best one we've had so far. We need to fix up another get-together."

He could feel Mike's grin. Finn stayed silent.

Mike continued. "I've tasted her now and I want more. I'm sure she does too. We got on well that first night. Did a lot of things. I bet you it's not a one-off for her. Anyway, she's too old for you. I had a text from her this morning. Did you?"

"No. What did it say?"

" '*Thanks Mike. See you again.*' "

"Did you reply?"

"Yes."

"And??"

"That's between her and me. You know that."

That clench in his stomach again. Finn knew he was being cuckolded. But did he want it? He'd never before felt conflicted over a woman.

"Okay Mike, let's leave it for now. We have an exhibition to curate, and you need to check on the Walker."

Mike laughed. "I'll be checking today. And I want to run through the figures with you. We need to cut back on our spending. That was a bloody expensive weekend. Okay, my friend. Back to work. Talk soon."

The phone went dead before Finn could reply. He had calls to make and meetings to set up. Madeleine could wait. For a moment.

Madeleine had no intention of waiting. Her night with Mike had been another eye-opener for her. Maybe it was because he was more her age, maturer than Finn. Finn was a superb lover. But Mike had given her another measure, taken his time even more, gone deeper. She didn't trust him for one moment, but she wanted to see him again. Find out more. Finn had wanted her to be with Mike. And she would be. Pandora's box was open.

CHAPTER 17

Emily had called her several times to meet up, and Madeleine had felt terrible about neglecting her best friend. They arranged to meet at their local pub.

Madeleine saw Emily running towards her and held her arms open to give her an enormous hug.

"I've missed you so much!" she said.

"Maddy, where on earth have you been?"

Madeleine grinned. "I've a lot to tell you".

They found a quiet corner table and gave their orders to the barman. Emily leaned towards her and tried to be cross. "So why haven't you been returning my calls? I've been worried."

"I'm sorry, my love. It's just there's been a lot happening. Forgive me?"

"Okay, but I want to know everything. The last time I saw you, you were off to meet Shammie's friend. What was his name? Frank? Some Irish name."

"Finn. What I'm going to tell you is between us. Promise me."

Emily's face brightened. "Of course. This sounds good...tell all."

Emily listened, transfixed, as Madeleine told her what had happened. She hid nothing. Emily's expression became more and more incredulous. This was Maddy? Her best friend? Sensible, lovely Maddy?

"I just don't know what to say. Fucking Hell would be appropriate, I guess."

Madeleine looked concerned and took Emily's hand. "Are you shocked? Have I been an idiot?"

Emily said nothing for a moment.

"Not shocked, exactly, but..."

Madeleine's heart sank.

"Maddy, I love you and always will. It's just a lot to take in... they aren't married, are they, these guys?"

"No, God no. They're the most un-married men I've ever met! Em, you don't approve, do you?"

Madeleine was crestfallen that her friend didn't understand the freedom she was experiencing and felt a distance come between them that had never been there before. Emily tried to backtrack, saying she was just concerned for Madeleine's welfare, that she might get hurt by these playboys.

"So, you do think I have been an idiot," said Madeleine.

"No, my love. Not an idiot. Just...oh, I don't know. It's a lot to take in. What's going to happen now?"

"I'm meeting up with Mike on Saturday. I haven't told Finn, though I bet Mike has. Finn wants to meet too, but I've put him off. I know now that Finn has a thing about his lover being with other guys. I thought at first it was a fantasy, a bit of hot sex role-play. But then it happened for real. And though I've never come across such a thing before, Em, I think I'm going to enjoy it. It makes me feel... I dunno, special."

"Just be careful, Maddy. I'm sorry if I'm struggling a bit with this. You know I want the very best for you."

"You don't think I'm a pervert, do you?"

"Sweetheart, the last thing you are is a pervert. I just need a bit of time to take this in. And...a bit at a time, okay? Just don't keep me out of the loop." She took Madeleine's hand. "I trust you to look after yourself. I love you and I want the best for you."

"I swear, Em. I won't leave you out again. I'm so sorry. I just got a bit carried away. It was so exciting! Actually, it was more than exciting. I feel alive and desired for maybe the first time in my life. Never in my wildest dreams did I think I'd have sex with a lover like Finn, let alone Mike as well. I'm happy, Em. Really happy."

"Then I'm happy for you Maddy. I really am. But tell me, how was it for you going back to Greece?"

Madeleine paused. "To be honest, it wasn't easy. Luckily, I didn't go anywhere I'd been with Justin. A lot has changed in Athens since we were there. Anyway, enough of me. What have you been up to?"

Nothing much had happened in Emily's life, a life that Madeleine used to envy. A part of her now almost felt sorry for her best friend.

CHAPTER 18

Finn had wanted nothing from a woman other than sex for a long time. It was so easy for him to seduce. He knew the impact of a positive mind-set, core confidence and self-esteem; how his smile could captivate; how to dress to attract, how to lead. Being brought up in the shadow of an abusive relationship where his mother dominated every aspect of his father's life, had made him scared of any real emotional attachment. Why on earth would anyone want it? If his father had taught him anything, it was how <u>not</u> to be a man. But now, Madeleine had come into his life...

He slept fitfully, unable to get her out of his dreams. It wasn't just the smell and the taste of her he longed for. He'd missed no one so much. She'd gone along with his fantasies and enjoyed them. She had got inside his head. He loved the way she was challenging him. Something in him was shifting. Maybe this is what love felt like? It was a novel experience.

His work was suffering, and Mike would soon hassle him. Maybe he should go to Dublin and see Flora. Spend a few nights with her. Get Madeleine out of his system. He mustn't fall for her. Except...except if he loved her, wouldn't the intensity of being cuckolded increase exponentially? He could be taken to new levels. Maybe he should encourage Madeleine to meet more men? She seemed open enough. He should tell her it was what he wanted. What woman wouldn't like the freedom to see other men within a relationship? No, he must get a grip. He was being stupid. She'd be bound to meet someone her own age and have a deep, loving relationship with him. She wasn't the type of woman to sleep around. She was meeting Mike again, but this was just a phase. He needed to deal with his obsession. It was dominating him, messing with his head. He had to admit he needed help.

But not yet, not quite yet.

His phone rang. Damn. Mike was gloating. "I'm seeing Madeleine again tonight. Really looking forward to it."

Finn tried to sound matter of fact. "What time are you meeting her?"

"8.30. Meeting her in Swift."

"Will you text me?"

"I always have, haven't I?"

"Yes, you have. Where will you go then?"

"I know how to press your buttons, my friend. We'll decide after a few drinks...dinner...my hotel. One or the other...or both. Where are you going to be?"

"I don't know. Maybe I'll go to the Club."

"Good idea. Take it out on the new woman you told me about."

"Maybe. I'll see. Just..."

"Just what, Finn?"

"Just be good to her." The phone went dead.

* * * *

Madeleine noticed the taxi driver looking at her in the mirror. A good start. She grinned to herself.

She was feeling sexy, stylish, attractive in the fitted backless dress she'd bought. Above all, she felt confident. For the first time ever, she had gone to a manicurist and had her nails done. She had dressed to show off and not just to Mike. As she arrived at Swift, she slipped off her coat and left it in the cloakroom. It was going to be a long night, and she was thankful not to have work in the morning. Fuck it. This was her time.

She made her way to where Mike was sitting, knowing all eyes were on her. She was wearing heels and stockings and had risked going braless, which made her even more aware of her body and the effect it was having on others. She felt so in control. Mike was standing there, his mouth open. It felt good. Very good.

"Maddy, wow. You look...." Before he had a chance to say more, she kissed him and then tapped his cheek.

"Hello Mike, who were you texting?"

"Finn. He wanted to know if you were okay."

"Am I okay? I look what..."

"You're stunning."

"Thank you, Mike. This is a great place."

They sat down and she kissed him again. She knew her dress was riding up, her stocking tops and thighs showing. "I hope you're ready for a long night. Don't let me down, Mike."

Mike took a deep breath and grinned. "I won't let you down, Maddy."

She looked at him with half-lidded eyes. "You'd better not. Or I'll have to get Finn over too."

He frowned. "Do you want that tonight? He's sitting at home feeling very sorry for himself."

Her cheek dimpled. "Good. Let him wait. I'll see how it goes with you first."

Swift was Mike's favourite bar in Soho, with curved seats where a couple could be very close. It specialised in whiskies, cocktails, and intimacy. A perfect place for seduction.

The waitress handed them menus and waited for their order.

"Would you like a cocktail?"

She looked briefly at the menu. "I'd love champagne. I'm in the mood for bubbles."

"Great. I'll join you. Two glasses of champagne, please."

They sat close together, and Mike stroked her face.

"Athens was good for you."

"You were good for me, Mike. Finn too of course. And yes, Athens is a special place. You know I've never ever done anything like that before?" She gazed at him with her deep brown eyes. She was feeling close to him.

"I know. But no regrets, I hope?"

"Not a single one. I feel great."

Mike's phone pinged. "I'm sorry. I'll switch it off. Oh, it's Finn. Shall I see what he says?"

"Of course." She smiled. "I want to know. Show me."

He handed her his phone. *'Say hi to her.'*

"Don't answer," she said.

He switched the phone off.

"How is Finn? I've only had a brief chat with him since we got back. He was a bit abrupt," she said.

"Maddy, you know, he's in love with you."

Her eyes widened. She was taken aback. "Really? Oh, that's crazy. I'm very fond of him, but I'm not in love. And he shouldn't be, either."

"You've made a big impact on him."

"Well, I'm glad. He has on me. But there's no way I want a full-blown relationship with him. Or you, for that matter."

He stroked her arm. "Look at me, Maddy. I have no wish to be anything to you other than a lover and friend, someone with whom to have some great sex."

She held his gaze and her lips parted slightly. "Here's to great sex. Talking of which, where are we going?"

Mike took her head in his hands and kissed her hard. Her response was immediate and urgent as she pulled him towards her. A woman passed by and glanced at them, eyebrows raised. Breathless, Mike broke off from their passionate kiss.

"People are watching."

Her eyes flashed. "Good. I love it."

The waitress came over with the champagne. They picked up their glasses and she turned to him.

"Cheers, Mike!"

They looked into each other's eyes. "To you, Maddy. You're a revelation."

A revelation? She loved that. She clinked his glass. "Good. I want to be. So, what's the plan?"

Mike laughed. "Well, I thought a couple of drinks here, then dinner, and I've booked us a room for later."

"I like it here. Let's stay a bit. Kiss me again."

Madeleine was feeling free, out of control and perfectly in control. Alive! So very alive. Reckless, open, breathless. She could express herself and be wanted. Never would she allow herself to be mistreated and ignored again. She now knew she could make her own choices. Mike squeezed her hand. "You're being looked at."

She tossed her head. "I know."

She snuggled up to him and nuzzled his neck. "Let's go dancing."

He frowned. "I'm a crap dancer."

"You can hold me tight, can't you? Press me against you?"

"Are you serious?"

She stroked his cheek. "Yes. I know a bar where there's a dance floor. A friend had a party there and I've always wanted to go back. Come on. Let's go there."

"Maddy, don't you like it here? I really am a crap dancer."

She sat back. She was loving the self-confidence she felt. "Well, if you can't dance, I'll have to find someone who can, won't I? Come on, it'll be fun. I want to dance. And you'll love it too. Let's have another drink and go."

Barrio was full when they arrived. Mostly younger people out for a good night. Groups of friends, some couples, a few single men. They walked through to the dance floor. The music was loud and there was a free table. He pulled back a chair for her.

"You sit, Mike. I'm going to get us drinks."

He put a hand on her shoulder. "I'll get them, Maddy."

"No. Stay where you are. I'm having a cocktail. You?"

He sat down and looked up at her. "Surprise me."

As she approached the bar, she looked at who was there. Some couples, a few friends, and a man on his own, tall, late thirties, good-looking. She tapped him on the shoulder and as he turned, looked into his eyes. "Excuse me. I need a drink." He looked at her and grinned.

"What are you drinking, gorgeous?" An American drawl.

She gave him a coy smile. "Cocktails."

He threw his head back and laughed. "My kinda woman! Okay, my treat. I'm Jamal, by the way. What's it to be?"

"Oh, that's very kind of you, Jamal. Thank you. I'm Madeleine. I'll have an Old Fashioned and a Manhattan."

He put a hand on her back and looked down at her. "That's such a cool name! You have a friend here?"

Madeleine held his gaze. "Yes, we're over by the dance floor."

His eyes twinkled. "Even better. I'll bring them over."

She put a finger to his lips. "Thank you. We'll be waiting."

She knew he was watching her as she walked slowly through the bar, making sure her hips swayed. This was so much fun.

"Where are the drinks?" asked Mike.

She grinned and sat down. "A guy bought us cocktails. He's going to bring them over."

Mike looked puzzled. "He's bought one for each of us?"

"I guess he's assumed my friend is another woman," she said impishly.

He frowned. "Maddy, for God's sake. I don't want another guy joining us!"

"Mike. Don't be such a stick-in-the-mud. I'll just let him dance with me in exchange."

"I'll dance with you."

She grinned. "I thought you couldn't dance."

"I'll dance."

She kissed him hard. "Yes, you will. And so will he. He's a good-looking guy, and I'm having a great night. You wouldn't deny me, would you? I love dancing."

The man was approaching with two cocktails, looking round the room for her. She waved and he stopped in front of the table, staring.

She beamed at the man and got up. "I hope you like dancing. I'd like to thank you."

She took the cocktails, put them on the table, took his hand and led him onto the floor. The music was fast, and she held his eyes as they moved to the rhythms. She glanced across at Mike. He was sipping the Manhattan, his eyes fixed on her. It was the Old Fashioned for her, then. Just an old-fashioned girl.

The music slowed and she moved closer to Jamal. "You're a good dancer."

"And you're a hot woman. Who's the guy? Your husband?"

She put her arms round his neck. "Just a friend. Two cocktails, two dances."

He put his arms round her and stroked her bare back. She pressed closer to him. His hands moved down to her buttocks and squeezed them. She guessed Mike wouldn't be happy. Too bad. She'd make it up to him. The music was sultry, sensual. Bob Marley's Turn Your Lights Down Low. Their bodies were tight together. He was very aroused. So was she. He pulled her even closer as she looked up at him and put her arms round his neck.

"Kiss me."

His kiss was hard and open. Her tongue pushed into his mouth. The music stopped. She pulled away and gave him a beaming smile. "Thank you for the drinks."

He was breathing heavily. "Can I see you again?"

She briefly held his hand. "Maybe."

He pulled a card out of an inside pocket. "Any time you feel thirsty, call me." He turned and strolled back to the bar.

She walked over to Mike, who was sitting back in his chair, arms folded.

"Ahh. That was nice! Now come on, Mike, don't spoil our night out. Come on, kiss me."

Mike felt a grin coming but tried to keep an annoyed face. Finn would have loved it, loved watching her display. He'd enjoy telling him about it later.

"Still want to dance?" he asked.

She grinned. "Yes please."

Mike's dancing surprised her. She'd imagined him to be a jerky dancer, but he was letting the music take over. Good for him. She let him take the lead, following his moves.

She noticed the cocktail guy was dancing with another woman and during a slow dance, manoeuvered Mike close to them and kissed him passionately. She knew his body. He was hers at least for the night. She knew he was amused by the game she'd played, and it had turned her on. The bar she'd brought him to wasn't far from the hotel. Another hour of dancing, then straight back to the hotel and room service. Their appetites were building. They needed to eat.

Tick.... tock....

★ ★ ★ ★

Finn knew Mike wouldn't respond to his text. At least not straight away. It was part of the game. He knew the bar Mike had taken Madeleine to. He'd been there himself with several women, and it always set the mood. He wondered what Madeleine was wearing, what preparations she had made to make herself ready for sex. She'd choose colourful, transparent, sexy underwear. That was the easy part. He imagined how she would have taken a dress out of her wardrobe and held it against herself, slipped it on, turning one way and then the other. She'd have put it back and taken another, repeating the process probably ten times before finally choosing the first dress she'd tried on. He imagined her wearing a red backless dress that hugged her body. He didn't know if she had one and if she hadn't, he'd buy one for her. Fun, alluring, so sexy.

He thought about going to the Club but decided against it. He'd stay at home, his imagination playing heady games with his mind, a gnawing ache in his stomach and a huge temptation to masturbate at the thought of his Madeleine being fucked by his best friend. Pain and pleasure. Early on, he had discovered that his sexual predilection had a name. Cuckold. Cuckolded. A word for the hurt which was so intense it could only be relieved by the pleasure of sexual release. All those years ago in Dublin, he had told his girlfriend, during sex, of his excitement when she flirted with other guys in front of him. "You want me to fuck them, too?" she'd asked. That's how it had started. She had always told him when she'd been with another man. Lovemaking was more intense when she described her exploits in detail. The intensity had come to a head when she left him for an older man. The pain had been exquisite, and a release. Other relationships had followed, but it was the ones where he could be open about his needs that gave him the greatest pleasure. There were periods in his life when he could enjoy sex without his fetish. He nearly married a lovely woman he cared for hugely, but eventually he had reverted, and the relationship fell apart when she didn't respond to his fantasy pillow-talk and found it disgusting. Wasn't she enough for him? How could he really love her if that's what he wanted? She wouldn't be part of it, even as a fantasy. She was a one-man woman.

It was two hours before Mike texted his reply.

'She looks stunning. Loves the bar. We're going dancing. Have fun.'

He knew there was no point in answering. Mike would have switched his phone off immediately. No interruptions. He wished Mike had told him what she was wearing. But that would come later. He longed to touch himself, but the denial increased his desires. He lay on his bed and switched on his laptop. Maybe some porn. Some cuckold stories. But there was nothing he could read that would be headier than his own feelings.

CHAPTER 19

Maxine and Julia snuggled together on the sofa.

"I think something is up with Maddy," said Julia. "She told me she'd gone to Athens with the art-dealer guy she met in Liverpool. And his business partner. She just seems a lot more, I don't know, free."

Maxine laughed. "Interesting. Free in what way? You think she's had both of them?"

"Well, who knows?"

Maxine re-filled their glasses. "Have you ever thought of having two lovers at once?"

Julia was shocked. "No! You are an amazing lover. I don't need anyone else. Why would you ask?"

Maxine shook her head slightly. "Nothing really. Just wondered. Loving you is fantastic, obviously. But sometimes, well… I guess I just don't want us to get into a rut. Turn into a dull, middle-aged couple."

Julia stared at her. "Do you find me dull? Is that what you're saying?"

Maxine flushed. "Don't be silly, my beautiful darling. I love you. You're anything but dull. But I don't want us to ever get stale. It happens. Suddenly you get bored in a couple, however much you love each other, look for distractions elsewhere. It happens too often." She hesitated. "I've seen friends split up because they don't have honest conversations. We promised we'd always be open with each other. No secrets. So, all I'm saying is we should be aware. And if either of us feels an attraction to someone else, we should tell each other."

Julia chewed on her lip. "Are you attracted to someone else?"

Maxine gave her a gentle smile. "Not right now. But I have been."

"While we've been together?"

"Yes. But I didn't do anything about it."

Maxine reached out to touch her, but Julia stood up and took a step back. "Who was it?"

Maxine got up and lifted Julia's chin. "Look at me. You remember at Angela's party last week, there was a girl there called Chloe? Late twenties, I guess. Blonde. Very feminine."

Julia looked away. "Not particularly. There were loads of people there."

Maxine's hand dropped to her side. "Well, it doesn't matter. I'm surprised you didn't notice. Anyway, she gave me her phone number and wanted to meet up. If I'd been single, I'd have called her. Oh darling, don't look so worried. I'm not going to call her. But I didn't want to hide it from you. Come here."

A tear trickled down Julia's cheek. Maxine reached out, wiped it away and held her close, stroking her hair. "Listen my darling, you're the one I love. I will never betray you. But I will never lie to you either. Haven't you felt attracted to anyone else?"

For a minute Julia leaned into the hug, then stood back, holding Max's hand. "I've never thought about it. I guess I've never allowed myself to be. Max, I appreciate you being honest with me, but this hurts. I wish it didn't, but it does. Tell me you're not getting bored with me? I love you so much. I couldn't bear anything happening to us."

They looked at each other, holding hands.

"I love you with all my heart, you know I do. And it's because I love you, I'm being open with you. So come on, there must be someone you've felt a little frisson with?"

Julia snuggled into Max's arms and kissed her. "No. No one." A small smile. "I have eyes only for you. But if I do, I promise I'll tell you."

★ ★ ★ ★

Julia had commandeered the small spare room in Maxine's flat to write. It was a squeeze and not as conducive to writing as she had wanted. She was making what she hoped were the final amendments to her novel. She wanted to let go of this one and work on the new ideas that kept swirling around in her head for her second book. She'd listen to Madeleine and Catherine's advice but was feeling more and more that she wanted this new book to be something different. Maybe that should be the third book. She'd always have a twist at the end she hoped would keep her readers guessing. At this stage, she did not know what it might be. She'd been three quarters through the first one before the ending had come to her. She was distracted. She started thinking about money. Despite Max's City job and her generosity, she didn't want to feel like a kept woman. She'd treat herself to lunch. If her book was as popular as Catherine had suggested it might be, there'd be more lunches out. Maybe they could move to a bigger apartment, and she could have a proper room of her own to write in.

Max's revelation had taken her aback. It had never crossed her mind to look at another woman. Or a man. She had fantasized from time to time about being with a man again. A hard body to compare with Max's lovely, soft, ample one. She remembered the first time they had kissed. Such an incredible softness. And the first time she had tasted another woman's sex. So wet, open, gentle, inviting. And God, did Max know how to use her fingers and tongue! So much better than any man she'd been with. Her mind drifted to Madeleine. She'd ask her out for a drink and see how she was doing. The last time they'd had lunch together had been unexpectedly fun. It would be good to see her outside work. She'd like Max to get to know her too. They were the same sort of age.

God, she loved Max.

CHAPTER 20

Sunday morning. Finn lay in bed feeling exhausted. Just as well he didn't need to get up early. He wished he knew which hotel Mike had taken her to. Drinks, dinner, a night of sex with his Maddy. Other women had told him Mike was a good lover. Liked to be in control. A confident man who knew what he wanted. They liked that. He wondered if she'd let him do whatever he wanted. Mike liked anal sex. Liked to be a bit rough sometimes. He hoped Mike hadn't crossed boundaries with her. He doubted she'd have let him. Maddy knew what she liked. The threesome in Athens had been a revelation. He and Mike had taken turns, resting after an orgasm while the other took over. She had been insatiable, switching positions, working on them both using her hands, lips, and tongue to restart them. And the orgasms she'd had! One of their best days of sex. The look on her face as she eventually drifted into a deep sleep had told them both she was happy.

He waited another hour. Still nothing from either of them. He'd shower and go out for brunch. Buy a Sunday paper. Catch up on news. Try and forget. If nothing by midday, he'd text them both.

His phone rang. It was Shammie.

"Finn, I'm bored. I need a distraction. What are you doing right now?"

"Shammie, wonderful to hear from you. I'm at a bit of a loose end too."

She laughed. "You? Loose end? Unlikely. Anyway, want to come over? I'm home alone."

There was silence for a moment.

"Finn?"

"You know what? Yes. I'd love to come over. Give me your address. I can come over about 5. Okay with you?"

★ ★ ★ ★

Shammie sucked in her cheeks and checked herself in the mirror. She looked good. Full-bodied. Like the bottle of wine she had opened. One of Jacob's good ones. Nibbles ready. Fresh sheets on the bed. She hadn't spoken to a soul for twenty-four hours and had been toying with the idea of calling Finn all week. Jacob was away. Why should Maddy have all the fun? She needn't know. She was playing the field and wasn't that into Finn now. He was fair game. She could make sure Finn wouldn't tell her. Anyway, Maddy wouldn't be the only woman he was fucking. Guys like that; sex mad. So tempting.

The bell rang. She opened the door.

"Hello Finn, come on in. Hey. What's the matter? You look exhausted. Are you okay?"

He grimaced. "I could do with a hug."

"Come here." She embraced him in a far more motherly way than she had intended.

"Hang up your coat and come through."

She sat down on the sofa next to him.

"So, Finn, what's all this about?

He leant forward, covering his face with his hands.

"I'm sorry. I know this isn't what you were expecting. But it's all your fault. It's Maddy."

"Is she okay? What's happened?"

He sat back and looked at her. "She's fine. It's me. It's just… I think I'm falling in love with her."

Shammie grinned, relieved. "For God's sake Finn. Really? Is she in love with you?"

He clasped and un-clasped his hands. "No. Quite the opposite. She sees more of my business partner, Mike now."

She sat open-mouthed as Finn told her about the relationship with Mike and the things Maddy had got up to.

"You've had a threesome in Athens, and they have cuckolded you? Well, Maddy, you little minx! She hasn't told me a word about this. Finn, I have to say I'm not sorry for you. Hats off to Maddy, though."

Finn finished his glass of wine. She poured him another.

"I thought you'd be more sympathetic, Shammie. I've hardly slept a wink. I told you because you know Maddy so well. What should I do?"

The last thing she'd expected from Finn was for him to treat her as an agony aunt.

"Finn, Finn, Finn. You must know this is just Maddy spreading her wings. You've done something brilliant for her. I had no idea you had such a sensitive side. I guess you haven't come across a Maddy before, have you? Not your usual woman, is she?"

"No, she isn't," he said.

She kissed him lightly on the lips. "So, no point taking you to bed then."

He gave her a hug. "I'm sorry, Shammie. I just needed to talk about her to someone who really knows her. Do you mind?"

She stood up. "Have you eaten today?"

"Not really," he said.

She took his hand. "Come with me to the kitchen. Bring the wine and glasses. I'll cook us something and we can talk. Maybe I can raise your spirits. And your pecker.

CHAPTER 21

The trees on Putney Common were turning rich gold in the late afternoon sun. Conkers, immaculately clean and shining, had split open on the paths. Emily had called Madeleine to apologise for the way she'd responded to her revelations.

There was no need. If anything, Madeleine should be apologising. She told Emily about the night with Mike. Emily started to ask questions, but Madeleine stopped her. She was still processing what had happened, what was happening. She couldn't quite believe what she'd done, how she'd dressed, how she'd behaved. They strolled, arm in arm, kicking the leaves, sending the conkers rolling for their lives. Together they took in mouthfuls of crisp, clean air and exhaled heavily, laughing, friends together, at one with each other as they walked towards the pub.

They found a table at the back and ordered food.

"Em, sweetheart, are you okay? You look down." Madeleine reached across and put her hand against her cheek and Emily held it there, feeling comforted.

"It's your fault."

Madeleine looked concerned. "Oh no. I thought we were okay. Want to talk about it?"

Emily shook her head. There was a tear in her eye. "I guess I'm a bit jealous of your life. I shouldn't be, God knows. You've not had it easy. But yes, I am envious of your life now."

Madeleine reached both hands across the table, and she took them.

"It's just a phase, Em. I'm just letting go of stuff that's been bottled up for years and using Mike and Finn to help liberate me. It's a total release. So please don't be envious. How are you and Jack?"

It was Emily's turn to be open. Since Maddy had told her about this new life of hers, Emily had felt depressed, conscious her life with Jack was unexciting. She'd snapped at him a few times and Jack had disappeared into his study. It was Emily who usually initiated sex, but it was so dull. Emily felt they should do something while they still could. Surprise each other. Surely Jack must feel the same? But he was engrossed in the research for a new academic paper. They knew each other inside out, too well. Or so she thought. She wondered if Jack had any sexual fantasies she didn't know about. She knew his favourite ones were watching a lesbian couple or a threesome with two women. So predictable. Maybe he watched porn in his study. If he did, what would he be watching? Something she'd like too, she hoped. Christ, did he masturbate in there? She'd ask him. Tell him she watched porn, even though she didn't. Maybe she should. It was so easy to hide secrets. They had shared everything in the early days. Their hopes and ambitions both as individuals and as a couple. They had achieved most. Maybe that was the problem. She couldn't remember the last time they had sat down and talked. Certainly not about sex. Really talked. And if he wouldn't? Marriage counselling? No thank you. She didn't know how to fix things.

Emily wiped the tear from her eye. "It's just so dull with him, Maddy. I love him to bits. You know that. But jeez.... maybe I need a young stud, too."

Madeleine couldn't help laughing. "I'm sure that could be arranged."

"Your Finn?"

"Why not?"

"I couldn't do that to Jack. I've got to find *something* to wake him up. And I don't fancy a threesome with another woman, even if it is his thing."

Madeleine leant forward. "Forget about his thing, Em. What's yours? I remember you at that party when you must have had sex with at least three guys."

"That was years ago in college."

"Yes, but you loved it."

She almost smiled. "I did, didn't I...." she said.

Madeleine paused. "You know what Finn loves? Knowing I'm having sex with Mike."

Emily's eyes widened. "You're kidding. Really?"

"Yep. Loves it."

"That's weird."

Madeleine leant back and ran her fingers through her hair. "Weird or not, it's his thing. So, you never know what might be the one thing that can spice up your life."

"Do you watch porn?" Emily suddenly asked.

"Yes. Sometimes. Do you?"

Emily shook her head. Madeleine leant forward, speaking quietly. "Why not? It's not all videos. There are some hot stories online. And there's books by Nancy Friday and Erica Jong, of course. I hate seeing you down, Em. You know I'm here for you. Anytime."

"Thanks, Maddy. I know you are. I'll be fine, it's just a wobble, I'm sure.

Madeleine called Finn as she walked home, but there was no reply. She tried again when she was in bed. His phone went straight to voicemail. She hoped he wasn't playing some sort of silly game. Mike had told her again he thought Finn was in love with her. She had to put an end to that. The last thing she wanted! Silly boy. She'd call Shammie in the morning and fix up to meet her and maybe some other friends. It was about time they all had a night out again. She pulled the duvet up to her chin and dropped asleep.

She watches as he bounces, twists, spin down the cliff.....
Three hundred feet below, circles ripple out across the sea....

Her scream echoes off the mountain and like him, disappears....
She's sobbing, sobbing, pulling her hair....in agony.

She woke, tears streaming down her face, her knuckles in her mouth to stop herself screaming. Not again, please, please not again.

Tick.... tock....

CHAPTER 22

The walk to work cleared Madeleine's head. She and Catherine sat round the office table working through options for Julia's book. Catherine had spoken to three publishers; all trusted Catherine and there was strong interest. Timing was key now.

"Maddy, I want you to come to Frankfurt with me next week and help me pitch. I need to introduce you to more people in the business and with the two of us, we can get round more of them. Julia's book will be our priority, but our complete list needs to be more prominent. We'll share a room if that's okay. It's not a cheap event."

She hadn't expected this. It would be an excellent opportunity to have a break from Mike and Finn. "No, that's fine. I'd love to come. Thank you. And it'll be good to get away for a few days."

"Great. We'll get your flight organized. Sorry it's short notice. Call Julia and update her."

Madeleine went out for her lunchtime walk and called Shammie. The phone rang for a while and went to voicemail. A minute later, Shammie called her back.

"Hi Maddy, my love. Sorry, I had a late night. Just getting up." She sounded breathless.

"You been up to no good? Is Jacob away?"

"He is, as it happens. How are you?"

"Well, I won't ask. I'm great thanks. Off to Frankfurt next week for the book fair. I was hoping we could meet up before I go. Give me some evenings that work for you and I'll WhatsApp Em too."

"Hang on. Let me check." The phone went silent for a moment. "Thursday or Friday will be best for me."

"Great, I can do both. Keep them free. You okay? You sound a bit distracted."

"No, I'm fine. Been a busy morning. Big kiss. Bye."

CHAPTER 23

After getting no answers to his calls and texts to Finn, Mike called his friend Alf and arranged to go for a bevvie with him at The Roscoe Head, their favourite Liverpool pub. He was annoyed with Finn, and he could let off steam with his oldest friend. They sat down together, and he took a large swig of beer.

"He's being a proper meff, Alf. He's never behaved like this before. Maddy's got to him, that's the problem."

Alf put down his pint. "But he hasn't got to Maddy, has he?"

"Would she be dancing with strangers in clubs and fucking me for hours on end if he had?"

Alf grinned. He loved hearing of Mike's exploits. "Maybe you need to get him up here, and we'll give him a good talking to. Get him away from London and her. We'll take him to Town House and get him laid."

Mike guffawed. "I'm not so sure. It'll take more than a swingers' club to sort him out. It's his heart that's leading him, not his cock."

Alf was far more interested in Mike's time with Madeleine. "So, you had a good time, eh? Tell me everything. Any pics?"

"None of the sort you like."

"You think she'd go to the Club?".

"Hard to tell at this stage. I wouldn't rule it out. She enjoys a bit of pain, and she's certainly not averse to showing off."

Alf's face lit up. "I bet that Mistress Jasmine would love her. Have you suggested it?"

Mike shook his head. "No, I was waiting for Finn to ask her, but I don't think he'll do that now. We'll see how things go in the next couple of weeks. Another bevvie?"

★ ★ ★ ★

Finn called back two days later.

"Where the hell have you been, Finn? Have you forgotten we're running a business? Rachel's been trying to call you and we need to meet. I'm not happy."

"I'm not happy either, Mike. Don't fucking shout at me. Yes, we need to talk, and not just about business. I'm sorry I've not answered your calls. I needed a bit of time to try to get my head straight. How's Maddy?"

Mike sounded surprised. "You haven't spoken to her either?"

There was a moment's silence. "I spoke to her briefly this morning."

Mike was not willing to put up with Finn in this mood. "When she left me on Sunday, she was floating on air."

There was silence. Then, "I want you to stop seeing her," Finn said.

Mike suppressed a grin. "Does she want to stop seeing me? Doesn't seem like it to me." He was enjoying this.

"Please Mike. This isn't a game for me anymore. Maddy's special. There are plenty of other women, for God's sake. One of her friends would fuck you for sure."

"What friend?"

"Forget it. And forget Maddy. Please. I'm going to meet up with her tonight, and I want to tell her how I feel. Give me a break, okay?"

Mike was tiring of Finn.

"I don't know what the fuck's happened to you. Just stop being a muppet. I suppose you're going to tell her you love her. You'll be making a complete prick of yourself if you do. She'll laugh in your face. Or is that what you want, my cuck? Is it? The ultimate humiliation?"

Finn ended the call.

He stared at himself in the mirror. He was looking good. Soon he'd be with Maddy. He'd seduced her once and he could do it again. Liverpool.... Athens.... No woman could have such a great time without feeling something, could she? It hadn't just been sex. Maybe the first night. But that walk on the beach when they talked about so many things, the romantic candlelit dinner in his favourite Liverpool restaurant, the tender sex. Okay, it hadn't all been tender. But that was the best, wasn't it? Switching from gentle to raw sex and back again? Sleeping in each other's arms. Whispering good night to each other. Yes, she loved sex with Mike. She was having fun. But it would change. Shammie had understood how he could be in love. Maddy was very lovable. Who wouldn't love her? He picked up the orchid he'd bought her and went outside and hailed a taxi.

He had chosen a restaurant in Soho. Simple, intimate with great food and wine. A perfect place to bring a special woman.

* * * *

Madeleine was immersed in her work with Catherine when she suddenly looked at her watch.

"Oh no. I'm sorry. I'm meeting a friend for dinner and I'm already late. I can rearrange. It's not that important."

Catherine stretched and stood up from the table. "No, you go, Maddy. We've got a lot done. Enjoy your evening. I hope you come in tomorrow morning firing on all cylinders!"

"Don't worry, I will."

She called Finn. "I'm so sorry. I'm running late and only just leaving work. It'll be at least 30 minutes before I can get there. Do you want to wait?"

Of course he'd wait. He ordered a bottle of wine and some olives. He was getting used to waiting.

She went to the bathroom and put lipstick on. She wasn't dressed for dinner, but that couldn't be helped. Finn wouldn't mind. She hoped he wasn't expecting a night of sex because there was no way it was going to happen. It would be good to see him and have a meal but not a late night. She walked to the tube and headed to Piccadilly Circus.

She spotted Finn at the back of the restaurant looking at his phone. "Texting Mike?"

"Maddy. You're here. So lovely to see you." He stood up and embraced her.

"Here's a little something for you." He picked up the orchid from beside his chair and handed it to her.

"Finn, this is beautiful, thank you. Where shall I put it?"

A waiter came over, took her coat and offered to look after the plant for her. She sat down opposite Finn, settled into her seat, tossed her head, and flexed her shoulders.

"I'm sorry I'm late. It's been a long day. I'm off to Frankfurt next week with Catherine for the book fair and we had to get a lot of stuff sorted out. It's a big deal for us, and I'm looking forward to getting away. It's lovely to see you but I'm afraid I can't be late home tonight."

He reached for her hand, but she moved it away. He sat back, hiding his disappointment.

"Maddy, even a short time with you is a delight. Have some wine."

"Thanks, I'll have one glass. I'm sorry I'm not really dressed for dinner. You're looking good."

She wasn't feeling relaxed. Finn gave her his best smile. "Maddy, you're exquisite, however you're dressed or not dressed." He paused for a moment. "I assume you had a good time with Mike?"

She frowned. "Hasn't he told you?"

"No, we haven't really spoken."

She looked at him. "That's surprising. I thought this was what it was all about for you?"

He waited a moment. "Maddy, I need to tell you something."

"Uh-oh. This sounds serious." She was right.

"I love you."

She stared at him. "You love me? What are you talking about? This was supposed to be just fun. Nothing else."

He tried to hide the disappointment. "Do you think you could love me?"

"No! Well, I don't know. No! Definitely not."

"I don't believe you, Maddy. We've had such amazing times together. So close and loving, so intimate. I know things got a bit out of hand with Mike, but he just wants your body. I want the woman you are, in every way. I love your mind, your spirit. And I don't want to share you with him anymore. I don't want to share you with anyone."

He reached over and took her hand before she could move it. "I love you, Maddy. I want to get to know you and you get to know me. The real me. Not the playboy, the womaniser you know me as. That's just a front. I've met no one like you before. Give me a chance. Please."

She pulled her hand away. "Finn, you love women and the chase. Don't deny who you are. You're not in love with me, and I don't want you to be. Anyway, you're far too young. And how could I ever trust you?"

He shook his head. "All you've ever seen is one side of me. I accept that. But you can trust me. Let me prove it to you."

"Finn, after the experiences I've had with two so-called full-time relationships, I have no desire to get involved in another one. Sex is fine, not commitment. You understand?" She got up. "I'm sorry, I should go. This is not what I was looking for."

He put his hand on her arm. "Maddy, please don't go. Please. I'll change the subject. Talk about anything you want. Tell me about Frankfurt. The food here is great. Please. Stay."

She hesitated. "Okay. But no more declarations, please. And I can't stay long."

"Thank you," he said softly.

MADELEINE

When Madeleine got home, she threw her coat over the banister, kicked off her shoes and poured herself a whisky. The food had indeed been good and once she had put Finn straight, they'd talked about everything that had happened between them and with Mike. It had helped to clear her head and confirm that what had happened had been great for her. But now, she needed some balance. In a just a few months, she had changed from being a dull, bored middle-aged ex-wife to a woman who gave herself willingly to men for sex in hotels and went dancing and picking up men. One thing she knew for sure was that she had taken control for the first time in her life. She had discovered things about her body that she'd never known. She was surprised that pain was an aphrodisiac for her.

What else was likely to happen? She'd done everything she could to bury the memories of what had happened with Justin, the man she had thought was the love of her life. Only the nightmares remained. Her time with Richard now felt as if it had never existed. The one thing she really worried about when she allowed herself to think about it, was whether she could truly love and be loved. All her relationships had scarred her. Could she ever trust anyone enough to open her heart to another person?

CHAPTER 24

Madeleine arrived at the pub first. Prosecco was waiting for Emily and Shammie. She stood up and hugged them both as they arrived together. "My darlings, so lovely to see you."

She poured them both a drink and they clinked glasses. She noticed Shammie was looking a bit uncomfortable.

Emily said, "You must be looking forward to Frankfurt."

"I am, Em. I need to get away for a few days. Life's been getting a little complicated."

"Oh, good!" Emily grinned.

Shammie shuffled in her seat and asked, "Good complicated or bad complicated?"

"I don't know. Both. Let's just say things haven't turned out quite as I expected."

"Stop being so enigmatic. Tell us all," said Emily.

Madeleine looked from one to the other. "Em, you know a bit about it. Shammie, you know I met up with Finn and he introduced me to his business partner. What you don't know is, I've slept with both several times, separately and together. It was good fun, until Finn told me he's falling in love with me."

She looked at them both. Shammie was staring at her drink.

Emily started to laugh. "It's supposed to be us women who are the emotional ones. I assume you don't love him?"

"No Em, I don't. Shammie you're very quiet. What's up?"

Shammie took a sip of her drink. "Maddy, we've been friends a long time, right? Finn came round the other day. He was in a mess. He told me everything. I know he's in love with you. I also told him not to be an idiot."

Madeleine looked at her, frowning. "He told you everything? What everything?

Shammie was looking even more uncomfortable.

"About you both in Liverpool, about Athens, about Mike, about his thing he has with Mike. I felt like a mother confessor."

Emily looked from one to the other.

"Why didn't you tell me, Shammie?" asked Madeleine. "I'd have been pre-warned. Wouldn't have had to have an embarrassing dinner with him last night."

"I should have done. I'm sorry. He stayed the night."

Emily looked shocked. "With you?"

"Yes. He drank an entire bottle of Jacob's best wine and fell asleep on the sofa."

Madeleine's eyes narrowed. "On the sofa..."

"Yes Maddy. The sofa. I covered him with a blanket and when I woke in the morning he'd gone."

Madeleine fixed Shammie with her eyes. "You slept with him, didn't you? I rang you that morning and he was there, wasn't he?"

"Okay, yes, I did but we didn't have sex. He just wanted to sleep. Like I said, he was a mess."

"And in the morning? He didn't fuck you? Really? This is Finn we're talking about. Well?"

"Maddy, I didn't think we needed to tell you. Besides, you said yourself it wasn't serious..."

Madeleine put down her glass. She was shocked at how much anger she felt. Why should this bother her so much? She felt betrayed and yet had no reason to be. Finn was a free man. Shammie openly had sex with others. So did she.

Madeleine grabbed her coat. "Fuck you, Shammie. Sorry, Em. I have to go. I'll call you."

Shammie put her head in her hands. "Shit. I sure mis-read that."

* * * *

The next evening, Madeleine was sitting next to Jack on the sofa in Emily's sitting room. The three of them had had dinner. Jack got up to go to his study. He patted Madeleine on the shoulder. "I hope you two can get this Shammie thing sorted out. Such a pity."

Emily stroked his arm. "We will. Behave yourself, darling." Jack snorted.

"Thanks, Jack. Sorry to spoil your evening."

He winked at Madeleine.

"No problem Maddy. Good luck in Frankfurt."

They waited until Jack had gone upstairs. Madeleine squeezed her friend's hand. "You've got a good man there, Em."

"I know," Emily said, settling in beside Madeleine. "I'm going to be brutally honest, Maddy. I think you're being hypocritical. You might be a bit hurt, but come on, you're making far too much of it. The way you're reacting is almost funny, given your love of threesomes and your rejection of Finn's love."

"Am I? Yes, maybe I am. I was surprised at how I reacted. But it was a shock. I don't know, Em. Sometimes I wish I'd never got into all this. Just for once in my life, I wanted to have some private fun while I sort my life out. Is that too much to ask?"

"I know. I get that. But come on. We all know Shammie's over the top."

"Would you have slept with a guy I was sleeping with?"

"Of course I wouldn't. And certainly not without asking you first. But this is Shammie. She knows she's upset you and wishes she'd never have done it. As she said, she mis-read the situation." Emily poured them both another glass. "At least she's trying to make it up to you."

Madeleine took a sip. "Thanks, Em. This must be the last one. I'm flying to Frankfurt in the morning."

"Maddy, let her sweat if you want to. But do nothing you'll regret. Sleep on it. Wait til you get back. She behaved stupidly, but she's a good friend and she's sorry."

Madeleine nodded. "I know. I'll get over it. But I'll find it hard to trust her again. And sure as hell, I'll never trust Finn. He's in love with me and he fucks a friend of mine? What a joke. I'll deal with him when I'm ready. There is one thing I want you to do. Call Shammie and tell her she must never tell Finn I know they slept together."

CHAPTER 25

The three days in Frankfurt had been exhausting. Up early, doing pitches, lots of conversations, late parties. A constant merry-go-round. Madeleine's admiration for Catherine had grown enormously. She had had no idea how much regard Catherine was held in and how hard she worked. The bidding for Julia's book had been intense. And profitable. A deal had been struck late on the last night.

The next morning while they were waiting for the flight back to London, Madeleine rang Julia.

"Jules, good morning. I've got some news for you. How does a three-book deal sound? How does £100,000 sound?"

There was a sharp intake of breath. "Maddy, tell me this isn't a joke."

She grinned and looked across at Catherine. "It's no joke. HarperCollins, no less. The contract will be ready to sign on Friday."

She could hear Julia's excitement. "Maddy, thank you. Thank you! This is amazing. What time on Friday? I love you! Please thank Catherine too. I love you both. £100,000! I can't believe it."

"Believe it, Jules. You earned every penny. But I must warn you. The hard work starts now. You've got two more books to write."

For a moment there was silence.

"God. Okay. I'll do anything you want. Fuck. This is everything to me. £100,000! Fuck. I'm going to celebrate. I'll have a party on Friday. You and Catherine will be the guests of honour! Please say you can come."

"I'm sure we can. I'll let you know what time to come in for the signing. Well done, Jules. Go and tell Max." She ended the call and turned to Catherine. "That was fun!"

Her phone rang. Finn. He could wait. So could Mike. She had a lot of thinking to do and she felt like a change. She'd ring Barbara as soon as she got back to London.

★ ★ ★ ★

Julia was shaking when she put down her phone. She had always believed in her writing. She loved doing it. But £100,000 was beyond anything she had dreamed of. She thought back on all the experiences that had shaped the novel, her university days and nights, her shifting sexuality, the writers she worshipped, especially the women writers, and Maxine who had opened her real self and loved her though the tough times and the good. And lovely Madeleine, who had believed in her and helped to shape the final version.

She poured herself a coffee and, shaking, called Maxine. "Darling, I'm going to be published. It's happening. HarperCollins has paid £100,000 for three books."

"Oh my god! That is amazing. Congratulations. I'm so very proud of you."

"Can we throw a party on Friday?"

"Of course! And I want to hear everything! But I must go to a meeting. Talk later. I love you. Well done!"

★ ★ ★ ★

Catherine and Madeleine were waiting for her when she arrived at the office to sign the contract. They both hugged her, and their colleagues applauded as Catherine opened a bottle of champagne. "Not too early I hope, Jules?"

Julia was grinning. "Hell no. Bring it on!"

Catherine filled all their glasses. "Congratulations. We're all so excited for you and for us. Here's to this book and many more. Maddy will take you out for lunch. Unfortunately, I have more meetings. Congratulations again, Jules."

"Thank you, Catherine. Thank you so much for everything you've done."

CHAPTER 26

Maxine had taken the day off to help get the flat ready for the party. Thirty-five people were invited, and Julia had no idea how they would all fit in. A few of her friends from Liverpool had been able to come but most were from their circle in London. The majority were women, mainly gay. She hoped Catherine would fit in.

Julia was surprised by how affectionate Madeleine had been over lunch. The conversation had been intimate and open. They had both talked about their sex lives as though they'd known each other forever. Maddy had told her she was involved with two men. She'd asked her about her relationship with Maxine and what it was like to have sex with a woman. They'd had enough to drink for the questions and answers to be explicit. Maddy intrigued her, and she couldn't deny an attraction. When Madeleine had kissed her cheek and held her hand as they parted it was a connection that excited her. Was this what Max had felt with the blonde woman?

After her lunch with Julia, Madeleine had gone home to work. Before she got to her desk she'd lain down on the sofa and given herself an orgasm to relieve the sexual tension. Her thoughts shifted from Julia to an amorphous body and back again. It hadn't taken long.

* * * *

The party was in full swing when Madeleine arrived. The loud music was Motown, which she loved and wondered who had chosen it. A woman she didn't know opened the door. Butch. Friendly. Catherine was already there, holding court, surrounded by several young, admiring women and one man. Budding writers, excited by Julia's success and wanting some of the same.

"Maddy! So good to see you. Wow, you look amazing." Julia hugged her and gave her a brief kiss on the lips. "I love your outfit. Come on in. I'll introduce you to some friends, but first I want you to meet my darling Max at last."

Julia took her hand and went into the sitting room. Max was pouring some drinks.

"Max, this is Madeleine."

Maxine looked up at the stunning woman, her own age, with rich, full auburn hair, wearing black tailored suit trousers, a tight dark green polo neck top tucked into the trousers, black heeled boots, and silver earrings.

"You're Madeleine? Sorry, that was very rude of me. I just wasn't expecting...it's so good to meet you at last. Thank you for everything you've done for Jules. I'm so proud of her."

Madeleine leant forward and kissed her on both cheeks. "So am I. It's been a pleasure to work with her. She has a big future ahead."

Maxine turned to Julia. "You never told me...."

Julia grinned. "Well, now you know, darling. Give Maddy a drink. I'm going to introduce her to more people."

Maxine watched as Julia took Madeleine's hand and led her towards a group of her Liverpool friends. Such incredible legs and hips. She had always imagined Madeleine as being interesting but bookish. She noticed others in the room were looking at her too.

Madeleine hadn't been to such a lively party for ages. It was lovely to be in the company of women. And Catherine was obviously enjoying it too. A lot. Seeing her passionately kissing a dark-haired woman had been a total eye opener.

A small group of scousers, old friends of Julia's, proud of their city, proud of Julia who had introduced her as 'my brilliant editor', had gathered round Madeleine. The butch woman who had opened the door was from Liverpool. "Jules tells me you've been to our great city recently. Like it?"

Madeleine was enjoying being the centre of attention. "I've only been there once but yes, I absolutely loved it."

The woman beamed. "You should come back and party with us, Maddy the Brilliant Editor! We'll all show you a good time."

Madeleine laughed. "I'd love to!" An entire group of gay women together. Another potential experience? But did she need to go to Liverpool for that? Looking around at all the smiling faces, she didn't think so.

She felt a hand on her arm and turned to see Maxine holding a bottle of wine. "Can I fill your glass?" Max had a deep, almost gravelly voice.

"Thanks, Max. Great party. But I must eat something first or I'll be doing something I might regret."

Maxine took her by the elbow. "Come into the kitchen. The food's there. So, having a good time?"

"Oh yes, I am. Lovely people."

Maxine picked up a dish of cocktail sausages and offered her one. "You're quite a hit Maddy. Several girlfriends have asked who you are. Have you ever been with a woman?"

Madeleine gave her a quizzical smile. "A straight question like that deserves..."

"A slap in the face?"

She liked Maxine's directness. "No. Of course not. No, I haven't."

Maxine held her eyes. "Ever thought about it?"

"Yes." A faint smile.

"I can introduce you to a few friends if you want."

Madeleine turned away, filled a plate with chilli con carne and rice and looked back at Maxine, her eyes shining. "You're not what I expected," she said.

"Nor are you," said Maxine.

"It's a pity you're taken."

"Yes. It is." Maxine touched her shoulder gently, lingering long enough to send a shiver through her body. "Let's see…"

Over Maxine's shoulder she saw Julia looking at them then turning away. "Julia's not happy, Max."

Maxine nodded. "It's okay. Don't worry. I'll talk to her."

She shook her head. "I'm sorry, I don't know what came over me. I will not get involved, Max. Julia's very important to me."

Maxine touched her arm for a moment. "She is to me too, Maddy."

Madeleine left the kitchen, saw Julia looking at her and walked over. "I'm sorry, Jules. I don't quite know what happened there."

"It's okay. Max seems to be going through a bit of a frisky stage right now and it's not all aimed at me."

Madeleine was annoyed with herself. "I'm sorry if I upset you. I'd never hurt you. Anyway, I've got my hands full!"

Julia took a deep breath and looked straight at Madeleine. "You know…. I fancy you, too."

Madeleine held Julia's gaze. "I loved our lunch. I thought about you afterwards."

Julia blushed. "I thought about you, too."

Julia took her arm. "I want to show you where I write. It's my private space. Totally private."

⋆ ⋆ ⋆ ⋆

Julia was still asleep when Max came in with a breakfast tray. She put it on their bed and drew the curtains back. "Hey, baby. Time to wake up."

Julia groaned and pulled the covers over her head. "Not yet please."

Maxine plumped up the pillows. "Sit up and have breakfast. I've brought you coffee, orange juice and toast and marmalade. Your favourites."

"God, my head hurts."

Maxine sat on the bed and stroked Julia's tangled hair. "I'm not surprised. You really let go, didn't you."

Julia slowly sat up and shook her head. Maxine took her hand and spoke softly. "Listen, darling. I saw you go into the study with Maddy. You were in there long enough to have written another novel. I was very jealous, and, yes, I felt angry. But I've thought about it, and I don't blame you. She's one hell of a woman."

Julia picked up the mug of coffee and looked at Max. "You don't mind?"

Maxine pursed her lips. "I can't say I'm deliriously happy, but I don't want it to affect us. I just want you to be honest with me."

Julia looked down and fiddled with her hair. "I'm sorry. I got carried away. We'd had a hot lunch together and it just sort of carried on. It was sex. Just sex."

"Was it good?"

"Yes, but nothing like as good as us."

Maxine chucked her under the chin. "Don't involve us, Jules. To be honest I *am* a little jealous."

She looked concerned. "Please don't be, my darling. I love you."

Maxine stroked her face. "I meant I'm jealous you had her. Dammit! I wanted her too."

"Oh."

They sat quietly together on the bed.

"Are you going to see her again?" asked Maxine.

Julia handed the tray to Max and slipped back down under the duvet. "Yes, I guess so. She's my editor."

Maxine stood up with the tray. "You know what I mean," she said.

Julia covered her head with a pillow. "I'd like to."

Maxine put the tray on the floor and pulled the pillow off Julia's face. "Okay. Invite her round for dinner. Just the three of us."

Maxine pulled the duvet off Julia and looked at her naked body. "How would you feel about it?"

Julia paused. "I think I'd like it."

Maxine undid her gown. "Good. Me too. One thing, Jules. Don't ever see her for sex without telling me you're going to. Never, ever do anything behind my back."

She got onto the bed and kissed Julia greedily. Julia moaned and pulled Maxine on top of her.

"I love you so very much."

CHAPTER 27

Finn woke, feeling angry and ashamed. He knew he should apologize to Mike. After breakfast, he called him.

"I'm sorry. I've made a complete prick of myself. Maddy doesn't love me and never will. You were right."

"Good. At last. Okay. You know what we should do. It'll help you, too."

He knew exactly what they should do. "The Club?"

"Yes. Let's get her there and see how far this sexual exploration of hers will go. You must take control of yourself, Finn. Let's get back to normal."

Finn sighed. "So, shall we take her together? That'll make her more likely to come. I doubt if she'll come with just me."

Mike thought for a moment. "Maybe we should take her to a munch first. Ease her into it. Introduce her to a few of the regulars so she realises they're not all weirdos. She needs to meet Mistress Jasmine in advance too. Listen, I'll handle this. Leave it to me. Just keep the next two weekends free."

He was relieved Mike would take the lead. Madeleine hadn't answered any of his calls. She'd just texted to say she was busy and would get back to him. He needed to fight back, to stop Madeleine from destroying him. It was time to find another woman to play with. Someone less high maintenance. He'd go back to Browns and see if the woman at the bar was around. He'd seen her there a couple of times and guessed it was a hunting ground for her too.

It would be fascinating if Madeleine agreed to come to the Club. A test for Mike as well. If he succeeded, good for him. If he failed, it might pull him down a peg or two. Either would be good. For the first time since he'd had that painful dinner with Madeleine, he was feeling better about himself.

He found the woman at the bar in Browns, and after two glasses of champagne, she came to his room. It had been too easy. She'd stayed the night and they'd fucked again in the morning. But it was meaningless, and when she left, Finn was glad to see her go. He'd tell Mike about her but right now, it was all about Madeleine. He didn't enjoy having to wait any more than Mike did. He knew they had sown a seed in her mind and if anyone could persuade Madeleine to come to the Club, it would be Mistress Jasmine.

He dressed and walked down to the bar. He had to concentrate on work. Sitting at his favourite table, the one where he'd first sat with Madeleine, he ordered a croissant and coffee for breakfast, picked up his phone and started on the list of calls he had to make. It was time to move on. Time to do some deals.

* * * *

When Mike rang Madeleine and told her he'd sorted Finn out, he could sense the smile on her face. Now he had to persuade her to meet Mistress Jasmine.

"I'm going to be in London on Thursday, and I'd love to see you. Do you know what a munch is?"

There was a giggle down the phone. "A cow eating?"

Mike laughed. "What do you know about BDSM?"

"Not much."

"Okay. A munch is where a group of people into the BDSM scene get together in a pub or a club for a social. If you saw them sitting together, you'd have no idea they all had this particular method of self-expression. Finn and I are going to one on Thursday evening. It's in Clerkenwell. Interested?"

Madeleine's reply was instant. "You must be joking!"

"Maddy, I know enough about you now to guess you might just enjoy it. What do you have to lose? You've not turned down a challenge yet! Come on, we'll look after you."

She shook her head. "Okay, for you, I'll think about it."

* * * *

They were waiting for her at the bar when she arrived. The pub was full, with men and women talking and drinking, muzak in the background. Mike saw her come in and nudged his friend.

Finn got up as she approached and took her hand. "I'm so glad you could come. And I'm so sorry I made such a fool of myself the other night. You're looking great. Nice choice of dress!" Madeleine was wearing the black turtleneck dress she'd worn for her first meeting with him.

"Thanks, Finn. Hello, Mike."

She looked around. "So where is this munch?"

"It's here."

"Yes, I know that but where? Do we go downstairs, upstairs?"

Mike grinned. "Look around you, Maddy. This is it."

She looked puzzled. "But everyone seems so …normal. Are they all into this stuff?"

In unison, Mike and Finn said, "Yes."

She laughed. "So, what happens now? And which of you two men is going to buy me a drink? I'll have a gin and tonic, with ice and lemon."

As she sipped her drink and looked around, Mike pointed out a tall, black-haired woman about her own age, sitting surrounded by a group of men and women.

"That's Mistress Jasmine." he said. "She's a Dominatrix. Everyone sitting with her is submissive. The man sitting to her right is her slave. She's the Queen Bee round here. Nothing much happens without her approval. I want you to be introduced to her, Maddy. Finn, you know her best. Go and have a word with her."

Madeleine finished her drink and laughed. "She's called Mistress Jasmine?"

Mike put a hand on her arm. "No laughing, Maddy. Shhhh."

Madeleine studied the well-built woman, a soft, pink leather jacket round her shoulders over a crisp white shirt, with matching pink leather trousers. She looked like she could fit easily into any surroundings, intriguing anyone who looked at her. Interesting.

Mike ordered another drink for her and together they watched as Finn walked over and stood waiting by the group. At first no one took any notice of him but then the woman raised her hand for silence and beckoned Finn over. Finn whispered in her ear and the woman looked across at Madeleine and spoke to Finn. He nodded and walked back to where Mike and Madeleine were standing.

"She wants you to come over, Maddy."

Madeleine looked at him. "No way! Really? Why?"

Finn's face was anxious. "She likes the look of you. It's quite an honour to be invited over. You must go."

She looked at Finn. "What do I say?"

Mike glanced at Finn. "Just go and stand by her and wait till she speaks to you."

Finn gently touched her hand. "Go on, Maddy. A new experience for you."

"Jesus Christ. Okay."

Madeleine picked up her drink and walked over. Mike and Finn watched as the woman sitting on Mistress Jasmine's left stood up and offered Madeleine her seat.

Mistress Jasmine turned and looked into Madeleine's eyes.

"Finn tells me you're interested in the scene."

"I guess I must be, to be here."

There was a murmur amongst the submissives and the woman who had stood up said, "You must address her as Mistress, even at a munch."

The Mistress smiled and Madeleine could feel a strange sensation as she stared back into her dark eyes.

"She obviously has a lot to learn. Don't be hard on her."

The Mistress picked up Madeleine's hand and stroked it.

"Your first lesson, Madeleine, is to call me Mistress. Do you agree to that?"

Madeleine heard herself speak. "Yes, Mistress."

"Good. So, you have no experience of our world?"

"None, Mistress."

The woman's voice was soft. "And you'd like to learn?"

"Yes, Mistress."

She dropped Madeleine's hand. "Okay. You may leave now. Go back to Finn and Mike. I'll be in touch."

Immediately Madeleine got up and walked back to the bar. She felt in a daze.

"That was weird. She's going to be in touch."

Mike put his arm round her, and Finn said "You have no idea what an honour you've been given, Maddy. I've never known that to happen at a first munch."

Madeleine shook her head. "It was like I was under a spell."

Mike stroked her cheek. "Maddy, BDSM isn't just physical. It's as much in the mind. She's a high-level hypnotist. It looks like you're going to be granted an audience."

Madeleine exhaled. "Christ. So, what happens now?"

"You wait," said Finn.

Madeleine had never needed a long hot bath, candles, and a large glass of whisky as much as she did when the taxi dropped her off home. She slid into the water and put the glass on the chair next to the bath. The candlelight calmed her, and the scent of her favourite bath oil eased her mind. She breathed slowly and deeply, letting the tensions evaporate. She could hear her mother's voice in her head: 'Be careful what you wish for.' What the hell had she done? Sex with two men, a threesome, sex with a woman and now a meeting with a Dominatrix. She giggled. 'Be careful what you wish for.' Too right. She was past being careful. But best not to wish for much more. She already had enough. She was in control, wasn't she? She had sorted Finn out. But Julia. That had been a surprise. And Maxine. She'd crossed two red lines. Never mix work with pleasure and never get involved with a married man. Or woman. It was always a disaster. She must ring Julia and put things straight before Catherine found out anything about it. The book was too important for them all for her to mess up. The last thing she wanted was to hurt Julia and Maxine. She'd apologise. She'd made a mistake. Shit. But it had felt so good with Julia. So soft. Feeling a woman's fingers inside her, sucking on a woman's nipples, tasting Julia's sex on her fingers… It had to be a one off. And now she'd fallen out with one of her best friends. Over what? A man, for God's sake. She had totally over-reacted. If she was honest. Shammie sleeping with Finn was a relief. It had taken the pressure off her.

She took a large mouthful of whisky and closed her eyes, letting the warmth of the bath soothe her body and her mind; she drifted into sleep. Outside, the clouds were building into a thunderstorm. She was deeply asleep in the bath when the sky cracked open releasing a bolt of lightning, immediately followed by an enormous bang of thunder that woke her from the falling nightmare that had invaded her mind again.

Tick.... tock...

CHAPTER 28

After the Monday morning meeting, Catherine asked her to stay behind.

"That was quite a party Julia and Maxine threw. I wish I could say it's not my business, but it is. Please don't get involved with Julia in any way other than professionally. It was so blatant. Can't you see how it looks? I don't need to spell it out, Maddy, and I don't want to have to mention it again. This is an official warning. Understood?"

Madeleine looked at the floor. "Understood." Catherine walked off to her office.

She sat at her desk feeling like a naughty schoolgirl. Humiliated. Dammit. She'd been so stupid.

Her phone rang. It was Julia. Why the hell hadn't she rung first and taken the initiative?

"Hi Maddy. How are you?" Her voice was upbeat.

She bit her lip. "I'm so sorry, Jules. That should never have happened - on so many levels."

Julia was smiling. "Hey, it's fine. I enjoyed it, didn't you?"

"Yes, but please let's not let it happen again." Nervously, she asked, "How's Max?"

Julia's voice was relaxed. "Oh, she's cool. She knows what happened. We talked about it, and we want you to come and have dinner with us. When are you free?"

Madeleine couldn't help sounding surprised. "What did she say? Was it okay?"

"Yes. It's fine. So, please say yes."

She was silent for a moment. "I really don't think I should. It's sweet of you both but you're too important a client for me to mess things up."

Julia was persistent. "Please Maddy, relax. It's cool. Really. Shall I have a word with Catherine?"

"No, no, no. Don't."

"So, you'll come for dinner? Max is a great cook and wants to get to know you better." She could feel the smile in Julia's voice.

She shook her head. "Okay. Yes. But only for dinner. Anything else is out of the question. How about Friday?"

"Perfect. 8pm?"

"What can I bring?"

Julia laughed. "Just bring your sweet self."

Madeleine had a pile of emails to answer and slowly made her way through them. Jane Fitch from HarperCollins wanted Catherine, Julia, and her to meet at their offices for a planning meeting in two days. She called Julia back. A professional call. No flirting. Thank goodness.

Her phone rang again.

"I'm busy, Finn. What is it?"

"I had a call from Tim this morning. Mistress Jasmine's slave. We've been invited to a private party she's holding at her flat. This is not an invitation to turn down, Maddy."

She shook her head. "Forget it, Finn. Call her back and tell her I'm sorry but I don't want to take this any further. It's not for me. I've thought about it and it's a step too far."

Finn was almost begging. "Maddy, I can't. You don't say no to her. Please, Maddy. I'll lose so much face if you don't come. And what do you have to lose? You wanted adventures, didn't you?"

Madeleine snapped back. "I'm up to my eyes in bloody adventures, Finn. I can't do any more."

"Please, Maddy."

"No, Finn. Sorry, I must go." She ended the call.

★ ★ ★ ★

She was at home watching a movie on Netflix when her phone rang.

"Hi, Mike. Hang on. Let me put this on pause. Okay. Now let me guess. Finn's called you and asked you to persuade me to meet up with this Mistress."

Mike laughed. "Yes, that's one of the reasons I'm calling. The other is to ask you out on Friday night. Let's go dancing again. Get some free drinks."

"Sorry, can't do Friday. I'm out for dinner."

Mike voice became serious. "Who's the lucky guy?"

"No guy involved. It's two women."

"Even better. Tell me more."

She groaned. "You're such a perv, Mike."

"Okay. So how about Saturday?"

She raised her eyes to the ceiling. "Maybe. I'll see how I feel. I'm not going to meet this Dominatrix, Mike. You can beg all you like."

"I never beg. Don't you know me by now?"

She laughed. "Touché. Mike come on; it isn't my thing."

There was an amused tone to his voice. "I beg to differ, Maddy."

"You're begging, Mike?"

Mike guffawed. "Yes, okay, I'm begging. Come on, we've had fun so far, haven't we? You've not done anything you don't want to, have you? And this will be the same. I can promise you an interesting evening. Trust me."

"I wouldn't trust you for a second."

Mike snorted. "That's unfair. Come on, we've had nothing but fun together. This will be more of it. Finn and I will be there. I promise you, you'll come to no harm."

Mike could sense her smile.

"I'll let you know. Let me get back to my movie." She ended the call and picked up the remote control.

CHAPTER 29

Seeing Julia disappear with Madeleine into the study had been far more of a shock than Maxine had let on. She'd felt jealous, and it had hurt. It was the surprise that Julia would do such a thing that got to her. Maxine had had to stop herself opening the door to the study. She knew others had seen it too. Most would have thought it was just a work thing. Maybe Julia had felt it was okay after their conversation about other people. She wished Julia had told her about the attraction. But then she hadn't told Julia about the blonde. Evens. Sort of. At least their conversation over breakfast had been honest. They'd fallen into bed at three in the morning and the sex had been passionate and intense. She felt their relationship had grown stronger. She loved Jules so much. And now she was going to be a published author with a healthy income, in the short term at least. She was proud of her love. So very proud.

When Maxine came back from work, Julia was cooking a meal for them. The table was laid with lit candles on it. A bottle of red wine, ready, open.

"Welcome home, my darling. How was your day?"

She looked quizzically at Julia. "Are we celebrating?"

"I received the first instalment today! But this is to say, 'I love you', and I'm sorry about what happened."

Maxine took off her coat and put it on the sofa with her bag. "Come here, you." She took Julia in her arms and nuzzled her neck.

"Darling one, we need to talk boundaries before Friday. We're both attracted to her, after all. She's sexy and intelligent and interesting. How do you think we should play it?"

Julia kissed her hard. "I think we can play it by ear. I'm sure it'll go well whatever happens. Anyway, tonight, let me spoil you, baby. Sit down. I'm cooking your favourite. Just how you like it. Have a drink."

Julia poured a glass for each of them and looked lovingly at her. Max stroked her cheek. "Spoil me, darling. I'm all yours."

* * * *

An intense week of work had finally ended. Publishers had signed up two other authors and Catherine had pulled forward deadlines and really pushed Madeleine to meet them. A punishment? Madeleine hoped not. But she did sense a bit of frostiness. Maybe it was because Catherine had let in a crack of light onto her secretive private life. Madeleine was not going to tell her where she was going to dinner tonight.

She showered, washed her hair, then shaved her legs and armpits and trimmed her bush. She normally only did this if she was going to have sex. It must have become a habit because that wasn't on tonight for sure. No mixing business and pleasure. A red line.

She chose a long green jersey dress, a delicate silver necklace, small green earrings, light grey eye shadow, a touch of rouge and a delicate lipstick. Stylish, not seductive. She dressed for her mood.

She rang the bell and Julia opened the front door. Madeleine thrust the bottle of wine in front of her like a barrier.

"Thanks, Maddy. Come on in."

The flat was softly lit and the smell from the kitchen was mouth-wateringly delicious. Maxine came out of the kitchen and gave her a warm hug.

"It's so lovely to see you! Here, take off your coat and come and sit down."

"Thank you. It's lovely to be here. And whatever you're cooking, I want some. I'm hungry."

Julia hung up her coat. "I told you Max was a superb cook. Make yourself at home. Red or white?"

Madeleine sat on the sofa. The lamps were dimmed, and soft jazz was playing. A bowl of nuts was on the table in front of her. Down the hall she could see Julia's study and beyond it their bedroom, the door open, softly lit too. Did they always entertain like this?

Julia sat next to her. "I love what you're wearing. The colour really suits you."

Slightly nervously, Madeleine looked down and brushed the front of her dress with her hand.

"Oh, thank you. Yes, it's becoming one of my favourite colours. Yours is lovely too."

Julia was wearing a black crepe dress with a strap over her left shoulder, leaving her right shoulder bare, the tattoo on display. "I splashed out and treated myself. It's Max Mara. It feels wonderful."

Without thinking, Madeleine said, "You *are* wonderful!"

Maxine came out of the kitchen and sat opposite them.

"Maddy, I just wanted to say what happened the other night is fine. Jules and I have talked it through. We don't have an open relationship, but we are always going to be honest with each other if we have feelings for anyone else. I just wanted to get that out of the way."

Madeleine breathed a sigh of relief. "Thank you for saying that Max. And what happened won't happen again. We were both a bit drunk."

Max reached out and took her hand. "Listen, when I said it's fine, I meant it. You're an attractive woman, Maddy. Julia had every right to be attracted to you. I am, too."

Madeleine blushed. "I don't know what to say."

Maxine and Julia smiled at each other. "We just didn't want to hide anything. There are no expectations on you, Maddy. We just want to get to know you better and enjoy your company. I hope you'll enjoy ours too."

She looked at them both grinning at her. "Wow. Okay. Thank you, I guess."

Julia took her hand and kissed her on the cheek. "You okay?"

"Yes. Yes, I am" she said. "And thank you both for your honesty. I feel... flattered. And more than a little surprised."

Maxine raised her glass to them. "Cheers, Maddy! Cheers, my darling! Here's to friendship and fun."

They all lifted their glasses. "Friendship and fun." Maxine stood up. "Okay. Have some snacks. We'll eat in about fifteen minutes."

* * * *

Maxine was still in bed. It was her turn for a lie-in. Julia looked around the kitchen. They normally cleaned up after a dinner party before they went to bed. What a night it had been. So totally unexpected. They'd hoped for it of course, had made love that week imagining Madeleine with them. Rarely did reality live up to fantasy, but this time it had. Madeleine had left as dawn broke, kissing them both before she went. They'd all needed to sleep but that had been impossible. Watching Maxine with another woman had been a revelation. Max had loved many women and been loved by them. Julia could see why. Openly kissing Madeleine in front of Max and seeing the excitement in her eyes had made her bold and wanton. She had found a freedom she'd never known before. A freedom to be herself without jealousy. And such a love for Max. The kitchen could wait. She went back down the hall and slipped into bed. She could smell Madeleine on the sheets and the pillows. But most of all she could smell and taste Max, who lay asleep beside her. Julia slipped two fingers inside Max, who stirred, opening herself. Slowly, gently she started to stroke her lover. They had all day.

CHAPTER 30

"Before I reveal all, Em, my love, I want to know how you and Jack are doing," said Madeleine.

Emily groaned. "He was watching porn."

"I knew it. How did you find out?"

She snorted. "I just checked his browsing history. So easy."

"What was he watching?"

"Women with big tits and guys with enormous cocks. So disappointing."

"Does he know you know?"

She bit her lip. "Yes. I confronted him with it. He was so sheepish. Just like a schoolboy."

"What did you say?"

"I just told him if he wanted to watch porn it was ok, but to do it with me."

"Is he ok with that?"

"Oh yes. I've discovered something about him I never knew."

Madeleine raised an eyebrow. "Oh, do tell."

"He thinks he may be bisexual."

"Jeez. How do you feel about that?"

She looked a little sheepish, then, "Fine. I rather like the idea."

"Why?"

She licked her lips. "I fancy a threesome with a couple of guys. I told him if he wants to explore, he can do it with me. That night we had the best sex we've had for ages. So that's my news. Can you beat that?"

Madeleine looked across at her. "Actually, yes."

"Hell, Maddy. What have you done now?"

Madeleine leant forward. "I had a threesome. With two women. And I loved it!!"

CHAPTER 31

It took ten rings for Finn to answer his phone.

"She's just called. I told you she'd go for it."

Finn was astonished. "She said yes?"

Mike was elated. "Yep. Mistress Jasmine is very pleased. We're in her good books. The party is next Saturday in her dungeon. About twenty people, mainly subs. Maybe a couple of other Doms."

"Does Maddy know what to expect?"

"No, of course not. Do you know what to expect?"

Finn laughed. "No. Her parties are always unpredictable. I hope she'll be in a good mood."

Mike sounded certain. "She will be. She was very pleased with Maddy. She always likes to meet new potential."

"Have you told Maddy what to wear?" Finn asked.

"I will if she asks. It might be amusing to let her turn up in something inappropriate. Mistress will soon put her right."

Finn wasn't so sure. "Do you know where Maddy is? She doesn't answer my calls now."

"Dinner with friends last night, apparently. She blew me out for tonight too. Our Maddy needs a bit of Mistress Jasmine."

* * * *

Mistress Jasmine's slave Tim was on his knees, naked in front of her, painting her toenails. She was sitting on her sofa, her iPad on her lap, checking her emails. A busy week ahead. So many people wanted her services. So many grovelling men and occasionally single women and couples. They came to her for stress relief and visiting her was the only way they could be true to themselves and their needs. Others wanted to play out a fantasy, let go in role play, escape into another world, be humiliated or experience pain at such a level that it flooded their bodies with endorphins. Above all they wanted to submit, hand over control, feel helpless, their bodies and minds in the hands of a Dominant Woman who could do whatever she liked to them. The control was sexual, never coercive. Bless them. She had regulars who she had got to know as friends. She was very fond of them. She loved her financial subs, the ones who would buy her lovely, expensive gifts, perfume, jewellery. One had even bought her a car. But best of all were the ones she controlled with her mind. She could easily hypnotise most submissives. Get deep inside their heads. Do pretty well anything she wanted with them. She always sat with them before a session started, talking softly, kindly, mothering them, asking them questions, letting them admit all their dark, shaming secrets and needs to their Mistress. She didn't care what the secrets were. The darker the better. They loved to tell her and with this information, she could control them. It was so simple. And tonight, a new prospect, Madeleine. It was rare such a woman came her way. She'd make sure she felt at ease. There was no alcohol at her parties. She wanted everyone to have a clear head. Drunkenness was instant banishment, and no one wanted that. Finn and Mike were coming too. She enjoyed their company, and they were good friends. Both were Doms and that pleased her, took a bit of pressure off her. She'd let them work on a couple of her subs while she started to get to know Madeleine. Her initial thought had been that she was submissive. But she wasn't sure. Madeleine had a strong side to her. Well, time would tell. Her guests were due in an hour.

Tim knew exactly what he had to do. He carefully trimmed her nails and applied nail varnish to her feet and hands. She was impatient today, a sure sign this was an important meeting for her. He'd checked all the equipment was exactly as she wanted it. All the food was neatly set out and there was plenty of ginger beer, Her favourite drink at parties. How he hoped she would use the new crop on him. But he knew her focus would be on this Madeleine. It wasn't often she was so interested in a newcomer. She must be special. He'd make sure the newcomer was well looked after. If Mistress was pleased with him, maybe she'd allow him to wear a pair of her special knickers.

★ ★ ★ ★

Mike had been most unhelpful on the phone. Madeleine still didn't know what to wear for Mistress Jasmine's scary party this evening. She assumed most people would be in tight or revealing clothes with little or no underwear. But to hell with that. She was much more inclined to wear jeans and her chic leather jacket. If she did, she'd probably be the odd one out. Maybe a dress would be a good compromise. There was no need for her to feel like a sacrificial lamb. Mike and Finn wouldn't let her come to any harm, and she could always say no. Mike told her there'd be nothing alcoholic to drink, only soft drinks and nibbles. So Jasmine wasn't much of a host. And that slave was such a creep.

Barbara had called at lunchtime, in London for a few days. Sadly, she wasn't free that evening or Madeleine would have had a good excuse not to go to the party. They arranged to meet for tea in Soho the following week and that had put her in a much more positive mood. It was so lovely to hear from her. Madeleine was still wracked with guilt after her night with Max and Julia. Talking it through with Barbara might help.

Mike and Finn were waiting outside the pub when the taxi dropped her off. Mike was wearing a hideous long black leather trench coat making him look horribly like a stormtrooper. Finn at least had on a more stylish black leather jacket. Both wore black t-shirts and jeans. She shook her head and quickly kissed them both. She wanted to get this over with.

The flat was in the basement of a long Georgian terrace. An expensive block. As they walked down the steps, a security light came on. Finn knocked on the door.

A short bald man wearing a pair of women's knickers opened the door and greeted them. He took their coats, and they followed him along the corridor. Madeleine suppressed a giggle. Walking behind Mike and Finn, she entered a room where Mistress Jasmine was sitting on what looked like a throne. The walls were painted black and discreet lighting gave the room the feel of a medieval dungeon. Twelve men and seven women in varying states of undress were standing around chatting to each other. Mistress raised her hand and they fell silent.

"Mike, Finn, so good to see you. And Madeleine! Please come and say hello to me."

Mike took Mistress Jasmine's hand and kissed it. Finn followed. She waved Madeleine forward.

"I've been looking forward to meeting you properly. Let me have a look at you. Turn round." Suddenly Madeleine felt nervous and did as she was told.

"Such a lovely dress. Everyone, this is Madeleine, my favoured guest for this evening. You will all take care of her. Whatever she wants, she gets. Understood?" There was a murmur of approval. Maybe this wouldn't be so bad after all.

Jasmine clapped her hands. "Now everyone, I want you all to introduce yourself to Madeleine and tell her why you love coming here."

As slave Tim offered bowls of nibbles to the guests, each one in turn described who they were, what they did for a living, why they were here and how they loved Mistress Jasmine. It was fascinating. Most of them were in creative jobs, some unemployed and two in senior positions in big companies. The youngest looked to be in her early 20s and the oldest in his 60s. None of them seemed particularly exceptional. Just normal people with a peculiar interest. She had never been surrounded by near naked people chatting about everyday things. She supposed this must be what it was like on a nudist beach. Except everyone was here with a need to be submissive or to dominate and apparently a need for pain and punishment as well as praise. Was that what she wanted, too? Had she subconsciously been drawn to this way of life? She noticed Mike and Finn deep in conversation with Jasmine.

She chatted with a few of the other guests and then felt a hand on her shoulder and turned to see Mistress Jasmine.

"Come with me, Madeleine. I want to find out more about you."

Mike and Finn glanced at each other and watched as Madeleine followed Jasmine out of the room, down the hall and into a room with a large freestanding wooden cross. Jasmine stood face to face with her, leaving no room for any personal space. Madeleine could feel Jasmine's eyes locked on her, could smell the sweetness of her breath. Madeleine felt like she was melting.

"Keep looking at me, Madeleine. I'm going to go inside your mind. Is that ok?

Madeleine hesitated.

"We're not going to do anything you don't want to do. You can stop me at any time. Just say 'red' and I'll stop. Do you understand?"

Madeleine nodded.

"Good, then take off your clothes."

She was transfixed by Jasmine's stare. Slowly, she lifted her dress over her head and stood in her underwear.

"Keep going."

She reached behind her back and undid her bra. She kicked her shoes off and bent to slip off her knickers.

"Put your hands behind your head. Stand up straight."

Mistress Jasmine walked round her. She had never felt so exposed. Every part of her was open to inspection. She felt Mistress Jasmine's hand stroke her bottom.

"Spread your legs. Why are you wet, Madeleine?" she asked softly.

Madeleine shivered. "I can't help it."

Jasmine was staring into her eyes, so close.

"No Madeleine, you can't help it. And why can't you help it?"

She felt transfixed. "Because I want it, Mistress."

"What is it you want, Madeleine?" Jasmine's voice was so firm, so kind, so soft, so demanding.

"Please Mistress, I don't know."

Mistress Jasmine continued standing inches in front of her, staring into her eyes. She felt Jasmine's fingers take hold of her nipples and squeeze them, harder, harder.

"Tell me, Madeleine. What do you want?"

Tears came into her eyes. The pain was excruciating and euphoric. Mistress Jasmine's mouth came close to hers. She could taste Mistress's honey breath as she was kissed, and her nipples slowly twisted.

Suddenly, through the pain and pleasure, her mind filled with Justin's face, twisted in shock. She shook her head, trying to fight off the image.

"I want to be yours, Mistress."

Gently Mistress stroked her face with the back of her hand and pushed her hair back. "Good girl."

Mistress Jasmine left the room and Madeleine slumped to the floor. She was shaking and crying, her mind flooded with memories of Justin. No, she didn't want this! And she didn't want to be hers! What the hell was she doing? The door opened and Finn came in and put his arms round her. She held on to him, sobbing. Slowly he got her to her feet as Mike came into the room. Together they helped her dress. She was still shaking. She had wanted it. She had wanted the humiliation and the pain. What was this about? The last thing she needed was to be reminded of Justin.

She shook her head and wiped her eyes. Mike put his arms around her and held her. "Okay, let's go."

The taxi stopped outside her house. Not much had been said on the journey back. She sat between Mike and Finn and held their hands.

"I don't want to be alone tonight. Please stay with me and hold me. Just be gentle." They got out and Mike paid the taxi.

She unlocked the front door."I'm going to have a shower. Pour yourselves a drink."

Mike gave her a hug. "Okay. Take your time."

The hot water helped to ease the pain in her nipples. She could still see Mistress Jasmine's eyes focusing on hers and shook her head. It would take a while to forget those deep, black eyes. That voice - gentle, strong, demanding. No arguing. Just submission. The pleasure of the pain. She closed her eyes and the memories that had shocked her and caused her to slump to the floor flooded back. Memories of the collapse of love, of abuse, of death that she had done everything she could to bury. Until now she'd succeeded; the only outlet for her memories was through the nightmares. Could she ever trust a man again? Richard had helped her re-build trust but had then destroyed it. She needed loving more than at any time in her life. She pressed her hands against the sides of the shower, convulsed in sobs.

In bed, she lay still between them, letting their hands gently caress her. She was exhausted and closed her eyes. Please, no nightmares.

Mike and Finn quietly left the house in the morning, leaving Madeleine to sleep in. A neighbour in the next-door front garden looked at them both as they walked down the path to the front gate. They waved and the man frowned. They headed for a cafe in the nearby parade of shops. A warm fug and the smell of coffee and bacon embraced them.

Mike picked up a menu. "We fucked up there, my friend. We shouldn't have taken Maddy home so soon."

Finn signalled to a waitress then turned back to Mike.

"Jasmine was not pleased. What the hell happened between them? We're going to have to do some serious apologizing to Mistress. I'll arrange for a large bunch of flowers to be delivered."

Mike nodded. "Good. Yes, we sure are. Maybe that woman you fucked the other night could be an offering."

Finn looked at the menu. "I have no idea, Mike. Right now, I want a strong coffee and to forget about it all. Let's just let things sit for a while. I hope Maddy will be okay."

"She will be. She's tougher than you think."

He nodded. "I know."

The waitress came over and Finn gave her the smile. "What would you recommend? We both have huge appetites."

CHAPTER 32

Madeleine lay with her head in Emily's lap, her eyes closed as Emily stroked her hair.

"Oh Em. Why the hell did I ever agree to this madness?"

Emily replied softly, "Because you needed to. You've done nothing wrong. You'll be fine."

"When Mistress Jasmine was hypnotising me, I had memories of Justin I've tried to bury for years and never think about again."

"What memories, my love? You loved him so much," said Emily, continuing to stroke Madeleine's hair.

"I did, but I've never told you this before. Justin wasn't everything you thought he was. He was great at first, wonderful in every way. But then he started to change. When Justin and I were alone in the flat and he'd had a bit to drink, he would sometimes accuse me of flirting with someone. He could be so jealous. And then he'd just lose it."

"Lose it in what way?"

"He'd shout and scream at me. Accuse me of the most awful things, of flirting with everyone, that I didn't love him anymore. I almost came to believe that I must be a terrible person, that everything was my fault."

"Oh, my poor love. But you know it was never your fault. I know how much you loved him. You were totally faithful to him." Madeleine's body started to shake, and she buried herself in Emily's lap. "My love, what is it?"

"I wasn't faithful, Em. You remember Billy, the guy on the same course as us? I slept with him, just once, just a stupid one-night stand. I had to tell Justin. I couldn't lie to him. As hard as he tried, he couldn't get it out of his head. We had so many arguments. He threatened to leave me. I told him I'd do anything to keep us together. I begged, begged his forgiveness. At first, I didn't blame him. I'd hurt him so much. But then it got worse. He started to control me. It was so subtle at first. Comments on what I wore. Making me believe I hadn't done something I had done. Putting forward reasons I couldn't go out without him. He hated me going out, with you especially. He was convinced you were leading me astray. He'd check my messages and emails. He made it seem like everything was my fault. I could feel the love I'd felt for him for so long slowly disappearing. But I could never, ever lose him. Everything had to be my fault."

Emily looked concerned. "Maddy, why didn't you tell me any of this? I could have helped you."

"I should have. I know that now. But I thought I could deal with it. If I told you, then somehow it would be true. I thought our love was strong enough, that we could work it out. That's why we went to Greece. And look how that ended."

"Yes. Do you know, there's something I remember about his funeral. It was what, twenty-two years ago, now? You never cried. Everyone else was distraught. But you sat quietly in the corner at his wake. People came and talked to you, and you smiled like you were comforting them. Do you remember?"

"Yes. I was in a sort of a trance. It just felt unreal. The love of my life. Gone. It was impossible. It *was* my fault, Em."

Emily shook her head. "Don't blame yourself, my love. Of course it wasn't. It was a terrible accident. It had nothing to do with you. You'll be okay. I promise. I'll look after you."

Madeleine opened her eyes and looked up at her.

"You won't tell a soul, will you. I've buried all the memories and I want to forget it again now. Blocking out what happened lets me get on with my life."

Emily continued to stroke her friend's hair.

"Sweetheart, no one will ever hear anything from me. I hate what he did to you. It's hard to forgive him for that. To be honest, it makes me bloody angry. The Justin I knew was a fun-loving guy. I know why and how you loved him. But I wish I'd known everything, Maddy. I could have helped you. Fuck it. Why didn't you tell me?"

CHAPTER 33

Jasmine woke from a restless night and called Finn.

"There's something about Madeleine I need to discover and I'm going to find it. I want her phone number."

Finn was disconcerted. "Mistress please, let me ask her first."

For a moment there was silence. "Are you disobeying me?"

"No, of course not, Mistress. But don't you think I should ask her?"

Instantly Jasmine replied. "No. Give me her number. Now."

* * * *

Madeleine was relieved to get back to work. She was still feeling raw after her experience with Mistress Jasmine. It would take time, but she would move on. She was strong. And Emily was always there to help. Such a good friend. Her mind wandered to Maxine and Julia. That had been quite an experience, but at what potential cost? If Catherine ever found out, it would be a total disaster. As for Mike and Finn, what on earth was she going to do with them? God knows, the sex was fun, and she'd needed it. She must take some time to think what to do next, keep in control of her life.

Her phone rang. Number withheld. She cancelled the call and went on reading a manuscript she'd been sent. It was funny. She could do with a laugh. The phone rang again. Number withheld. Why did these wretched people keep calling about the accident she'd never had?

"I haven't had an accident, and please don't call again."

"Hello, Madeleine." She felt the hairs on the back of her neck stiffen. "Before you ask, Finn gave me your number. Don't put the phone down. I just wanted to check how you are."

She bit her lip.

"Just a minute, please."

She went out into the corridor.

"I'm okay, Mistress."

The voice was firm but kind. "Good. Now listen to me. I want us to talk. Just the two of us. Like friends. When are you free? It's okay, you can drop the Mistress for now."

★ ★ ★ ★

There were only a few people in the café, and she immediately spotted Jasmine sitting quietly reading at a table in the far corner. Her distinctive face with its long nose and full, wide mouth, was instantly recognisable, but the smart pale green suit was unexpected. Her hair was tied back in a bun. Jasmine looked up and put her book down as she approached.

"Sit down, Maddy. May I call you Maddy?"

Madeleine sat opposite her and nervously played with her hands under the table.

"Would you like a coffee or a tea?"

Jasmine's face had a kindly look.

"Coffee, please. A flat white."

Jasmine raised her hand, and a waitress came over immediately to take the order. She gave a little curtsey and went off to get their drinks.

Jasmine gave a grin. "Another of my friends, Maddy. She's quite delicious naked." She paused and looked directly at Madeleine. "Tell me what happened the other night."

Madeleine scratched her head. "I, I'm not sure. You hurt me and I didn't like it."

Jasmine looked at her quizzically. "Really? Your body was telling me otherwise. Now tell me the real reason. And look at me."

A tear moved slowly down Madeleine's cheek. "I was embarrassed. I've never done anything like that before. I was scared."

Very quietly, Jasmine asked, "What were you scared of, Maddy?"

The tear reached Madeleine's chin and she wiped it away. "I just didn't know what I was getting into. It was too much."

Quietly and firmly, Jasmine continued. "Maddy I'm very, very good at what I do. I'm a professional. One of my skills is mind control. I know the deepest secrets of many people. You'd be amazed at people's lives and the things they've done and been through. All the people at my party, including Finn and Mike, have secrets that would astound you. But whatever I'm told, I lock away. No one else will ever know. So Maddy, look at me."

Jasmine reached across and lifted her chin. "Look at me."

Madeleine stared into her eyes. She felt herself going lightheaded, floating.

"Tell me, Maddy. Tell me what happened."

Her face crumpled. "I saw my first love."

Jasmine's eyes widened and fixed hard on her. "Go on, Maddy. Tell me who your first love is."

The tears were in full flow now. "His name was Justin. I was hiding from him. He was so angry."

Quietly, "Why was Justin angry?"

Her hands were shaking. "I'd done something awful."

Jasmine took her hand. "What had you done, Maddy?"

Almost inaudibly, "I'd cheated on him. I never meant to. I loved him so much."

"Why did you cheat on him?" Jasmine asked, softly.

"We'd been invited to a party and Justin didn't want to go. We'd had a row. He was always jealous of me. He'd stopped me going to so many things and I'd had enough. For once, I stood up for myself and went on my own. I got drunk and slept with a guy."

"Did you tell Justin?"

"Yes."

"Why?"

"We were always honest with each other. I couldn't hide it from him. It hurt him so much."

"Where's Justin now?"

She paused and swallowed. "He's dead."

Jasmine's eyes stared at her, unblinking. "When did he die?"

Her breaths were coming in short and sharp. "When we were twenty-two."

Jasmine's voice became sterner. "Poor boy. So young. I want you to come and see me again. You'll do that, won't you Maddy?"

Softly, without hesitation, she replied. "Yes, Mistress."

Jasmine sat back and took a sip of coffee. Madeleine blinked several times and looked around the room. Jasmine was smiling.

"How's the coffee, Madeleine? Have you been here before?"

"No, never. It's good, thank you."

Jasmine's voice had become matter of fact. "That was a lovely chat. I understand you a lot better now. Love can be so complicated, can't it?"

Madeleine's brow furrowed. "Yes, love. So complicated."

Jasmine's eyes sparkled. "It has so many nuances. I'll see you again soon."

Jasmine got up and left the cafe. The waitress came over.

"I'm so glad you two have met up again. Do you remember me?"

Madeleine looked at her. "You were at the party."

The waitress gave a coy smile. "Yes. I'm sorry you left early. I was hoping we could play."

Madeleine frowned. "Play?"

The waitress wet her lips with her tongue. "Yes. Next time, I hope. Don't worry about the bill. It's covered."

Madeleine stood up to leave and grabbed the table to stop herself falling. She felt anxious, uncertain. Why on earth had she told Jasmin so much?

CHAPTER 34

Barbara knew something was wrong the moment Madeleine walked into the café in Soho. She was looking pale and tired despite obviously doing her best to look bright. She stood up and opened her arms. Madeleine breathed a sigh of relief and let herself be held.

"It's so good to see you, Barbara."

Barbara helped her off with her coat and they sat down opposite each other. She leant across and gave Madeleine's hand a squeeze.

"It's good to see you too. But are you okay?"

Madeleine gave a slight smile. "I've had a tough weekend. But I'll get over it. They do a superb cream tea here. I'm going to have one. Will you join me?"

"Sounds lovely. I hope they do Jasmine tea. It's my favourite." said Barbara.

Madeleine squirmed.

"What's wrong?"

"Nothing. I'm okay."

The waitress took their orders and they looked at each other, happy to be together again.

"It's been too long, Barbara. The time just flies by."

Barbara sat back. "That usually happens when you're having a good time. Are you?"

Madeleine nodded. "I had a great time after I left you in Athens."

Barbara lifted her hands and clapped, her bracelets jangling. "Brilliant! Tell me everything!"

Madeleine bit her lip and smiled coyly. "Let's just say the three of us had fun - together and separately."

"Brava. I'm so happy for you." Then she leant forward. "And how's it going now?"

The waitress laid out the scones, cream, jam, and a large pot of tea.

Madeleine filled both cups before answering. "Good question. It's not gone quite as I expected."

"In a not so good way?"

Madeleine spread the cream on her scone. "That about sums it up. I thought it would just be simple, but it's got a bit complicated, some parts are intense... oh it doesn't matter now, it's just so lovely to see you."

Barbara leant forward and patted her hand. "I'm a good listener, if you need it."

Madeleine nodded. "Yes, you probably are. But for now, I want to hear all your news. I assume you're back in Ledbury and settling in for the winter with your friend."

Barbara pursed her lips. "Well, that was what I was hoping for, but she decided she wanted to make a life in India with a woman she met out there, so I'm feeling a bit lost right now. I had a Dear Jane letter waiting for me when I got back."

"I'm so sorry. Had you any inkling of this?"

She nodded. "I always thought it might happen. Stella loves India and she has great friends there. I hope we'll always be able to stay in each other's lives but right now I need some space to deal with it."

Madeleine grunted. "Seems like we're both having to face up to some realities."

Barbara took another bite of her scone and wiped a crumb from the corner of her mouth. She'd put the jam on first and Madeleine the cream. They looked at each other and laughed.

"Barbara, in my admittedly somewhat limited experience, when one door closes, another opens. That's what I hope, anyway."

Barbara felt a stir of curiosity and pleasure as she nodded in agreement.

For nearly two hours they talked and laughed, forgetting their problems.

"Maddy, how about you come and stay? I'd love to show you where I live, and we can go on some great walks in the Malverns, get some country air in your lungs."

Madeleine could think of nothing she'd like more.

CHAPTER 35

Emily and Maddy were coming round for dinner and Shammie was cooking her favourite meal for them.

The doorbell rang and she ran to open it. "Come in, come in. It's so lovely to see you both. Maddy, you look amazing. You too, Em."

She hugged Emily, then looked at Madeleine. They grinned and hugged.

"Something smells good, Shammie. Angela Hartnett again?" asked Madeleine.

"Always Angela. If only I were a lesbian."

Emily looked at Madeleine and laughed. "Me too, Shammie."

Shammie took their coats. "Okay, you two. Go through to the kitchen and help yourself to wine. The bottle's open. I've raided Jacob's cellar again. I want to hear all the gossip. Maddy, next to the bottle is a little something for you. To say sorry."

"I've got something for you too, Shammie. I'm sorry, too."

Madeleine opened the small package. Inside was a beautiful grey cashmere scarf. She looked at her friends. "Ha! Guess what I've got for you, Shammie!"

"You haven't got the same thing?!"

"Yep."

All three burst into laughter as Madeleine and Shammie ceremoniously exchanged the two identical scarves.

Madeleine put hers around her neck. So soft. She'd love wearing it.

This was going to be a Jasmine-free evening. She wasn't ready to talk to her friends yet.

CHAPTER 36

Julia and Madeleine found a quiet cafe-bar away from the office to work on ideas for the next novel. They'd timed the meeting to give them a couple of hours to work before Maxine would join them. They sat closely side by side, their thighs touching. The sexual tension between them threatened to explode. Their fingers would touch and spark, but they denied each other any release. Plot. Synopsis. Ideas. Two hours of planning ahead of them.

"If my first book was anything to go by, this synopsis will fly out of the window as soon as I write. The characters will take control. I had no idea how the last book would end until I was halfway through."

"I know, Jules. But this one is going to be much more difficult. The publishers need a synopsis as soon as possible. Planning will help. What's it going to be about?"

"I'm going to use my main character again but do something a little different."

"Don't make it too different. You have a winning formula, Jules."

Julia flexed her shoulders. "I know. But the third one is going to be different. I'm going to write about something that's been on my mind for a while. Domestic abuse."

Madeleine paled. "Are you sure? What do you know about it?"

"Thankfully, I haven't experienced it directly, but there was a lot of it about when I grew up. I've been researching it and I want to write about it. One of my best friends in Liverpool had it all through her childhood. Her father totally controlled all of them. It ruined her mother's life. What do you think?"

Madeleine was fighting back nausea. How was she going to deal with this? She got up. "I must go to the toilet."

It was ten minutes before she came back.

"That was a long pee! I've scribbled some notes. Want to see?"

"Not now, Jules, if you don't mind. Are you sure you want to write about that? You must be so careful. It's not an easy subject to read about. Can't you think of something else?"

Julia looked puzzled. "Maddy, is this a problem for you?"

"You're free to write about whatever you want. It's just that it's a painful subject for many people. It's so important not to write anything titillating."

"I won't. This is going to be dark. I have a shattering end in mind that I'm not going to tell you, Maddy. I want this to be as much of a surprise to you as anyone."

Madeleine looked at her sideways. "You never cease to surprise," she said.

"That's good, isn't it?" Julia asked.

Madeleine took her hand. "Sometimes, Jules. Sometimes. Okay, let's get working on your next book. We'll deal with the third one when this one is done."

★ ★ ★ ★

"Well, you two look cosy." Maxine was standing by their table.

Julia got up and hugged her. "Hello, my darling. My god, the time's gone quickly. We've had a great meeting. How's your day been?"

Maxine took off her coat and hung it over the back of a chair. "Long and boring. I've been imagining the two of you here and couldn't wait to join you. Hello, Maddy. So good to see you again."

Maxine leant over and kissed her on the cheek.

"Good to see you too, Max. Coffee?"

Maxine sat down and stretched her legs. "No. I want a large glass of red wine. And crisps."

Madeleine waved to the waiter. "Let's get a bottle. We've done enough work for today."

Maxine let out a sigh of relief. "It's so good to be out of the office. Maddy, I hope you'll come back for dinner."

The dinner lasted all evening and into the early hours. Madeleine phoned Catherine to say she'd be working from home in the morning. The response was frosty. It was getting on for 11 a.m. by the time she got home and started to work.

Madeleine had been the focus of Maxine and Julia's lovemaking. They had both concentrated on extracting every ounce of pleasure from her body. They had fed off it, discovering every erogenous zone she had and many she'd never known about. They had used ice cubes on her nipples and pushed them inside her. She had been tied to the bed with soft scarves while they had sat over her and made love to each other. She had wanted to kiss and lick the bodies that hovered above her, but they had denied her. Their fingers circled and teased her bringing her to within a second of an orgasm and had then pulled away. They used their toys on her and themselves. She had screamed in frustration and then in ecstasy as at last she had come. And come again. The intensity was far greater than anything she had experienced before, even with Finn and Mike. The three of them had slept curled together until dawn and Madeleine had woken to Julia opening her with her tongue.

Madeleine sat at her kitchen table and slowly drank a strong mug of coffee. She loved the intense sex with Maxine and Julia. Was it the softness of their bodies that added to her pleasure? She had her own sex toys but sharing theirs had raised the level of intimacy. She loved the taste of a woman. Loved the taste of a man, too. Maybe she wouldn't finish with Finn and Mike quite yet. They had their uses. She wondered if she'd ever meet someone she could really love, start a proper relationship with, rebuild her life. A proper, normal relationship? She wasn't sure she knew what one was any more. She'd been married to a gay man and had sexual encounters with men and now women. Was this what Richard had experienced? Was she surrounded by normality and was she the exception? She wasn't sure anymore. Her best friend wanted what she was experiencing. Did she want what her best friend and her other friends had? What was married love anyway? Just something to get bored by. Best to take her pleasures where she could. Could she live with a woman? Why not? She thought of Mistress Jasmine. What an extraordinary woman she was. What a strange way of life. What had happened to her to turn her into a Dominatrix? Something must have driven her to need to have so much control over others, to enjoy inflicting pain for pleasure. It couldn't just be the money. Was she hiding from a trauma? Whatever it was, she must make a good living from it. Jasmine would be earning a lot more than her, for sure. She wondered if she'd ever hear from her again.

Enough. She was exhausted but she had to work. If she didn't, Catherine would be on her back again.

CHAPTER 37

Tim opened the front door to the new client, a good-looking man in his early sixties. He had paid his Mistress's £200 tribute in full and on time.

"Go down the hall. Mistress is in the last room on the right. Knock and she'll tell you when to enter."

The man knocked and waited outside the door. He had seen pictures of Mistress on her website dressed in a tight-fitting Grecian style white dress split to the waist, bare arms, a glimpse of underwear, large breasts tightly confined. Long black wavy hair. Deep red lipstick. Her hands on her hips, her painted nails long and beautifully manicured. So exquisitely powerful. He had emailed her with his needs, and they had discussed them on the phone. He knew she understood, and he could confess everything to her and be punished. Nothing would go outside these four walls. He felt safe here. Any moment now he would be in Her presence and for an hour he could let go.

She was sitting on the sofa when he entered. She patted the seat next to her and told him to sit. She was dressed head to toe in black shiny latex with the highest heels he had ever seen, just as she'd said she would. She spoke to him gently and softly.

"Now George, let's have a little chat before we start. Have you visited a Mistress before?"

His head bowed, he replied. "Yes Mistress. Many years ago. I'm very nervous."

She patted his hand and continued in her silk voice. "Don't be nervous. Remember, I understand you. And I'm going to get to know you a lot more. From everything you've told me in your emails, you've been a very naughty boy and you deserve your punishment. You should be thoroughly ashamed. You do deserve it, don't you George?"

He sniffled. "Yes, Mistress. I do."

Jasmine stood up and looked down at him. "Yes, you do. Before we start, I'm going to give you a safe word. Unless you use it, I will continue with your punishment until I decide it matches your sin. Is that clear?"

The man could hardly speak. "Yes, Mistress."

Her voice was stern. "Good. Now go and get undressed in the room over there. You'll see another door leading into my dungeon. When you're undressed, go in there and wait for me. Touch nothing. Is that clear?"

Faintly he replied. "Yes, Mistress. Thank you so much."

The man got up and went into the room to undress. George had such a boring kink. She'd beat the hell out of him for that. She picked up her phone, searched for Madeleine's number and called. George could wait and sweat for a few minutes.

Madeleine was drifting to sleep. She buried her head under the pillow and let the phone ring out. Nothing would disturb her early night. The phone rang again. She let it go to voicemail and checked to see who had called. Unknown number. Shit. It must be Jasmine.

She checked the voicemail. 'Always answer my calls in future. Is that understood? I will call you tomorrow.'

That unmistakable voice. To be obeyed. Her hand slipped between her legs, and her body instantly responded.

★ ★ ★ ★

The Monday morning meeting was full of excitement. What a week it had been. They had all worked so hard and Catherine was full of praise for everyone. They discussed their diaries and went through the week to come. So much to do. Madeleine had two evening book launches she had to go to. Catherine would come with her to one of them and wanted her to meet a new author she was interested in signing. She'd value her opinion of him.

Madeleine's phone rang. Number withheld.

"I'm sorry Catherine, I have to answer this."

Catherine was annoyed. "Please Maddy, call them back."

"It's my sister. My mother isn't too well." She got up and left the room.

"Good morning, Madeleine. I assume you heard my message."

She hesitated. "Yes, Mistress. I'm in a meeting. Can I call you back?"

For a moment, silence. "Do you have my number?"

"No."

"Then how can you call me back?"

"I can't, Mistress." She felt foolish.

Jasmine's voice was strong and decisive. "No Maddy, you can't. I want you to come and see me on Wednesday evening. Just the two of us. 7.30."

She hesitated again. "Mistress I have a work event I have to go to on Wednesday evening."

"What time will it finish?"

"About 9.30."

"Then I want you here at 10 p.m. Is that understood?" The phone went dead. She took a deep breath and went back to the meeting.

"Is your mother okay?"

Madeleine looked blankly at Catherine. "Oh, yes. Thank you. She's had a fall but nothing serious, thank goodness."

Catherine stood up. "Good. Okay everyone, let's get on with it."

They all got up from the table. "Maddy, hang on. Are you alright? You look like you've seen a ghost."

She shook her head slightly. "Do I? No, I'm fine thanks."

Catherine was looking concerned. "Having an elderly mother is a worry. I've been through it. If you want to talk, let me know."

She touched her arm. "Thank you, Catherine. I appreciate that. I'm sure she'll be okay."

★ ★ ★ ★

Daunt Books in Marylebone High Street was Madeleine's favourite venue for a book launch. When she arrived, she noticed Catherine talking animatedly to a good-looking man. Early sixties, she guessed, slightly balding, casually dressed in jeans, a white open-necked shirt, and a dark blue jacket. She walked over to them.

Catherine held out her hand. "Maddy, just the person. I want you to meet Giles. Giles Hawthorn. I told you about him on Monday. You might have read his first novel, Elegant Doubts. It came out last year. Giles, Madeleine is my right-hand woman. I never sign anyone without her approval."

The man beamed. "Madeleine, I'm delighted to meet you."

For a second, she glanced at his lips. "Thank you, Giles. It's lovely to meet you, too."

Catherine put her arms around them both. "Maddy, I'll leave you with Giles. I'd love the two of you to get to know each other. Fix up a proper meeting. Giles is near to finishing his second novel and I'm very interested in him."

Catherine walked off and joined another group of people. Giles was standing close to Madeleine.

He raised his glass. "Cheers, Madeleine. It's a real pleasure to meet you."

"Cheers. You too." They clinked glasses and their fingers touched. Electric. They looked at each other and laughed.

"Catherine told me you were Julia McGuigan's editor. A lot of people have been talking about the deal." He was looking at her eyes, then her mouth.

"Yes, it was a great deal for a first novel. Catherine helped so much. She really is the best." She held his eyes.

"I'm getting to know that. I hear her name a lot."

"Well, I hope you'll sign with us too," she said.

He bit his lip. "I've already made up my mind to do that."

Madeleine laughed. "Good."

He looked around the room. "Do you know many people here?"

"Yes, it's my job."

He shook his head. "Of course. Silly question. What are you doing after the launch? We could talk properly."

"I'm meeting a friend, I'm afraid," she said.

"That's a pity, I'd have loved to take you to dinner."

Her eyes sparkled. "I'd have loved that too, Giles, but I'm afraid this is a friend I can't say no to."

Damn you, Mistress Jasmine.

He tried not to show his disappointment and gave a half-smile. "Are you married? With somebody? I'm sorry, I don't mean to…."

She laughed. "It's Okay. I was married, but no longer."

He looked relieved. "Okay. Then may I ask you to dinner another night? How about tomorrow?"

"I'd love that. Thank you." She opened her bag. "Here's my card. Call me."

"I will."

He tore a sheet of paper from a small notebook and wrote down his number and gave it to her. Two women were hovering close to them. Madeline put a hand on Giles's arm. "I'll leave you to your fans. Talk later."

She stayed as long as she dared at Daunt's. She had to go. But first she'd buy a copy of Elegant Doubts.

★ ★ ★ ★

A cab was approaching as she walked out of the bookshop. She'd be on time, if not early. Would she be allowed to be early? She asked the driver to drop her off at the corner of the block and walked slowly back towards the flat. Her heart was pounding. She should have told Emily where she was going, but it was dead on

10 p.m. No time to call. She walked down the steps; the security light came on and the front door opened. In the doorway stood the young woman who had waited on them in the cafe, totally naked.

"Hello, again. Mistress is waiting for you."

The girl closed the door and walked ahead along the corridor. Madeleine followed, watching the sway of her naked hips. She was exactly as Mistress Jasmine had described – delicious. Mistress Jasmine was sitting on a black leather sofa. She was wearing a soft red leather dress with a zip that ran the length of the front. She looked magnificent.

"Hello, Madeleine. Right on time. I like that. Come and sit next to me. Pussy, take Madeleine's coat, then go and get us a ginger beer each."

Pussy curtsied. "Yes, Mistress."

Jasmine looked at Pussy and then at Madeleine. "I've trained her well."

Madeleine felt extremely overdressed. She had had to dress both for Daunt's and for Mistress Jasmine. She'd tried to find something perfect, but it was impossible. She sat next to Jasmine, who turned towards her and put a hand on her knee.

"Where have you been this evening?"

She flushed. "I've been to a book launch, Mistress. I'm not sure if I'm dressed appropriately for you."

Jasmine put a finger under her chin and lifted it up, so their eyes met.

"Don't worry. We'll soon deal with that. I love your scarf. So soft."

"Yes, a friend gave it to me."

Jasmine raised an eyebrow. "A close friend?"

"Someone I've known for a long time. She gave it to me because she'd upset me."

A faint smile played on Jasmine's mouth. "It's a good feeling, isn't it, when someone makes amends like that."

Almost inaudibly, Madeleine replied "Yes, Mistress."

Jasmine's voice was strong. "Maddy, we've started to get to know each other. You're a truly fascinating person. A beautiful, striking, interesting, intelligent woman. A rare woman. Do you agree? Look at me when I speak to you."

She lifted her head and gazed into Jasmine's eyes. "Thank you, Mistress. It's not really for me to say."

Jasmine softly stroked her cheek. "I'm an excellent judge of character. Believe me, I'm not just complimenting you. Even Finn's high praise didn't do you justice."

The door opened and the girl came in holding a tray with two ornate glasses of ginger beer, and a beautifully presented plate of snacks.

"Put them down on the table, Pussy, then come and give Madeleine a kiss."

The girl obeyed and bent over in front of Madeleine. Pussy's mouth was open, waiting for Madeleine's tongue, and they kissed. Madeleine wanted to cup the small, firm breasts in front of her. The girl stood up, walked towards the corner of the room, put her hands behind her head and stood motionless facing the wall.

"She kisses well doesn't she, Madeleine?"

She licked her lips, the taste salty. "Yes, Mistress."

Jasmine brushed back the hair from Madeleine's face. "Would you like her as your plaything?"

The answer was immediate. "Yes, Mistress."

Jasmine laughed. "She comes at a price, Maddy. Let's see if you're prepared to pay it. Look at me."

She turned towards Jasmine. Their eyes locked and she felt the warm drifting feeling she'd felt in the cafe.

Mistress Jasmine stroked her hand and said softly, "Did you often cheat on Justin, Maddy?"

The rhythmic stroking of her hand continued. "No, Mistress! It was just once. I felt so guilty."

Jasmine's eyes gazed at her unblinking. "How did he find out?"

In a whisper, she replied, "I told him. He could tell something was wrong. I couldn't keep it from him."

Jasmine's voice was so gentle. "It was wrong of you to cheat on Justin, wasn't it Maddy?"

Almost inaudible, "Yes, Mistress."

Softly, "What happened next?"

Her voice caught. Tears filled her eyes. "He just stared at me. His face was white. Then anger. So much anger. He told me to leave."

"Did you leave, Maddy?"

She started to cry. "No, Mistress." Tears fell down Madeleine's cheeks as she answered.

"Why not, Maddy." The sobs were building.

"I begged and begged and begged him to let me stay."

Jasmine was unmoved. "Did he, Maddy?"

Whispering, "Yes, Mistress. But he said I had to do whatever he said."

"He controlled you, didn't he?"

She wept and her body shook. "Yes, Mistress."

"That wasn't good, was it?"

"No, Mistress. I hated it. But I loved him. I really did."

She felt Mistress Jasmine put her arms round her.

"Thank you, Maddy. This is going to help you. I promise."

Madeleine laid her head on Mistress Jasmine's shoulder. Never had she felt so weak and helpless.

"Pussy, come over here. Comfort Madeleine. Make her better."

Mistress Jasmine stood up and went out of the room. The girl came and sat next to Madeleine, put her arms around her, stroked her hair and softly kissed her.

"Don't be frightened of Mistress. She'll look after you, but she needs to know all your secrets to do that. She knows everything about me, and I've never felt safer. My Dad hurt me. But here I'm safe. I love her so much. Sometimes I do things wrong, and she punishes me. But I deserve it and even though it hurts so much, I love the feeling. Has Mistress flogged you yet, Maddy?"

She wiped her eyes. "No. I don't want her to."

Pussy looked concerned. "Oh, you mustn't mind it. I know I'm pleasing Mistress when she beats me. She also gives me to her friends. That's a real honour."

Mistress Jasmine came back into the room. She had changed into a black latex dress and high-heeled boots.

"Both of you, come with me."

They followed her into a room with a wooden leather vaulting horse in the centre.

"Pussy, we're going to show Madeleine what a good girl you are."

Mistress Jasmine strapped Pussy over the horse and tied her hands underneath it. The girl's legs were spread and tied to the feet of the horse with her backside up in the air. She was totally exposed.

Madeleine felt excitement and horror in equal measure.

"Madeleine, get undressed and come and stand next to me. I want to show you what we do. Have you seen a flogger before?" She shook her head.

When Madeleine was naked, Jasmine showed her a thick leather handle with twenty thin leather thongs about eighteen inches long hanging from it.

"I start with this. It will warm up her backside and get her ready for the cane."

Pussy wriggled on the horse and moaned.

"Be quiet, Pussy. I'll gag you if you make a sound."

Mistress Jasmine started slowly, moving into a figure of eight motion, gradually increasing the strength and speed of the flogger. Pussy's backside reddened. From time to time, Mistress stroked it and whispered in Pussy's ear. Then the flogging would start again, harder and with even greater intensity and speed. Pussy counted each stroke out loud as fast as she could, thanking her Mistress. When she had reached 100, Jasmine picked up two canes and gave one to Madeleine.

"I'm going to show you how to use this, Maddy. Then I want you to carry on until I tell you to stop."

The cane was springy rattan.

Madeleine watched as the caning started. There were greater gaps between each stroke than with the flogger but from Pussy's reaction, the pain was much more intense. The welts on her backside grew redder and each stroke left a long line. The marks deepened in colour, and blood blisters began to show.

"Okay, Maddy. Come and stand here. Hold the cane firmly."

Mistress Jasmine stood closely behind her and raised her arm with the cane. "Not too high. Use the wrist. Start slowly and build up. And don't worry about Pussy. She loves it. Off you go."

Mistress Jasmine stood back, her arms folded and watched as the first stroke landed on Pussy's backside. "That's good. Five more like that then harder."

She gave Pussy twenty strokes. She was sweating and the girl was moaning. Jasmine stepped forward. "Okay, that'll do for now. Undo Pussy and help her up." Madeleine undid the straps and helped the girl off the horse.

"What do you have to say, Pussy?"

The girl bowed her head. "Thank you, Madeleine."

Jasmine applauded. "Both of you. Come here."

They stood naked in front of her.

"Hands behind your heads. Spread your legs."

With both hands she reached between their legs.

"That's good. You've both responded well. Go and get dressed."

The girl left the room and Madeleine started to put on her clothes.

"Maddy, you've done well. Next time it'll be you."

Alarmed, she said "I don't like too much pain, Mistress."

Jasmine's nose twitched. "You'll start to like it. It's deep inside you. We'll start gently. You can go now. Pussy is staying here tonight."

She felt a pang of jealousy. "Yes Mistress. Thank you, Mistress."

Smiling, "I'll call you. You'll answer, won't you Maddy."

"Yes, Mistress."

Mistress Jasmine left the room. Madeleine finished dressing and walked out into the cool night air, a spring in her step.

CHAPTER 38

Madeleine spotted Giles through the restaurant window. He was sitting at a table towards the back, looking at his phone. His choice of restaurant had impressed her. Good, simple bistro food. Just what she liked. She stood for a moment, looking at him. It looked warm inside. Time to get in from the cold.

She had nearly reached the table when he looked up. He stood and embraced her, kissing her on both cheeks. She liked his bear hug. No uncertainty with him.

"It's good to see you, Madeleine. I'm so glad you could make it."

She kissed him on the cheek. "I've been looking forward to it."

The waiter took her coat, and she sat opposite him. He poured her a glass of wine. He was looking so happy. It made her happy too.

"I'm celebrating. I rang Catherine and she's agreed to represent me."

"Yes. She told me. I'm very pleased."

"So, we'll be working together."

Her heart sank. No mixing business and pleasure. She'd already done enough of that.

"Catherine wants to take the lead. She's very excited to be working with you."

Giles smiled at her, his eyes laughing. "And I'm very excited to be having dinner with you. Let's forget work for now. I want to get to know you."

Another person wanting to get to know her. This time, she wanted to get to know him, too. It had been nothing like this at the start with Richard.

"Let's order, Giles. Then we can swap stories."

They looked at the menu, hardly taking it in.

He nodded. "Okay. Do you eat meat? The beef tenderloin here is exquisite. So is the Bouillabaisse."

"Is this a regular place of yours?" she asked. His skin was a light olive colour, little wrinkles around his eyes, his hands large with a few liver spots on them. She wanted to touch them.

His face looked almost childlike as it lit up. "It's my favourite restaurant. That's why I chose it."

His voice had a slight lilt to it she couldn't place. "What are you having?" he asked.

"The tenderloin."

He looked her straight in the eye. "Then I'll have the Bouillabaisse."

The waiter took their orders, and they looked across the table at each other, taking each other in.

Giles put his hand on hers. "I'm so glad we met."

She liked the weight of his hand but pulled hers away. "Me too. So, tell me about you."

He told her how his parents had brought him up in Yorkshire. His mother was an Austrian refugee. With hindsight, he'd married far too young. He'd stood at the altar in his hired morning suit, wondering what the hell he was doing. Anyway, it was what you did. Train to be a professional, in his case a solicitor. Get married, buy a house, have a company car, a mortgage. The marriage had not been particularly happy. Thankfully they didn't have any children. He'd discovered that the man he thought was his father, wasn't and that he had a sister whom he had never met. He had been traumatised. Then he met someone on a course. They had an affair and fell in love. It shouldn't have happened, but she was very caring and loving and that was just what he'd needed. His divorce was hard, emotionally and financially.

He'd married the woman he loved, and they'd been together for fifteen years until she'd had an affair and ended it. He'd been prepared to carry on, work it through rather than go through another tough divorce. But she wanted to leave. As it happened, it turned out well. The life he had now was so much more fulfilling. He hoped theirs was too. He had no contact with either of them. He'd hated being a solicitor, but it had made him enough money to last him a year after the second divorce. It was during that time he'd started writing.

He'd written Elegant Doubts three years ago. He'd sent the book off to publishers and agents and it had taken eighteen months for it to be picked up. The rest was history. Aside from writing, he did some freelance legal work to pay the bills.

She listened with her chin in her hand, looking at him.

Their food arrived and they started to eat. She took a few mouthfuls of the tenderloin. He was right. It was mouth-watering. She sipped some wine, watching his pleasure as he ate.

"Any other relationships?" she asked.

He put down his knife and fork, a smile playing on his lips. "Just one of any substance. With a married woman. But it's over."

She raised an eyebrow. "How over?"

He looked down at his plate, then swallowed a mouthful of wine. "It was a painful break, but it's over. We're friends."

"So, it's not really over."

He looked straight at her, not missing a beat. "It is. It's over."

"And no other relationships since? No one ready to pounce?"

He put his head back and roared with laughter. "Ready to pounce? I love that. No, not as far as I know."

She wasn't sure she believed him. He was an attractive man. Not a great track record. She hoped to God this wasn't another Finn. But she felt sure he wasn't. There was a delicate silence as they continued to eat.

"How was the tenderloin?" he asked.

"As delicious as you said it would be. How was the Bouillabaisse?"

"As delicious as I said it would be."

She laughed and poured them both another glass of wine.

"Thank you for telling me about yourself."

He leant forward, his arms spread wide across the table. "I want to hear about you now, Maddy. But before you start, I just wanted to say how much I'm enjoying this evening."

She held his eye. "Thank you. I am too." She was having a surprisingly good time. She wasn't used to having a relaxed, easy evening with a nice man, especially one who seemed to be so disarmingly emotionally open. It felt like a date, but it wasn't. She certainly wasn't ready for that. It had never crossed her mind that she was 'dating' Finn or Mike.

"Okay. Tell me all."

She took a deep breath. "Like you, I married too young. I was 23, I'd been at University in Bristol. It wasn't a happy experience. My parents lived in a village in Oxfordshire. My dad was an unsuccessful artist. He left us when I was five. My mother brought us up. She was an alcoholic. They're both dead now. I was thankful to get away to Bristol Uni when I left school. I studied English because I loved reading, especially poetry. But I was in a relationship with someone who died and that really screwed me up. Richard, my ex, helped me through the mess. He was nice, well, he seemed nice but with hindsight was a bit dull, fifteen years older than me. He had his own estate agency and was doing well. He gave me stability for the first time in my life. He was ambitious and I guess he thought I'd look good on his arm. We got on well enough. He was a fantastic cook and introduced me to good food. We drifted apart sexually, and I began to resent the time he spent with his friends. One friend in particular. Paul. Anyway, to cut a long and boring story short, it turned out that he and Paul had been lovers for years."

He looked genuinely astounded. "God, that must have been awful."

She sighed. "It wasn't much fun. Why the hell I didn't realize sooner, I'll never know. I had a few hints over the years, but I laughed them off. Anyway, that was a while ago and we're divorced. Richard and Paul live in a house we owned in France. I have our house in Putney."

"That's quite a story. Do you have a lot of friends? Any lovers?"

She hesitated. How far should she go if this was to be a purely business relationship?

"I have a small group of very close friends, two in particular, who helped get me through it all," she said.

She looked away and then back at him. "Yes, okay, there've been a couple of people in my life." She felt good saying that.

"I see." He looked a bit taken aback. "Anyone serious?"

She looked at him, her lips parted, smiling. "No one serious."

He laughed and gave her a long quizzical look. "Good. Are you still hungry?"

She held his gaze. "I noticed a chocolate mousse on the menu. Go halves?"

"Love to. Like a coffee? Brandy? I want to hear what happened to you after Richard and Paul walked off into the sunset."

★ ★ ★ ★

What a marvellous evening it had been. Giles hadn't felt such a close connection with a woman for years. He was sure Madeleine felt the same. They had stayed talking until nearly midnight and then taken pity on the waiter who had openly looked at his watch. Giles had wanted to walk her home, but she'd said it was late and too far. They'd hugged each other and kissed lightly on the lips. He felt a passion for her and the electricity between them as they hugged was palpable. She'd broken out of the embrace and had started to walk towards a taxi rank. He'd run after her, taken her hand, turned her towards him and kissed her passionately. And how she'd responded! As though she hadn't been kissed for years. That couldn't be. It was impossible. He'd watched as she disappeared round the corner and then set off to catch his bus home.

CHAPTER 39

In Athens, the summer had melted away and the evenings were distinctly cooler. Mike had invited Madeleine to join him for a few days while he worked on the exhibition. He'd tried everything he knew to get her to come, but she had been too busy. She was adamant. No. Too much happening in her life to take time off at the drop of a hat. She'd meet up with him when he got back.

He'd come to Cafe Pinelope in Pangrati. He liked this area above the city centre. It felt local, away from the tourists who even at this time of year packed the Acropolis, Plaka, Monasteraki and Syntagma. It was an easy walk down the hill, past the old marble Olympic stadium and through the National Gardens into the city centre. He'd rented a small apartment in Pangrati as part of the cost-cutting exercise. The Liverpool exhibition hadn't gone as well as they'd hoped and for the first time since he'd started the business with Finn, he was feeling nervous. Ever since Madeleine had come on the scene, Finn hadn't been nearly as effective. He couldn't wish they hadn't met her. They'd had a lot of fun with her. But now she was more distant. They'd wanted her to share her experiences with Mistress Jasmine, but she wasn't forthcoming. They needed to talk with her and get things back on track. It felt strange for a woman to be ending things with them. He ordered a mushroom risotto and a beer. A quintet started to play. Rebetiko, the pretty waitress had told him. The mournful music of the working people of Greece. It matched his mood. He'd have an early night. Tomorrow would be another day.

★ ★ ★ ★

Several days passed without any contact from Mistress Jasmine. Madeleine resisted the temptation to go back to the cafe in Marylebone High Street to see if the girl was there. Giles had been to the office to meet Catherine and discuss his new novel. After the meeting, Catherine had told her Giles had wanted to make some changes that would delay it for a few weeks. She wasn't happy, but indecisive authors were nothing new. He needed to be handled carefully. She'd get him across the line, and all being well. they'd have another success on their hands.

Julia's novel was at the printers.They'd agreed the cover design after a struggle with Julia and HarperCollins. Why was it that these final stages always took so long and caused such stress? The PR Agency had presented its thoughts on the launch and that at least had gone smoothly. It was a pity they'd missed the Christmas market, but they had ambitious plans for the Spring.

Madeleine had not been in the slightest bit tempted to go with Mike to Athens. She'd loved the city and everything that had happened. But that was then. She'd moved on. Mike and Finn had been great for her, but now she wanted more than their strange, 'sharing' relationship. She was worth far more than that. Julia and Maxine had invited her to a party, and she'd stalled, promised to let them know. It was this weekend. She'd have to decide today.

★ ★ ★ ★

Julia looked fantastic in a red dress that left nothing to the imagination. Since her book deal, she had blossomed. Since her time with Madeleine, too. Maxine wasn't worried. She was certain of their love, and she was sure nothing would come between them. Maxine decided on a black jumpsuit. She looked in the mirror and put on her lipstick, wondering what Madeleine would wear. She was due to arrive soon for a drink before the party. Their close friends Abby and Margaret were celebrating Abby's birthday in a club they'd hired for the evening. She loved dancing and so did Julia. Did Madeleine? She had no idea. In fact, no idea about Madeleine at all other than sex with her was amazing. Did she need to know anything else? It was probably best she didn't.

The bell rang.

"She's here, darling. I'll go and let her in."

Maxine smiled. Julia would have first taste of those lips. Good for her.

She walked into the sitting room where Madeleine and Julia were holding hands. Madeleine was wearing a gorgeous simple loose fitting green dress. From the smudged lipstick, the kiss had been passionate. She poured the three of them glasses of white wine.

"Cheers, my loves! So good to see you, Maddy. Give me a kiss too."

As they kissed, Madeleine's phone rang. "Damn. Sorry." She searched in her bag for her phone and looked at the number. Julia glanced at Maxine. Maddy had turned pale. The phone continued to ring as she stared at the screen.

"Are you okay?" Maxine asked.

Madeleine glanced at them. "Yes, sorry. I must take this." She walked quickly down the hall to Julia's study and shut the door.

They looked at each other. "What's all that about?"

Julia put down her glass and picked up her phone. "I'll order the Uber. It'll take a while to come on a Saturday night."

Madeleine came back into the room. She was looking flushed. "I'm sorry. I can't come with you. Something has come up. I must go."

"My love, what's happened?" Julia asked.

Madeleine picked up her bag. "It's my mother. She's had a fall. She's in hospital."

"Oh Maddy, I'm so sorry. Look we don't have to go to the party. Would you like us to come with you?"

Madeleine shook her head. "Max, that's sweet of you but I'll be fine. You go on. I'm so sorry."

"Are you sure?"

Julia put her arms round her. "We'll miss you. Will you call and let us know how she is? We can give you the address. Please come if she's okay."

"I'll do that. Sorry, I must dash." Madeleine picked up her coat and walked out into the street to get a cab.

* * * *

Pussy walked down the hall and let Madeleine in. This time she wasn't naked. She was wearing a white basque with black stockings and high heels. Around her neck was a collar. She was heavily made up with thick black false eyelashes, exaggerated black eyebrows and black lipstick. Her makeup was smudged; she'd been crying. Madeleine followed her down the hall. Her backside was covered in dark red welts.

Mistress Jasmine stood in the room with her arms folded, wearing a black leather suit.

"I'm so glad you could come, Madeleine. I'm sorry about the short notice. I hope you weren't doing anything too important. Pussy has been a naughty girl. I will not tolerate disobedience. Tell Maddy what you did, Pussy."

Pussy sniffled, looking down at the floor. "I lied to you, Mistress."

"What about? Look at me." Her voice was chilling. Madeleine stood there, transfixed.

Pussy lifted her head. "I told you I hadn't been fucked this week."

"And it wasn't true, was it, Pussy?" Her voice was sounding angrier.

"No, Mistress." Pussy was shaking. She knew what her Mistress was capable of.

"And how did I know you were lying?"

"Finn told you he'd fucked me," Pussy whispered.

"Speak up, wretch! I want Maddy to hear this." Pussy started to sob and repeated what she'd said.

She looked at Madeleine. "Finn fucked her this week, Maddy. What do you think about that?"

Madeleine paled. "I don't know, Mistress."

She glowered at her. "Of course you do. Don't lie to me too, Madeleine."

Madeleine said the first thing that came into her mind. "I hope she pleased Finn, Mistress."

Jasmine turned to the girl. "Did you please Finn, Pussy?"

Pussy shuffled from foot to foot. "Yes, Mistress. He told me he was very pleased with me."

"Well, at least that's true."

She turned to Madeleine. Her voice was softer. "So Maddy, why have you abandoned Finn and Mike? They aren't happy. Mike told me you refused to go away with him."

Madeleine nodded. "Yes Mistress, I couldn't go. I'm too busy at work."

She came and stood directly in front of Madeleine. "Is that the only reason?"

Madeleine hesitated. "I want the truth, Maddy."

Quietly she said, "I've met someone, Mistress. He might be special."

Jasmine's jaw tightened. "Have you told Mike and Finn?"

A whisper. "No, Mistress."

For a moment there was silence. Then, "Why not?"

Madeleine took a deep breath, "I just haven't got round to it." From the corner of her eye, Madeleine saw Pussy shaking her head.

Jasmine turned and sat down on the sofa, crossing her legs. "Maddy, they are good friends of mine, and I don't like my friends getting upset. Who are you seeing?"

Madeleine clasped her hands together, feeling very alone standing in the middle of the room.

"Please Mistress, I don't want him involved."

Jasmine gripped her knees with her hands. "So, you're keeping secrets from him, are you, Maddy? That's not a good start to a relationship, is it? Are you ashamed of me?"

Madeleine looked at the floor and then up at her. "No, Mistress. Not at all. It's just it's new and it could be special."

Mistress grimaced and looked at the girl. "Special. Did you hear that, Pussy? Maddy has a special friend. Who else have you slept with, Maddy?"

"I haven't slept with him yet."

"That's not what I asked you, is it?"

"No, Mistress."

Mistress slapped her thigh and the sound reverberated round the room. "Who else have you slept with?"

Madeleine shook. "Please, Mistress. I can't tell you."

Pussy flinched.

The voice was like ice. "Tell me, Madeleine."

Almost inaudible. "I can't."

Jasmine got up from the sofa and slowly came over to Madeleine. Her eyes narrowed.

"Take off that pretty dress."

Madeleine glanced at Pussy, who almost indiscernibly nodded that she should obey. She undid a few buttons and pulled the dress over her head.

Mistress smirked. "Well, you are dressed for fun, Maddy. A lovely bra, matching green lacy knickers, stockings, and suspenders. That isn't what you normally wear, is it Maddy?"

She blushed. "No, Mistress."

She moved to within an inch of Madeleine's face. "So where were you going tonight?"

Such sweet breath. "To a party with friends, Mistress."

She looked deep into her eyes. "Special friends, obviously. Your boyfriend coming too?"

Madeleine swallowed. "No, Mistress. Just me and my friends."

Abruptly Jasmine turned away. "This is boring, Madeleine. Pussy, take her to the dungeon, undress her and strap her to the St Andrew Cross, then come back here and wait. I can't stand prevarication."

★ ★ ★ ★

Jasmine stood in front of the naked Madeleine; her eyes locked on her. Madeleine's arms and legs were held tight, stretched out on the wooden cross. The leather belt tight round her waist, buckled behind the cross, made her completely immobile. "I can do anything I want, can't I, Maddy?"

Madeleine was terrified. "Yes, Mistress."

Her voice softened. "Look at me, Maddy. You know what's going to happen now, don't you? Remember the safe word?"

Madeleine nodded and stared back into her eyes. She felt her cheek being gently stroked and was aware of herself slipping into a trance. She grew calmer.

Mistress's words soothed her. "You're that young woman again, Maddy. You've cheated on Justin. Justin's angry, isn't he?"

Her eyes were fixed by her Mistress. "Yes, he's very angry."

That soft voice again, "What happens when he's angry?"

"He screams at me."

"How does it feel when he screams at you, Maddy?"

"It's so painful…it hurts. Hurts so much. It makes me hate him. But I love him so much."

Madeleine started to sob. Her body shook and she felt the restraints bite into her wrists, ankles, and belly.

The soft voice continued. "You betrayed him, didn't you, Maddy?"

"Yes, Mistress."

"Should you have, Maddy?"

"No, Mistress."

"And he shouldn't have controlled you, should he?"

Faintly, she whispered, "No, Mistress."

"Maddy, I want you to tell me everything. Are you prepared to?"

Madeleine's head fell forward, then gave the slightest of nods.

Jasmine reached out and wiped a tear from Madeleine's face. A pause. "Now Maddy, tell me how he died."

Madeleine screamed and fought against the restraints. Mistress stroked her cheek and kissed her. "Tell me, Maddy. How did he die?"

"No, I can't!"

"You can, Maddy. Tell me. Whisper in my ear. Now."

Madeleine leant forward, her lips against Jasmine's ear. "We were on a Greek island. We were climbing up a long, steep cliff, up a mountain, the sea below. He was shouting, shouting at me."

Madeleine felt Jasmine's fingers tighten on her nipples. "Good girl, carry on."

"Please Mistress, I can't!"

Slowly, Jasmine started to twist her nipples. "You can, Maddy."

Madeleine's head fell back, and her body shook as the pain from her nipples brought her close to orgasm.

Jasmine kissed her deeply, then whispered, "Tell me Maddy. How did he die?"

"He was shouting at me and then I… I killed him. I killed him."

"How, Maddy?"

"I pushed him. He tripped. Lost his footing. And then he was gone. Gone."

"Gone?"

"Yes, over the cliff. Into the sea. Gone."

Madeleine slumped forward, her body limp. Quickly, Jasmine untied her and held her in her arms. Madeleine opened her eyes and Jasmine stroked her hair.

"How do you feel now, Maddy?" she whispered.

Madeleine stared at her. "I loved him, you know. I didn't mean to kill him."

"It's ok, Maddy."

Shaking, she said, "I'm so lonely, so messed up. I see him when my eyes are closed, when they're open. I smell his smell. I hear him laugh. I hear him cry. I can feel him all the time."

She kissed Madeleine softly on the lips and held her in her arms. "It's over now. You can let go. You must learn to forgive yourself. Stand up. I'll help you get dressed. Then Pussy will make you a cup of tea."

⋆ ⋆ ⋆ ⋆

Jasmine called a taxi and walked Madeleine up the steps and into the cab. That had been a heavy session; but so very interesting. Despite all her experience, Madeleine's story had shaken her.

It was no surprise to Jasmine that Madeleine had a deep subconscious desire to be punished. Feeling responsible for the death of her lover would have left deep emotional scars, which Madeleine had obviously never dealt with. What an astonishing secret to have been told! It was just as well that Pussy hadn't been there to hear it too. She could trust her now, but as with so many subs, a time would come when the little one would move on.

Had Madeleine killed Justin? It seemed like she had. She obviously thought she had. Jasmine idly wondered if a confession extracted under hypnosis was allowable in a court of law. Maybe she'd get that wretched solicitor chap George to find out for her. She should introduce him to Finn. It was remarkable how useful her subs could be.

CHAPTER 40

Barbara placed a vase of flowers in the bedroom Madeleine would be sleeping in. It was a comfortable, chintzy room with an en-suite bathroom and a window that looked out over the hills. On the dressing table mirror she hung a couple of necklaces she'd made for her. She hoped she'd like them and couldn't wait to see her wear them. She wanted her home to be a haven for Madeleine, who'd been on the verge of tears when she'd called, asking to be able to stay as soon as possible. Whatever was upsetting her, this house would be her home, a sanctuary, a place where she could take a deep breath and relax. She wandered through the rest of the house, checking everything was as she wanted it. Madeleine was the first guest she had had since Stella left. She and Stella had talked briefly on the phone, both wanting to stay friends, accepting any other type of relationship was over. It was strange, but the loss of Stella hadn't hurt as much as she expected. It felt rather that Madeleine had slipped unconsciously, quietly, and so quickly into the vacant place in her heart. She glanced at her watch. In an hour, she'd get the car and drive to the station to collect her. On the way back, they'd pick up fish and chips.

Barbara stood in the middle of the platform, wondering which carriage Madeleine would be in. Passengers started to get off, but there was no sign of her. She'd texted to say she was on the train, so what had happened? Then at the far end, she saw the guard slowly stepping onto the platform, helping a woman get down from the train. She ran to where Madeleine was holding onto the guard's arm. The suitcase behind her had toppled over.

"Your friend had a tumble on the train just now. She's a bit shaky."

"It was so silly of me. I have no idea what happened. Thank you so much for looking after me."

"No problem, you take care now," the guard said as he got back onto the train.

Barbara took Madeleine's arm and picked up the case. Slowly they walked out of the station and into the carpark. Barbara opened the passenger door for Madeleine, who sat down with a big sigh. She got into the driving seat and turned to her friend. "What happened, my love? You look white as a sheet! I'm going to get you home and tucked up in bed."

Madeleine gave a wan smile. "I'll be fine. It was just a silly fall. I lost my balance. It's so good to get away from London. I'm exhausted."

* * * *

Barbara was reading in the sitting-room when Madeleine came in wearing a nightie and gown, her hair tousled. It was nearly midday.

"Good morning, Maddy. You look a lot better. I hope you slept well. Come and sit and I'll get you a coffee."

"I've had the best night's sleep for ages. A coffee would be great." Madeleine sank onto the sofa and tucked her legs under her. "Oh, this is lovely."

She patted Madeleine's shoulder. "This is your home, Maddy. For as long as you want."

She made the coffee and brought it in on a small tray.

"I didn't know if you wanted milk or sugar. So here it all is."

Barbara sat down beside Madeleine and watched her as she slowly sipped her coffee. The colour was back in her cheeks. How she wanted to hug her. Whatever Madeleine was troubled by would come out when she was ready to talk.

Gently Barbara asked, "How do you feel about a walk after lunch?"

"That would be great. I was looking at the hills from the window this morning. Can we go up there?"

She reached across and squeezed Madeleine's hand. "That was just what I had in mind. We'll drive to Malvern. It's only a few miles away. There's a great walk along the top of the hills. You can see for miles. And on our way down, we can stop at a superb little wine cellar, owned by friends of mine. I'd like them to meet you."

They climbed slowly. By the time they reached the trig pillar on the spine of the hill, Madeleine was out of breath. Barbara helped her up onto the step. From the pillar they could see Worcestershire, Herefordshire, Gloucestershire, and the Welsh mountains stretching out before them. She reached for Madeleine's hand. "Well?"

Madeleine turned to her, her lips quivering. A tear rolled down her cheek. "Barbara, I feel such a mess. I just don't know what to do."

Bit by bit, over the next two days, Madeleine told her story. It wasn't easy for her or at times for Barbara to hear. For Madeleine, confiding in Barbara was cathartic, the relief palpable. For the first time in her life, she felt able to tell someone else everything about her parents, her fear of abandonment, her brother's accidental death and how it had traumatised her, her relationship with Justin, her marriage to Richard and the burden of Justin's death, her relationships since her divorce and her experiences with Mistress Jasmine. She felt so much more in control of her life, a free woman at last. A weight had lifted.

In Barbara, Madeleine had a marvellous new friend who knew exactly when to listen, when to hold her, when to talk. There was no judgment, no recrimination. She began to feel like mountain air, light and free.

They had several days of total relaxation and Madeleine finally started to think ahead about the future, and what it might hold.

She and Barbara got on so well, it was like coming home. They discussed plans for the summer, and Madeleine fantasised about taking a sabbatical from work and living for a while with Barbara on her island. She saw herself learning to make pots; Barbara was thrilled by the idea. Could she give up work for a bit? But what about Giles? He seemed worth getting to know… she closed her eyes and stopped her swirling thoughts; focused on the moment, the Billie Holliday song Barbara had put on, the candlelight.

The two women snuggled on the sofa together.

CHAPTER 41

Mistress Jasmine sat back, crossing and uncrossing her legs, allowing a glimpse of her underwear to the middle-aged man with a growing belly kneeling in front of her, wearing stockings, suspenders, and a purple thong. She stretched out a stockinged foot. He bent forward and licked it. His hands were tied behind his back.

"You're a miserable little worm, George. And yet, I allow you to look between my legs and clean my feet."

The man beamed. "Yes, Mistress, such an honour."

Jasmine pushed him away with her foot and he fell on his side.

The man started to get up and Jasmine pushed him over again.

"Did I tell you to get up?"

"No, Mistress." He resumed the kneeling position.

"Do you have a wife, wretch?"

"No, Mistress, but there is someone I really like."

"Does she really like you?"

The man bowed his head. "Yes Mistress, I think she does."

"I don't suppose you've told her about your dirty little secret have you, George?" The man sniffled. "No Mistress."

"I didn't think so. Pathetic. What sort of relationship can it be if you can't tell her?" The man bowed his head.

"Stand up, George."

The man attempted to get up and fell over.

Jasmine waited until he had struggled to his feet and said, "What kind of law do you practise, worm?"

"General legal advice for charities, Mistress".

"Do you now? Come and kneel in front of me."

The man knelt and stared, mesmerized, as Jasmine spread her legs again in front of his face.

"I may need some legal information in the future. I will expect you to provide it."

"Yes, Mistress."

"Now tell me the name of this new woman of yours, you wretched worm."

CHAPTER 42

Madeleine looked at her two oldest friends and took a deep breath.

"So, there you have it. Any questions?"

It had taken her nearly an hour to tell them what had happened. She had sat in the leather chair, then paced up and down the room, pausing occasionally to look out through the French windows into the garden. The friendly robin had perched on the watering can and stared at her, as if fascinated. Several times her friends had tried to interrupt, but she had told them to wait.

Emily and Shammie looked at each other and spoke at the same time.

"What the hell are you going to do now?"

"Why didn't you come to me, rather than Barbara?" said Emily, and then immediately felt bad and asked, "Are you okay, sweetheart?"

"Em darling, I just wanted to get away from everything and everyone and give myself some space. I had to get out of London. Barbara lives miles away, and I just knew I could take my time with her and get my thoughts straight. I wasn't excluding you. It wasn't personal. I'm so glad you both know everything now. As for what I'm going to do, I'm just going to take it day by day."

"My God, Maddy, it's a lot to take in," said Shammie. "Meeting Finn in Brown's that day… wow, look what it's led to… so much! But more importantly, what do you think Mistress Jasmine will do?"

"Just what I was thinking," said Emily. "Do you think she's going to cause any trouble?"

"Right now, I'm not sure what to do. It's possible I won't hear from her again."

"Not much chance of that, Maddy," said Shammie. "She'll try and control you, now she knows about Justin."

"I don't think so. Her whole thing is consensual. I'm sure she's not a blackmailer. I can't say I'm happy about her knowing but, you know something? It's freed me to have let it out and spoken the words out loud, instead of just in horrible nightmares."

Madeleine put both her hands out to her friends.

"I'm so sorry I never told you before. You understand why, don't you? I know you won't tell anyone, ever."

"Of course not! But what if Jasmine tells Mike and Finn?" said Emily.

"She wouldn't do that. I feel sure of it. She just wouldn't.," said Madeleine firmly.

"I really hope you're right," said Emily. "But what do you really know about her?"

A look of doubt fleetingly crossed Madeleine's face, but she quickly overcame it.

"I just feel sure. Weirdly, I trust her totally."

"Are you going to see her and Finn and Mike again?" asked Shammie.

"Maybe."

"And what about Julia and Maxine?" asked Emily.

"Well, I'll obviously see Julia professionally. As for the other stuff, I don't know at this point. Let's wait and see."

Shammie squeezed her hand. "However weird it's been with this Jasmine character, you must admit you've had an exciting time of it, with one thing and another. God, I'm almost jealous..."

Madeleine smiled. "You're not going believe this, but there's more... I need to tell you about Giles. He's lovely. This could be something important... but I'm not sure what to do about him just now. Jasmine has made me realise I'm hanging on to the past and I must deal with that. I'm not looking for a full-on relationship, and I suspect he probably is. Also, he's a client and I just shouldn't go there. I'm already on an official warning over Julia... oh God, it's so complicated!"

"If this Giles turns out to be worth keeping, you could always follow in my footsteps and have an open relationship."

"You're a superb role model, Shammie. I have a lot to learn from you."

Emily laughed. "I'm going to have a word with Jack. Now I know he's bi, maybe I'll indulge him and get some extra fun for myself."

"God yes, so many options," said Madeleine. She paused. "Sometimes I think back to my time with Richard. All those lonely years, the agony of incompatibility. Lying awake beside him, listening to him snoring. And those grudges he buried until he decided to bring them up. And now...fuck, never again."

"I love you, Maddy. I'm so proud of you." said Emily.

"Me too. Anyway," said Shammie, "what's everyone doing for Christmas?"

Madeleine hated Christmas. She had not a single memory of a happy Christmas time. Her childhood memories were dominated by her alcoholic mother. Richard had always put on a big show but only to entertain friends and colleagues. At Christmas parties, the enforced jollity and drunkenness made her look for the quietest corner, and she'd slip away at the first opportunity.

"What do you think, Maddy?" Shammie's voice cut into her thoughts.

"Sorry, I was miles away. Say that again."

"Em and I are thinking of a shared party. We could all host it. Invite Barbara so we can all meet her. Finn, Mike, Jasmine too. What a party that could be!"

"Barbara yes, no way the others!"

"Oh, come on Maddy. It'd be fun. I can just imagine the conversations. '*So, what do you do for a living?*' '*I flog submissives.*' '*Oh. how very interesting. What are you doing for Christmas?*'"

Madeleine tried to stop herself from laughing. "No way! But yes, I'm happy to co-host. Your place, Em, would be best. Can we just have our close friends? We could do a shared meal. Keep it simple. Sorry, but I've always hated Christmas parties."

"That's all going to change, Maddy. We're going to make this the best Christmas ever, so we're all ready for an incredible new year."

CHAPTER 43

The notes that Catherine had given Giles made sense. He had thought the new novel was done and had already started to plan his next one. He hated re-writing, but she'd put her finger on a problem he knew was there but had tried to gloss over. He wondered if Catherine had discussed the notes with Madeleine.

Madeleine.

He'd asked Catherine about her, but she'd been purposely vague and had questioned him on why he was asking. He said that he was just asking after her. She told him that Madeleine had taken a few weeks off. Needed a break. A break from what? He'd called and texted her. Madeleine's silence had started to make him worry. Surely, she wouldn't be ghosting him. It was astonishing how quickly this woman had got under his skin.

The manuscript that Catherine had returned with her notes was on the laptop in front of him. She'd given him a deadline of 31st December to get it re-written. He'd have to work every day. He could forget Christmas. A good reason not to join in with his brother's faux family fun.

A coffee first.

Then writing… writing… writing… discipline… discipline. Discipline. God, he'd loved that last session with Mistress Jasmine! He wished he hadn't given Madeleine's name when Mistress asked the name of his new girlfriend, but it had slipped out without thinking. Oh well. It wasn't much of a risk. London was a big place. He stretched his fingers and started writing. The tap, tap of the keyboard became mesmeric and he slipped into his creative world.

CHAPTER 44

The woman beside Finn stirred in her sleep and turned towards him. Browns Hotel bar had delivered again. The woman, who was staying at the hotel, had made the first move, and offered to buy him a drink. He wasn't objecting. It made a nice change not to be the pursuer. She knew what she wanted and had told him without any hesitation how she liked to be fucked and he'd delivered. It was six in the morning, and they hadn't had much sleep. She had to be on a conference call at nine so maybe he'd slip away now and go for a walk in Green Park before going home.

It was still dark in the room. Their clothes were mixed up in a heap on the floor and he quietly disentangled them. Two buttons were missing from his shirt where she had ripped it open. He stumbled as he put on a shoe, and she sat up.

"Trying to slip away, I see."

"Yes. Sorry to wake you."

"Leave me your number. You're good."

He wrote his number on a hotel compliment slip, kissed her on the cheek and quietly closed the door behind him, tipping the doorman as he left the hotel and headed for the park. He was feeling more like his own self, the self he was most comfortable with. He still thought about Madeleine but there seemed little point in losing sleep over her when he could have uncommitted fun.

CHAPTER 45

Madeleine took a deep breath as she walked into the office for the first time in a while. Catherine had allowed her to work from home, but it wasn't going to be possible to put things off any longer. She'd continued to use her dead mother as the excuse and felt horribly guilty about it, especially when they'd all sent her a huge bunch of flowers.

Catherine got up from her desk and smiled as Madeleine came in.

"Maddy, we've missed you. Grab a coffee and let's have a quick chat before we all get together. There's a lot to catch up on."

It was good to be back amongst familiar faces. She wondered why she'd been so nervous about coming back. Charlie, Helen, Catherine, and Madeleine. The team, sitting round the kitchen table, the usual Monday morning briefing like nothing had changed. But for Madeleine, everything had changed. The chat around her was about Christmas and presents and parties. In her head she could hear Mistress Jasmine's soft, persuasive, addictive voice.

Catherine's voice broke the spell. "Christmas may be close, but we have a lot to do before then. Maddy, it's great to have you back in person. Fill us in on where you've got to."

"First, I want to thank you all for your love and support over my mother. She's doing okay now and I'm so glad to be back. Working from home has some advantages but, well, it doesn't beat seeing your lovely faces. I've had several calls with Julia. She's doing research for her next novel. She's been sending me drafts and they're good. I've also been reading a lot of manuscripts that have come in. Most as usual are hopeless but there are a couple of gems that I'll be putting forward for discussion. So, it's been a productive time and I'm sorry I've been away for so long."

Charlie leant over and stroked her arm. "We've missed you, Maddy. Lovely to have you back."

"Okay. Thanks, Maddy." Catherine took a sip of coffee. "I want to give you Giles Hawthorne to look after. He's not easy to work with and seems to have been rather distracted recently. I think he'll probably respond better to you, Maddy. You okay with that?"

Giles. This was not what she wanted. On the other hand, if her contact with him was professional and it would have to be, it would help to put a barrier between them. It had been hard enough rebuilding a totally professional relationship with Julia.

"Sure, yes that's fine."

"Good. I'll call him and tell him. He's asked after you a lot and I know he respects you. Charlie, Helen, where are you with your projects?"

As soon as Catherine told Giles of the new arrangement, he was on the phone to Madeleine.

"Maddy, this is fantastic. How have you been? Where have you been? Are you okay?"

"Hi Giles, I'm fine thanks. Listen, I'm sorry I've been so distant. I had some personal stuff to sort out. How are you? And most importantly, how's the novel coming along?"

"I'm much better now! The novel is progressing well, but I've missed you, Maddy. Let's have dinner soon."

"Yes, happy to have dinner with you but I need to get one thing straight. I said right at the beginning that this had to be a professional relationship. Nothing else. I know we slipped after that lovely evening, but you must agree to this, or I won't be able to take you on."

He feigned a Yankee drawl. "Sure, anything you say, gorgeous. So, when are we gonna meet?"

"I mean it, Giles. I'll be in touch. Bye for now."

She worked through lunch, left early, and took the tube to Putney. It was bitterly cold, and the rain gusted along the pavement. She'd decided to cook a simple pasta, with a lemon, cream and parmesan sauce and ducked into the supermarket to pick up the cream she needed. Simple, tasty, and easy to make. Just what she felt like after her first day back in the office.

She opened the front door, and a comforting warmth embraced her. She shook the rain of her coat and hung it up.

Since her confession to Mistress Jasmine, she was sleeping more deeply through the night. The falling nightmares had not returned. She dreaded them coming back and wondered what she'd have to do if they did. Would it help to go back to Mistress, be helpless, punished for what she did? The orgasms she'd had under Mistress Jasmine's control had been intense. She'd wait and see how she felt. There would be no shame in going back to her. She had given herself willingly and if that's what she needed, so be it. She was beginning to feel comfortable with the new parts of her life, however unexpected or strange; she felt more in control than she ever had before.

CHAPTER 46

The last client of the day left, and Jasmine sat down with a cup of tea, kicked her heels off and put her feet up on a leather stool. The naked girl knelt beside her and started to gently massage Jasmine's feet.

"Oh, that's good. Thank you, Pussy. You've been a good girl today. Just do that for five more minutes, then go home."

"Yes, Mistress. But can't I stay with you tonight?"

"Not tonight, little one. Your Mistress needs to sleep. I want you to take tomorrow off. Mike and Finn are coming over. We have a lot to talk about."

"Yes Mistress. Is this about Madeleine?"

"Shhh. I've told you to forget all about her. Now, off you go."

* * * *

The train from Liverpool to London wasn't as full as usual and Mike had the table to himself. He plugged in his laptop, opened it up and checked it had connected to the wifi. His phone rang.

"Mike, I'll meet you off the train at Euston. Let's have a coffee and a catch-up in Pret before we go and see Jasmine. I've fixed up for us to go to the gallery at 5 o'clock to go over the final checks for the Rachel Grieves exhibition. Where are you staying tonight? If you don't have any plans, let's have dinner."

"Okay, that's fine. No plans for the evening yet. Thought I might try to see if Maddy's free."

"Have you spoken to her lately? I've called a few times but no response. She's playing hard to get. Thankfully, I've found a new distraction. I'll tell you about her when we meet."

"I've had the same brush-off, but I'm not giving up on her, my friend. I look forward to hearing about this new one. See you at Euston."

He called Madeleine, and it immediately went to voicemail. "Hi Maddy, it's Mike. I'm in London and free this evening if you'd like to meet up. Let me know." He hoped for a reply, but he wasn't holding his breath.

★ ★ ★ ★

"So, what do we do now?"

Jasmine, Mike, and Finn sat round a table in the café. Jasmine looked at them. "You must never let on that you know. You stay schtum with Maddy, okay?"

"If you say so. Of course, we must make sure it's the same Madeleine," said Finn.

"It is. I know it," said Jasmine.

Pussy came over with their coffees and cakes. Finn patted her on her backside.

"Good to see you, Sir," she said.

"You too, Pussy. Let's play again soon, okay?"

"Yes, Sir. Thank you, Sir. I'd like that. I'll leave you to your chat now if that's okay."

They watched as the girl walked back to the counter and washed her hands.

"I love that girl," said Jasmine. "Okay, so when are you two handsome men going to see Maddy again? Make it soon. I want to know if she says anything about what happened. If she doesn't want to come and see me again, I'll be really upset."

CHAPTER 47

Friends would soon be arriving for the Christmas party at Emily and Jack's home. Shammie and Emily's excitement was infectious, and Madeleine had relaxed, feeling her dislike of Christmas lessening. Between them, they had invited about 40 friends, including, at Shammie and Emily's insistence, Giles and Barbara. Much to the disappointment of her friends, Madeleine had put her foot down over Jasmine, Mike, and Finn. They were most definitely not invited. Maxine, Julia, and Catherine, however, were coming. Madeleine had not been sure about it, but if Giles was coming, she had little excuse not to invite them. She owed them hospitality.

The house felt warm and welcoming. Christmas decorations were up, food and drinks were laid out on the white tablecloths covering the dining table and the first of Jack's playlists of familiar, popular Christmas songs came softly through the speakers.

The bell rang.

"God, someone's here already. I'll get it," said Madeleine.

Barbara stood under the porch light, arms spread wide, a suitcase by her side. "I'm here! Hope it's okay I'm early." Madeleine stepped forward, enveloped in a huge hug and the sound of rattling bangles.

"Oh, it's good to see you, Barbara." Madeleine felt a kiss on the side of her head. They held each other, swaying in unison. "Come in, come and meet Shammie and Emily."

The introductions done, the four of them raised a glass of champagne to each other.

"Emily, Shammie, you're just as Maddy described you. I'm so happy to be here and meet you both at last."

"And you're even larger than life!" said Emily. "Thank you so much for helping Maddy. She told us what you did for her. We've all been friends for years and she's very precious to us."

"I hope you don't mind me saying that I feel like she's been a friend of mine for years too, though it's only been a short while," said Barbara.

"Enough! You're making me blush," said Madeleine.

"Barbara, let me introduce you to my husband, Jack," said Emily. "He's just finishing something off upstairs in his study. I'll show you the bathroom at the same time. I know you've driven from Ledbury, so come and freshen up."

Barbara followed Emily out of the room.

"She is something else, Maddy! I can see why you like her so much," said Shammie.

"She's a great person and really good fun."

"Attractive, too."

"Yes, she is."

"Maddy, you're blushing!"

The bell rang again. "You go this time, Shammie."

The sound of friends in full party flow reverberated round the room, drowning out the music. The champagne had long been finished, but the wine was flowing, and the food was disappearing fast. Madeleine felt an arm go round her waist and turned to see Giles. God, he was attractive. Damn!

"Maddy, at last. It's so good to see you. Thank you so much for inviting me."

"Giles, it's great to see you, too. How are you?"

"Somehow, I've finished the re-write. I've put my pen away now til the new year. I've no plans for Christmas, other than enjoying myself. This is my first party of the season."

"That sounds great. Come on, let me introduce you to a few people."

She spotted Maxine and Julia deep in conversation with Barbara, who'd put her arms round both their shoulders. Suddenly they roared with laughter and people turned towards them. "Barbara, you're wicked. We love you,' said Julia. "Maddy, where did you find this wonderful woman?"

"Isn't she great? I'm so glad you've met each other. I want to introduce you to another friend of mine. Not only a friend, but another writer and client. Max, Jules, Barbara, meet Giles Hawthorne. Giles, this is the amazing Julia McGuigan."

"Julia, at last. Congratulations on your novel. I'm so pleased to meet you."

"You too, Giles. I read your book. Loved it. This is Max, my partner. And Barbara, well, Barbara's a…." Julia hesitated.

"Barbara's a superb potter. We met in Athens. I'm very envious of her lifestyle," said Madeleine.

"Giles, great to meet you. Are you single?" said Barbara.

Giles glanced across at Madeleine. "Yes, as it happens, I am."

"A handsome, mature, creative, single man. So hard to find these days. Maddy, I'm amazed you haven't snapped him up."

"That would be most unprofessional, wouldn't it Maddy?" Catherine was standing behind her.

"Barbara, enough of that," said Madeleine. "Catherine, this is my friend, Barbara. I'll leave you all to swap life stories. I think you'll find them interesting. And keep me out of it! Giles, get some food before it all goes."

Madeleine squeezed Barbara's shoulder and turned to chat with other friends. She could feel Catherine's eyes on her. Had she seen or sensed something that was making her suspicious? She tried to think if she had done anything to give herself away. Could Catherine have seen Maxine and Julia both kiss her on the lips when she took them upstairs to the bedroom where everyone's coats had been put? Had she seen Giles kiss and squeeze her hand? No, she was being paranoid.

By midnight, people were starting to leave. Catherine hugged

Julia and Giles, wishing them both a happy and relaxing Christmas. "We all have a lot of work to do in the new year. Have you seen Maddy? I must thank her."

* * * *

Catherine's Uber was halfway down the road before she realised she'd left her scarf behind at the house. The driver turned the car round, and as Catherine got out, she saw the front door open. Madeleine and Giles were in the hall, kissing passionately under the mistletoe, their arms round each other. They stopped, laughing as Barbara, Julia and Maxine came down the stairs, coats over their arms. She watched as Julia, then Maxine kissed Madeleine too. Barbara was clapping and laughing. Slowly, Catherine turned and got back into the taxi. Never mind the scarf.

* * * *

Barbara's bedroom door was ajar when Madeleine got up. She tapped on the door and looked in. There was no one there. Pulling on a dressing gown, she went downstairs. Barbara had made a large pot of coffee, and two mugs were set out on the kitchen table. She was sending a text and looked up as Madeleine came in.

"Coffee's ready, Maddy. Shall I pour?"

Madeleine stood behind her and stroked her hair.

"How long have you been up?'

"About half an hour. I'm not one for lying in bed in the morning unless there's a good reason. How are you feeling? That was a splendid party. Giles has texted me."

"Really? What did he say?"

"He wants to take me out to dinner tomorrow night."

Madeleine felt a split second of jealousy. It must have shown on her face.

"Is that a problem, Maddy? If it is, please tell me."

"No, it's fine. As I said, I have a professional relationship with him, nothing else. You go ahead. He's a nice guy. Maybe a little possessive. You'll have to stay longer now."

"Oh dear, is he possessive? I can't be doing with that. Maybe I'd better say no."

"Don't be silly. He's interesting. Enjoy yourself. Now, tell me what you'd like to do today."

"I'd love to go for a walk and maybe go and see the Christmas lights. How do you feel about that?"

Madeleine took a sip of coffee. "Hell, yes why not. It's been a while since I've gone anywhere with a girlfriend."

"Girlfriend. I like that." Barbara got up, went over to Madeleine, and kissed her full on the lips. For a second, Madeleine froze. Then her mouth opened, and Barbara took her in her arms. There would not be a walk today.

⋆ ⋆ ⋆ ⋆

Barbara arrived at the restaurant and a waiter came over.

"Are you Barbara?" he asked.

She nodded. "Your friend is on his way, but he got held up. Can I take your coat? It's an awful night out there. Come and sit by the fire til he arrives. He tried to call you but couldn't get through."

Barbara took out her phone. It was switched off.

"Damn, what an idiot. Thanks, that would be lovely. Can I have a vodka and tonic?"

The fire warmed her, and the vodka put her in good spirits. She looked at the menu. Bouillabaisse. Her favourite. Good choice, Giles.

The door opened and Giles rushed over. "I'm so sorry. The bus got stuck in traffic. I tried to call you." He bent over and kissed her on the cheek. "Have you been here long?"

"I'm sorry, my phone was off. The lovely waiter has looked after me well. I want the Bouillabaisse."

"That's one of my favourites here. They do a great beef tenderloin too."

"So, you've been here before?"

"Yes, it's a favourite place. I came here with Maddy."

"You went out with her?"

"That's a bit of an exaggeration. To be honest, I'd have liked to but it's a purely business relationship now."

"Was that your choice?"

"No, it's hers. It was odd. She disappeared for a while. Something to do with her mother. Or at least that's what she told me. Not sure I believe her, though."

"Why not?"

"I don't know. Just...well, it was strange. When she got back, everything had changed. Anyway, why talk about another woman when I'm here with you. I've only met you once, but I feel a real affinity with you. I loved it when the first thing you asked me was if I was single."

"Giles, I'm not a woman who messes around. If I like someone, I make it clear. I really do like you. So, let's eat and see what happens. I want you to tell me all about yourself."

Giles told her the edited version of his story, a bit more guarded than he'd been with Madeleine.

Barbara listened quietly to his story, her eyes never leaving his face. This disarming man intrigued her.

"So that's me," he said.

Barbara sniffed, then smiled. "Bullshit. Okay, it's good bullshit. One day, I'm going to get to know the real you, Giles. But right now, I'm hungry. Let's order."

"Can't think of anything better," he said, relieved.

They talked, laughed, discovered a shared love of opera and Bob Dylan, flirted outrageously, ate three courses, and drank two bottles of wine.

"Coffee and a nightcap to finish off?" he asked.

"Where?"

"Well, here…or do you mean…?"

"I mean your place, Giles. I want you."

★ ★ ★ ★

In her deep sleep, Madeleine heard a bell ring. She stirred but didn't wake. Again, a bell ringing. She sat up and called Barbara's name. No answer. The bell rang again. She looked at her phone. Four in the morning. Again, it rang. The front door.

"Darling, I'm sorry I'm so late. I should have taken a key."

"It's okay, come to bed. I guess you had a good time."

Barbara took off her coat and kissed her. "Yes, let's go to bed. I'll tell you all in the morning."

Madeleine's alarm rang. Sleepily, she reached for Barbara. Naked, they snuggled, their bodies spooned together. Madeleine whispered, "you had sex with him, didn't you?" Almost imperceptibly, Barbara nodded and turned towards her. "Yes, I did."

Madeleine lay still, staring into her eyes. "Was it good?" "Yes." Madeleine turned away. "Just give me a minute, will you?"

Barbara got up and naked, went to the kitchen, made them both coffee and brought it back to the bedroom. She sat down beside Madeleine's foetal body and stroked her hair.

"I'm not apologising, Maddy. It makes no difference to how I feel about you. It's just how I am."

Madeleine wiped a tear from her cheek and turned to face Barbara. "It's okay. Just takes a little getting used to."

It didn't take long; Barbara always made her feel okay.

★ ★ ★ ★

On the concourse at Paddington station, Giles took Barbara in his arms, kissing her passionately. "We're going to miss you."

She smiled. "I'm going to miss you both, too."

She turned to Madeleine. "Maddy my love, thank you for everything. You're very special."

"Safe journey home. Come back soon, Barbara."

They hugged and kissed.

"I will. Just try and keep me away. I want to talk to you both about Christmas. I'll call when I get home. And now you two, stop being silly. Get to know each other properly, okay?"

She blew them both a kiss and got onto the train. Madeleine and Giles watched til it disappeared round the bend.

"Maddy, we need to talk," he said.

CHAPTER 48

"Finn, I promise you, we'll meet up in the new year. It'll be good to see you and yes, I'll come to the opening night. Yes, I promise. Now, I must go. Have a good Christmas and say hello to Mike, okay?"

Madeleine put the phone down. "Sorry, Giles. I've been avoiding him for ages. I had to take it."

She rolled over into his arms. "I cannot tell you how long it's been since I've had a proper lie-in on a Sunday morning. Let's stay here forever."

"I think Barbara might have something to say about that," he said. "So, who's this Finn guy?"

Madeleine pouted. "Oh, you know, just someone I know. A man." She smiled and kissed him. "So, what are we going to do about other people? Haven't you got a woman tucked away somewhere?"

"As it happens, no. Well, not the sort of woman you mean. Don't you want us to be exclusive?"

"I hate that expression. Anyway, we aren't exclusive, are we? There's Barbara. I don't think she's ever been exclusive in her life."

"This is bizarre, isn't it?" He sat up. "I wonder what's going to happen when we go to Barbara's for Christmas. Have you ever slept with two people at once?"

She laughed. "Yes. With Finn and Mike. And, er, also with Julia and Maxine."

Giles stared, open-mouthed. "Seriously?"

"I had a threesome with Finn and Mike in Athens. The weekend I met Barbara."

Giles lay back, arms behind his head. "Okay, I want to know everything about that weekend. And about Julia and Maxine."

"Everything? Are you sure?"

"Yes. Every detail."

"Okay, just as well we've got all morning. Wow, you're getting hard again. Mmmm!"

★ ★ ★ ★

The Christmas Eve traffic out of London was nose to tail. Madeleine had wanted to leave earlier, but Giles had overslept after a late night in a pub with friends and arrived at her house two hours late.

They set off in the hire car in silence. Madeleine swore at another driver who tried to cut in front of her. She turned to Giles.

"This is not a good start to what will probably be a strange Christmas. You could at least apologise for being late."

"I have apologised, twice. But, okay, I'm sorry. I'm sorry."

She glanced across at him and her eyes twinkled.

"That's better."

"Maddy, there's something we need to talk about. It's been on my mind. What are we going to do about Catherine? If she finds out about us, there's going to be hell to pay. You're going to have to tell her and get her onside."

"God knows how I do that. She called me after the party and wanted to meet up. I have an awful feeling she might suspect something. I put her off til after the Christmas holiday. I know I need to tell her. But not now. This is the first Christmas I've looked forward to for, well, my whole life. I just want to have fun!"

"I've brought some music to play. It's a playlist of my favourite tracks I put together for the journey. I hope you like them!"

"Sounds great, put it on." She reached across and put a hand on his thigh. "It's Christmas!!"

★ ★ ★ ★

The front door opened, and a smell of roasting lamb enveloped them a second before Barbara wrapped her arms around them both.

"You made it! My darlings, I'm so happy to see you. What a Christmas this is going to be. Come in, come in. Here, let me help you with your cases. And three bags of presents! What have you brought?! Wonderful, wonderful!"

The Christmas tree in the hall reached up to the ceiling, squashing the angel on the top. The white twinkling lights reflected off the hand-made baubles. Colourful paperchains hung across the ceiling.

"Leave your cases in the hall for now. If you need the bathroom, it's upstairs on the right. Maddy, can you show Giles? Then come and have some champagne. We can eat in about an hour. I'm so excited!" She skipped off into the kitchen. Madeleine and Giles grinned.

"You ready for this, Maddy?"

"God, yes. You?"

"Bring it on." He took her hand and followed Barbara into the kitchen.

The lamb was exceptional, the champagne superb, the wine, fruity and smooth. They sat together on the sofa, almost unable to move.

"I love feeding my friends. Just wait and see what we have for tomorrow," said Barbara.

Madeleine stretched out her legs and exhaled.

"Barbara, can we please have Christmas lunch in the evening? It's going to take me hours to digest all this. That was superb."

"Sure," Barbara laughed. Anyway, I don't think any of us will want to get up early on Christmas Day. Now, about sleeping arrangements...."

"I'd been thinking about that," said Giles. "Do you have a big bed?"

"Of course I do. There's also a king-sized bed in the second bedroom, the one you slept in, Maddy. I want us all to feel completely free to sleep where we want, with whom we want, whenever we want. And I hope you'll agree, there is only one rule. That we communicate with each other, be honest with how we're feeling, individually and together. If anyone feels uncomfortable, or left out, or jealous, we share it and talk about it. As you know, I had a relationship with a guy and a woman, but not all together. So, this is as new to me as it is to you. And I'm very excited by all the options we have. Tell me how you're both feeling."

Madeleine giggled. "You go first, Giles. I need a moment to think."

"I don't need a moment to think," he said. "This is every man's dream, fantasy if you like. Now I'm facing the reality, I'm feeling excited, happy …and a bit nervous. Maddy?"

"I'm feeling full. Sorry, that was flippant. I agree with you, Giles. It's exciting and a bit scary. But I know if we talk, hide nothing, we can make it work. And I want it to work in every way. It's not just sex, is it? It's the whole thing. How we share our time, how we deal with things we want and can't have, who we give priorities to. I hate jealousies, but they're inevitable. Barbara's right. We must talk together, be honest, be prepared to deal with the feelings of not just one other person, which is hard enough, but two others." She paused. "Gosh, right now, that feels almost impossible. But you know, for the first time ever, I feel I can be totally open and honest with you two. That feels so good."

⋆ ⋆ ⋆ ⋆

"Happy Christmas, my darlings! It's time to wake up!" Giles was standing naked by the bed holding a tray. Madeleine and Barbara yawned, nearly in unison and looked up at him.

"Wow, Giles! You've made breakfast as well?!" said Madeleine, blissfully. "Do I smell coffee and croissants?"

Giles laid the tray down on the bed, stood up and looked at the two naked women spread out in front of him. "I have, my beauties, and I made it with love. I'm living the dream."

Every morning, they checked in with each other and only once, when Giles had felt left out and hadn't owned up to it, had there been a row. They explored Ledbury and the Malverns, together and separately. Each had taken time out when he or she needed it. The bond between them grew as they talked and laughed, made love, experimented, walked, cooked with and for each other, and sat quietly, reading, or listening to music.

On New Year's Day, they had an early lunch, mostly in silence. Each was wishing this wouldn't end. They created a WhatsApp group for themselves and called it *We Three*. Barbara promised to come to London as often as she could. She felt fine that Madeleine and Giles would spend more time together. She'd make up for it when they were all together again. Her house was theirs. They talked a little about what would happen in April when Barbara was due to go back to Naxos. But that was then. This was now. Time to pack the car and go. Hugs, kisses, and smiles. They'd be together again soon.

* * * *

Madeleine, home alone, wandered around her house. She was torn between the delight of being by herself, with no one else to consider, and missing the hedonistic week where she had indulged herself in ways that a few months ago she'd have said 'no' to. Now it was 'yes, yes'. She giggled to herself. Was there anything she wouldn't say 'yes' to now? An overwhelming sense of freedom consumed her. She could say 'no', she could say 'yes', and she would decide which it was to be. No one else would ever decide for her again.

Where would this new relationship of three take her? She reflected on how all three threesomes, all different, had been so exciting, so liberating. Three. The perfection and strength of a triangle; the beginning, middle and end; father, son and holy ghost; mind, body, spirit; hear no evil, speak no evil, see no evil; on your mark, get set, go; the third eye; life, liberty and the pursuit of happiness; sex, drugs and rock n'roll; wine, women and song; liberté, egalité, fraternité; veni, vidi, vici. Two is interesting, but three? Three is compelling. Barbara, Giles, Madeleine. Had she found, at last, the best way to be?

CHAPTER 49

Madeleine sat ashen faced in her sitting room as Catherine paced up and down in front of her.

"I saw you, Maddy! How could you do this? I warned you over Julia. Now Giles too! It's unforgiveable! I trusted you. I asked you to keep it professional. I really value all the work you do. You know that. I couldn't run the business without you. That's the brutal fact."

"I'm so sorry, Catherine."

"Shh! Let me think. Is there anything else you want to tell me? I don't know – are you having a relationship with Charlie when you're out of the office…???"

Madeleine got up from her chair and stood in front of Catherine. "Please, Catherine, don't say that. I didn't intend for any of this to happen…"

"You're not a fucking child, Maddy. Why, why have you done this?

"The truth is, I got myself in a mess. Something from my past. Nothing to do with work. I swear that's true. And in freeing myself, I got carried away. I shouldn't have got involved with them. I'm sorry. I love the job. I love working with you. I know I messed up over Giles. But the fact is, I love him. We've found a connection and a way of life that works for us. It isn't a typical relationship. There's nothing else that has any bearing on work. Jules and Max are just friends now, and we have a brilliant friendship. That's it."

"Can you still work with Giles professionally? Can you be objective about his work? And what about Julia?"

"Yes, definitely. If anything, I'm more critical now. After all, being married to his agent never hurt Julian Barnes."

"And the mess you got yourself into? Is that sorted out?"

"Yes, it is."

Catherine took a deep breath. "Maddy, you may not believe this, but I do understand love. I know how it feels and I know what it feels like when it ends. I do want you to be happy and you haven't been for a long time. But.... I'm sorry. I cannot forgive this. I warned you after Julia's party not to get involved with her and you said you wouldn't. You lied to me over that, and now Giles. I have no choice but to fire you. I want you to do notes for me on everything you're doing, and I'll give you a month's pay. But that's it. I don't know how I'll manage without you, but I will. This breaks my heart, and I will compromise by keeping the facts to myself. You can even have a reference from me. But I can't trust you or work with you anymore."

Madeleine stared, shell-shocked, as Catherine went into the hall and put on her coat. She heard the front door open. Then Catherine, her voice shaking, said, "Collect your stuff on Monday afternoon when I'm out of the office. Goodbye, Maddy." The door banged shut.

Faintly, Madeleine said, "Goodbye, Catherine." She crumpled onto the sofa and burst into tears.

Madeleine wandered from room to room, dazed, vaguely tidying, emptying, stacking, loading. She watered the houseplants, switched on the television, stared vacantly at the screen, and switched it off. The phone rang twice and rang out. The third time, she picked it up.

"Giles, I..."

"Maddy, you okay?"

"Catherine fired me today. My job's gone."

"Fired you, why? Maddy, what the hell's going on?"

"Because of you and me. And Julia. Because I lied to her. I told her everything today. I wanted to be honest. I wish I hadn't."

"Oh, my love, that's awful. She can't just fire you! I'll call her, get her to change her mind. I'll leave the agency. I'm not having it. Anyway, she needs you. This is mad."

"I have to send her handover notes. She doesn't want to see me in the office again."

"She can't do this to you, Maddy. There are rules. Laws. Procedures."

"Giles, she's done it. I've called her three times since she left, and she won't answer. You must stay with the agency. Don't even think about leaving. I'll write up the notes for her and then I'll just wait and see. I don't know, maybe she'll change her mind. Emily's coming over in a bit."

"I'll come over too. I can be with you in an hour."

"No, darling, I just need to think. I'll call you tomorrow."

Madeleine threw the phone onto the sofa. "Fuck." She opened the French windows and stepped into the garden. A pair of pigeons flew up into a tree and started to coo.

★ ★ ★ ★

Three days after being fired, Madeleine had spring-cleaned the house, weeded the garden, gone for long walks and bought herself a new dress. She'd calculated she had enough money to last six months without getting another job.

Friends had rung her, consoling, hopeful, optimistic. Julia had called, distraught, not knowing what she'd do without her lovely editor. Barbara and Giles were coming for the weekend. So much great support. But none of it really helped.

She set off for a walk on the Common.

Joggers ran past her. She watched a woman much her own age throw a ball for her dog. No. She wasn't ready for that. She felt the Common belonged just to her. She stroked a big tree and loved the rough feel of the bark against her hands. As a child she had run naked through fields on her grandparents' farm. She remembered the whip of the corn against her body and how she would later admire and caress the red welts on her skin, feeling a strange, delicious pleasure. Jasmine had revived that pleasure. She needed relief from the pain of losing her job.

She wandered into a copse of oak trees and bracken away from the path and looked around, checking she was alone. Her jeans were tight, never easy to get on or off, but she quickly removed her coat, sweater, and bra. The oak tree was large and strong, unyielding, and she moved slowly against it. The bark bit into her belly and breasts. She could feel her legs weaken but it was the feeling between them she focused on. She stood still, tight against the tree, her arms wrapped round the trunk, and breathed deeply. She moved again. And again. This was a deeply buried, painful, beautiful ache, and she was going to relieve it. She wanted to touch but denied herself, squeezing her thighs instead. Her orgasm shuddered through her body, and she dropped to her knees.

Back home, she undressed and looked down at her body. Her belly and breasts were red and bruised. She picked the flecks of bark from her skin, had a bath, and gently rubbed lotion into her body.

* * * *

Mechanically, she made a tuna salad and switched on the television. Coronation Street. So much better to listen to other people's problems. Her phone rang. Unknown number. Jasmine was the last person she wanted to talk to. Or was she? She was wise in her own strange way. Hell. Why not?

"Hello, Mistress."

A man's voice. "Hello? Maddy? Maddy, it's Richard." For a split second, she had no idea who Richard was. Then she remembered the voice she hadn't heard for so long. She grasped the blanket she'd placed over her knees.

"Richard? I'm sorry, I wasn't expecting.... you sound a bit different. Is everything alright?"

"Yes, all good here. I don't know why but you've been on my mind, and it's been a long time, so I thought I'd call. Is that okay?"

"Yes, I guess so."

"Okay, that's good. So, what's this 'hello mistress' thing? Or shouldn't I ask?" He laughed, nervously.

"You can ask, so long as I don't have to answer. Why are you using an unknown number? How are you? How's life in La Belle France?"

"I'm sorry. I thought you might not answer if you saw my number. Life here is okay. We have our routines. We've been sort of accepted by the locals. They don't stare now when we walk down the street."

"You have your routines? That sounds exciting."

"Well, don't you?" He sounded annoyed.

"Sorry, that was bitchy. But since you ask, no, I don't think I do. My life is full of surprises."

"I'm glad for you, Maddy. I hope they're good surprises. You deserve it. I wish, how I wish, that I'd been more honest with you."

"More honest? Me too. You lied about the most important thing in our life together. It was just such a waste of time. But that's past."

"I know and I'm so sorry. Lying is so destructive. It's a lesson learnt the hard way."

Madeleine sighed. "Yes, it sure is. I lost my job three days ago because I lied."

"Catherine fired you? That's awful. You loved that job. What happened?"

"Do you really want to know?"

"Yes, of course."

"I had relationships with two of our authors. I lied about them. I crossed a line and Catherine fired me." Silence. "Still there, Richard?"

"Yes, still here. Well, that was bloody stupid."

"Well, thank you for your support. I know it was stupid, but I don't regret the relationships. I'm still in one of them."

"They are lucky guys, Maddy. I'm glad for you, I guess."

"Richard, you don't know the half of it."

"Okay, well, uhm, yes, you are full of surprises. How's Emily?"

"She's well. She's been an amazing support since you walked out. A total brick."

"I'd like us to be friends, Maddy. The truth is I need someone to talk to who I love and who at least cares for me and knows me well. I love Paul, and things are good but there are times it's bloody lonely here. And maybe I can help you too if you need it. Can we talk about it?"

"We can talk about it. So, I'm someone you love, then?"

"Of course you are. I love you as a friend and I hope that's what we can be. We've known each other for twenty-two years."

"I'm glad you called, Richard."

"Thank you. And if you ever need me, well.... I'm coming to London soon. Let's have lunch, dinner, whatever. I'd better go. Paul's coming back. Bye for now, Maddy."

She called Emily. "You'll never guess who I've just heard from."

"Who, who?? Jasmine??"

"No, even stranger. Richard."

"Bloody hell, Maddy. What did he want? Was it okay?"

"Yes, it was rather nice. He wants to be friends. Doesn't sound like he's living the life he hoped for over there. Anyway, what am I going to do, Em? I miss work so much."

"I know you do. It'll get easier, I promise. You have a good weekend with Barbara and Giles. Jack and I are off to meet a friend. Just to cheer you up, things are going really well with us. Talk soon. Love you."

★ ★ ★ ★

Madeleine's phone rang again. Finn. She hesitated, let it ring, then, sighing, answered it.

"Did you read it?"

"Read what?"

"The email. It's your official invitation to the London opening. Just like old times, eh?" She couldn't help a smile, remembering how she had felt when that first invitation had come in.

"I've got it in my diary, Finn. I've said I'm coming. I'd like to bring two friends. Is that okay?"

"Of course it is. I've invited Shammie and her husband, too. Just so you know. Tell me your friends' names, and I'll add them to the guest list."

"I'm glad you've invited Shammie. They might even buy a painting. Her husband isn't short of a bob or two."

"That's good to know, darling."

"Please don't call me darling, Finn. My friends are Giles Hawthorne and Barbara Beckwith."

"No problem. We're looking forward to seeing you. And, please, let's have a drink together soon, even just for old time's sake. Mike and Jasmine say 'hi', by the way."

"Say 'hi' to them too. See you there."

★ ★ ★ ★

Barbara and Giles arrived at Madeleine's house a few days later. They pressed her on what she was going to do.

"I don't know yet. I've lost my confidence. I feel so ashamed of how I behaved with Catherine. It was so unprofessional. I need time to sort myself out before I re-apply for jobs. I'll get there in the end. But fuck, it hurts. At least I hope I've learnt a lesson."

"You should come and make some pots with me. I get my best ideas when I'm on the wheel," said Barbara.

Over dinner, they discussed how to treat Mike and Finn at the exhibition the next day and what to tell them, and decided to say nothing explicitly, but not hide their relationship. If Finn or Mike were observant, which Madeleine knew they would be, they'd know.

★ ★ ★ ★

The gallery was packed when they arrived. Madeleine immediately recognised Pussy and Tim, Mistress Jasmine's slaves, who were serving drinks. Nervously, she looked around. Surely Jasmine wouldn't be here, would she? Maybe they shouldn't stay. Almost imperceptibly, Pussy gave a little curtsey of recognition.

"What can I get you, Madam?" she said.

"I'll have red, please. Giles, Barbara, what would you like?" Madeleine turned towards them. Giles was white as a sheet. "Are you okay, darling?"

"Yes, sorry. I'll have red, too."

"White for me," said Barbara.

They took their drinks and slowly pushed their way through the crowd.

"Are you sure you're okay, Giles?" asked Barbara. "You look like you've seen a ghost."

"I'm fine. Maybe I won't stay too long."

"Okay, well take it easy," said Barbara. "Now, introduce us to these lover boys of yours, Maddy. Where are they?"

Several of the paintings had red dots against them and one of the gallery staff was adding another to one of Rachel Grieves' larger works. The opening was going well.

"There you are, gorgeous!" Madeleine felt a hand on her shoulder and turned to face Mike. He bent down and gave her a kiss on the cheek. "You've been hard to get hold of. We've missed you."

"Mike, this is Barbara and Giles, good friends of mine. Barbara and Giles, Mike."

"So, this is the famous Mike," said Barbara. "We've heard a lot about you. And not all good. Some things very wicked!"

Mike looked at Madeleine, who was shaking her head.

"Maddy, I like your friend. Where have you been hiding her? So, how do you like the exhibition? Have you seen Finn yet? He's over there somewhere, doing what he does best, schmoozing. Why don't the three of you join us for dinner afterwards?"

"Thanks Mike, but we have other plans. It looks like it's going well. You go and work. We probably won't be here long."

"If you change your mind, let me know. You're good at that." Mike kissed her again and Giles flinched. "Call me and we can have a proper catch-up. Hey. Finn's coming over."

Giles put down his glass. "If you don't mind, I think I'll go outside for a bit. I need some fresh air." He turned and barged his way towards the door. "Okay, we won't be long," said Barbara to his disappearing back.

"Maddy, Maddy! How are you? So good to see you".

"Finn, this is Barbara. And this is," she said pointing at him as he opened the door and left, ".... was, Giles How's it going? The paintings look amazing."

"Yes, it is going well. Giles, eh? I feel sure I've seen him before somewhere."

"You won't have seen him before; I can guarantee that."

"Strange, he looks very familiar. Can't say I know a Giles. A George, maybe. Hey, there's Shammie too. Lovely!"

Barbara and Madeleine stayed for another ten minutes, chatting briefly with Shammie and Jacob who had bought one of the paintings, before leaving to find Giles.

Outside, he was nowhere to be seen. They walked around the block but there was no sign of him. Their calls went to voicemail.

"Has he ever just disappeared on you before, Maddy?"

"No, it's bizarre. Let's go home and see what happens."

Their cab pulled up at the house. Giles was sitting on the doorstep, his head in his hands. Madeleine crouched in front of him. "What's the matter, darling? Are you okay?"

He looked at her and then up to Barbara. "I guess it's good this has happened," he said. "I need to tell you something."

Barbara gave him her hand and he pulled himself up. "Let's go in," he said. "I need a stiff drink."

Barbara and Madeleine tried hard to keep straight faces as Giles told them about his fetish and his visits to Mistress Jasmine and a club, where he was known as George. He'd recognised both the young girl and Finn.

"Is that it?" said Madeleine when Giles finished.

"Well, you are a naughty boy!" said Barbara and burst into laughter.

"It's no laughing matter. I'm so ashamed."

Barbara put her arms around him. "Giles, darling, it's okay. So, you have a kink. Big deal. You're not alone. We all have something." She looked quizzically at Madeleine.

"Giles, I have something to tell you, too," said Madeleine.

CHAPTER 50

Madeleine's hands were shaking as she got the tray ready for tea. The last time she'd used a teapot was when they were together. She'd wanted to meet him in a cafe, but Richard had insisted on coming to the house they'd lived in. Why was she so stupidly nervous of her ex-husband coming to tea, for god's sake? Get a grip, woman!

She stared at the man standing in the doorway.

"Fuck, you've aged!" Instantly, her hand covered her mouth. "God, Richard, I'm so sorry. Come on in."

She took his coat and hat, put them over the banister and followed him into the sitting room.

"I know I've aged. You, on the other hand, look amazing. And this room is so different. I hardly recognise it. It looks good. Colourful. Like the new you."

"Yes, well, a lot has changed in so many ways, Richard. Sit down. Make yourself at home."

He smiled at her joke. "I'll try."

"I'm sorry, I don't know why I feel so nervous, saying silly things," she said.

"It's okay. I'm nervous too. Do you want to be mother?"

Madeleine flinched at the familiar twee phrasing she had always hated. "Don't say that. It freaks me out. Yes, okay. Actually no, you can pour! I will not revert to that role anymore, the little wife."

"You were never the little wife in my eyes, Maddy. Never. I was always so proud of you, so proud of who you were."

"It's a pity you weren't honest with me, then."

"It took me a long time to accept I was gay. It's not easy to admit that you're something you've fought for so long to deny. I thought if I married you, a woman I was so attracted to in so many ways, any feelings I had for men would disappear. I tried so hard, Maddy. I'm so sorry." His eyes filled with tears, and he pulled a handkerchief from his pocket.

She reached for his hand. "Richard, I'm sorry too. I've learnt a little about needs and fears I've buried all my life. I'm facing them and life is so much better for it. I know how tough it is to accept what's real and not live a pretend life. It must have been tough for you. But I hope you're happy now with Paul. How is he?"

"He's okay, thanks. Like me, he's got older. I was so relieved when I came out, Maddy. But now, we're both rather dull old men of habit. I never expected that. If I'm honest, it's almost a bit boring, sometimes. Ah, you remembered my favourite biscuits." He picked up a ginger nut and dunked it in his tea. "Thank you. Now tell me about you. What's happening in your life?"

"How much do you want to know?" she asked.

"Everything."

★ ★ ★ ★

"Barbara, he was lovely. Vulnerable and honest about his own life, and so kind and understanding about mine. Just like the Richard I knew at the beginning. I wasn't planning to tell him everything, but he asked and that's what I did. I can't tell you how good it felt."

"I'm so pleased for you. I guess it's a sort of reconciliation. How do you feel about him now?"

"He feels like a friend. Not one I'll be in contact with a lot, but one I know I can turn to if I need to. And the same for him with me. It's like we can close a chapter and truly move on."

MADELEINE

Madeleine had driven to Ledbury for the weekend. Giles had gone fishing with a friend. She lay on the sofa in Barbara's arms. "Life's good, isn't it?"

"Yes, my darling. It is. We have the whole weekend to ourselves. The weather forecast is good. What do you fancy doing?"

"Can you show me how to make a bowl?"

"Of course. I'd love to. We'll start with something simple but first, let's have some supper. I've got us a sea bass. I'm going to make my famous red wine jus."

"Thank you, Barbara. For everything. I love you."

CHAPTER 51

Finn was thrilled that Madeleine had agreed to meet him again at Brown's Hotel. He'd offered her dinner, but she said she was pushed for time. Seeing her again at the gallery had reignited his desire for her. He was confident he could get her back.

He stood at the bar, chatting with the barman when he felt a tap on his shoulder and turned. Standing in front of him were Madeleine, Giles, and Barbara.

"Hi Finn," they said in unison.

"Hello," he said, unable to hide his disappointment. "I wasn't expecting all three of you!"

"We come as a package, Finn," said Barbara.

"So I see. Would you all like coffee?" he asked, recovering his demeanour.

A waiter showed them to a table and took their orders.

"How are you, Finn? How was the exhibition? It looked amazing," said Madeleine.

"It's an enormous success, Maddy. Mike and I are thrilled. And so is Rachel. We're off to Athens next week. Want to come?"

For a moment, Madeleine felt the familiar clutch in her stomach.

"Finn, we've come here together because we want you, Mike, and Jasmine to know that between the three of us here, we have no secrets. Giles and Barbara both know about what happened between me, the two of you and Jasmine. We also know about Giles' visits to Jasmine and the Club. So, will you please tell them that we have no regrets about what happened. In fact, I'm very grateful to you all, but it's over now. And I also want to tell you that the three of us are in a relationship together and it's working out fine."

Finn looked briefly crestfallen but quickly regained his composure and smiled at Madeleine. She noticed the flicker of sadness in his eyes. Then his demeanour changed, and he burst out laughing.

"Maddy, from the second I met you, I knew you were special!" He shook his head. "Nothing surprises me about you. I think this is fantastic. Congratulations. I can't imagine what Mike and Jasmine will say, but as far as I'm concerned…." He hesitated. "Okay, for me I did once hope things could be different between us. But for you, I'm happy. So, what do you call this? Polyamory? Is that what it's called? Giles, you're one lucky guy."

Finn watched them leave, picked up his phone and called Mike.

CHAPTER 52

The sound of the anchor chain rattling into the water woke Madeleine from a deep sleep. She looked across at the bunk where Barbara was still sleeping and slipped out of her bed. Giles was awake on the top bunk. Madeleine gave him a quick kiss and whispered that she was going up to the deck. "I'll come with you. This must be Santorini," he said.

They watched the ramp descend, and passengers and vehicles disembark. It was still dark, and Giles put his arm round her against the pre-dawn chill.

"How are you feeling, my love?" he asked.

"I'm okay. This is where Justin and I got on." She shivered and snuggled deeper into him. "I'm cold."

★ ★ ★ ★

There were few tourists on Anafi in early April. The white and blue, small, simple apartment they had rented for a few days was perched on the side of the hill on the outskirts of Chora. Giles had gone to get some provisions. Madeleine and Barbara sat at a table on the bougainvillea covered veranda, looking out over the Aegean Sea. Ahead of them was one of the small islands that Apollo reputedly stood on to fire the lightning bolt showing Jason and his Argonauts the way to the island and to safety. Madeleine breathed in the scent of thyme that floated in the warm air. She closed her eyes and started to drift.

Giles's gentle kiss on the top of her head woke Madeleine. He put coffee on the table in front of them.

"I've found a place we can have lunch. When you're ready, let's go and eat and then come back for a siesta. We need it, after eleven hours on that bloody ferry."

"Thanks Giles. Just what I need." Madeleine took his hand. "I'll finish the coffee, then have a shower before we go."

"I'll join you, darling," said Barbara.

"It's a small shower. I doubt if you'll both get in there," said Giles.

"We'll manage, lover boy!" said Barbara.

Refreshed, they walked hand in hand up the hill into the town, stopping to look at the bougainvillea and the flowers that flowed out of pots beside doors. Resisting the tempting, narrow passages, they followed the main street until it opened onto a square. Giles pointed to the taverna where a woman waved to them, inviting them in. They chose a table looking over the sea and gave their orders.

★ ★ ★ ★

Madeleine picked at the salad in front of her.

"We hadn't planned to come to Anafi, you know," she said. "We'd been on Santorini and the woman whose house we stayed in, told us about it. She came from Anafi and her sister could put us up, so we said, why not? There was a ferry the next day and we got on it. When we came here twenty-three years ago, there were only two restaurants and most of the visitors camped on the beaches. We rather wished we'd known that, as we'd have done the same. We spent the first day naked together on the beach, swimming, lying, snoozing, feeling horny. It was the first time in a while we hadn't argued. Mount Kalamos looked amazing from the beach and that's where we decided to go the next day. There's a monastery at the foot and a tiny church on the top. It sounded perfect."

Barbara and Giles each took one of her hands.

"I thought I had my life planned out with Justin. And then with Richard. Neither worked out. Now I have the two of you. I couldn't have done this without you both. For the first time in my life, I'm with two people I totally trust."

"It's not a life I'd ever have thought I'd have, either. I won't let you down, Maddy," said Giles.

"Nor will I, my love," said Barbara. "I thought I'd got it made with Dimitri and Stella, but you two are a whole other planet!"

Madeleine took a deep breath. "Okay, let's do it tomorrow. I want to get it over with..."

* * * *

They got up early and made a quick breakfast. Giles put enough water in this rucksack for the three of them. Madeleine carefully put the wreath on her arm. By 8am, they were in the taxi driving the twenty minutes to Zoodohos Pigi monastery, where the track to the top of Mount Kalamos started.

They parked next to a wall where three donkeys stood motionless under a tree. A nun swept the path leading to the monastery, which was built on the site of the Temple of Apollo. Madeleine picked a sprig of wild thyme and threaded it into the wreath. Barbara picked a bunch of wild red poppies and gave some to Giles.

Silently, with Madeleine leading the way, they set off up the rocky path.

From time to time, they paused and looked out across the sea. Two emerald-coloured rocks reached out from the water. The path narrowed and steepened until, after walking for forty minutes, Madeleine stopped.

"They've put up a handrail." She slumped to the ground. "They've put up a fucking handrail!"

Barbara and Giles sat beside her, their arms embracing her. "We've got you," said Barbara. "Is this the place?"

Madeleine nodded and stood up. "This is it. Okay, let's get it done."

She took the wreath off her arm, then stopped.

"I can't do it."

"Why not?" Barbara asked.

"It doesn't feel right, commemorating him like this. The truth is, I hate him. I hate what he did to me. He made me feel so small. He destroyed me." Madeleine began to sob, and Barbara put her arms around her.

"Do you want to talk about it?" she asked.

Madeleine wiped her eyes and took a deep breath.

"He had a way of always making me feel I was wrong or doing something wrong. Every little thing was my fault. He was so clever. I'd tried many times to leave, but it's like he could sense it, and then he'd be nice to me, buy me a little present, tell me how he loved me."

"Maddy, I can only begin to imagine what that must feel like," said Barbara. "You told us you'd finally made up your mind to leave him. You were going to tell him up at the top."

"Yes, that's what I'd planned. But on the walk up, he kept pushing me, telling me to go faster. When we got here, I stopped to look out over the sea. He yelled at me to keep going. He was hot or something and wanted to get to the top quickly and rest. But in that moment, something in me snapped. I knew I couldn't go on like this. So, I said to him, quietly, calmly, that I'd had enough. I was leaving him. His face was white with fury. I can see him now. He came at me, grabbing me, his fist raised. He'd never been physical before. I was terrified. I pushed him away, and he tripped, fell back. I tried to catch him. But he just.... disappeared... over the edge...."

"Oh my God, Maddy, that's awful," said Giles.

"I looked over to see if he had stopped himself falling. Then I heard a splash down below and I screamed and screamed."

Madeleine paused, caught her breath.

"You know what the first thing I thought was? That it was my fault. That I'd killed him. I suppose I've always known rationally that it was an accident, but his voice in my head, telling me it was my fault… it's just so powerful. That's why I believed then, and for years, that I was guilty of his death. I blocked it out as much as I could over the years, but the nightmares kept bringing it back… it's like he won every single time, even now."

"But he hasn't won, Maddy," said Barbara.

"No. you're right. He hasn't. I have Mistress Jasmine to thank for that. She was the one who made me face it – even if I wasn't ready to tell her the whole truth. There's nothing I've hidden from you now. And you both, you've showed me I'm loveable, despite what I've done, that I can really love and be loved. I could never believe it before."

They put their arms round her and held her tight.

"Why don't we finish the walk you started?" asked Giles.

Madeleine smiled, turned, and started up the hill, Giles and Barbara behind her. Slowly, they picked their way along the path until they reached the top. The small church snuggled into the rock. Silently, they wandered around, taking in the 360-degree view across the island and the sea.

Madeleine walked over to the church and put the wreath against the door. Barbara and Giles placed their poppies beside it. They stood together, holding hands.

"There's one more thing you need to do Maddy," said Barbara. "Forgive yourself."

"How do I do that?"

"Just say it out loud. 'I forgive myself.' Come on. Do it."

Giles and Barbara held her hands. She stood, facing the sea, took a deep breath and in a tremulous voice, she murmured, "I forgive myself." Then she shouted it out at the top of her voice.

A feeling of calm and warmth spread through her body.

She felt like she was floating. And ready to fly.

EPILOGUE

Finn, Mike, and Jasmine rarely had dinner together, but Madeleine was a good enough reason to make an exception. Losing her from their lives was just not going to happen, whatever new relationships she was involved in.

Finn, however much he had persuaded himself to the contrary, was not ready to lose a woman he knew he could love.

Mike hadn't had so much fun in bed, or on the dancefloor, with a woman for as long as he could remember.

Jasmine wasn't happy that Madeleine had shown no interest in seeing her again. She knew Madeleine had deep-seated needs that she could help fulfil and was determined to explore them further.

Giles was of minor interest but could well provide a way to Madeleine. And Barbara sounded like an interesting prospect.

By the time they were served dessert, they had worked out a plan to ensure that Madeleine would not go far. They raised their glasses, smiles on their faces. "To Madeleine!"

The hook was ready to be baited. They would give her a little time to enjoy her new life before reeling her back in.

Tick.... tock....

ACKNOWLEDGEMENTS

It has been immense fun writing, producing, and publishing this novel and I hope those who read it have fun too.

A huge thank you to all those who read various incarnations of the novel and whose comments helped to shape it. A special thank you to Jean Rafferty whose professional advice was invaluable and to Sean Street for a conversation on sound in a Liverpool café.

A very special thank you to HS and AMP without whose encouragement, love, thoughts, persistence and advice, this novel would never have been finished.

Alex Simons
alexsimonsauthor@gmail.com
2023

Straw Hat
Books

Printed in Great Britain
by Amazon